Heart
of the
Beartooths

by

Dr. Sue Clifton

Daughters of Parrish Oaks, Book 3

Heart of the Beartooths

Cover Art by *Kim Mendoza*

The Wild Rose Press, Inc.
PO Box 708
Adams Basin, NY 14410-0708
Visit us at www.thewildrosepress.com

Publishing History
First Champagne Rose Edition, 2015
Print ISBN 978-1-5092-0292-8
Digital ISBN 978-1-5092-0293-5

Daughters of Parrish Oaks, Book 3
Published in the United States of America

She rounded a curve and stopped at a dense clump of willows overlooking the waterfall.

And there he was, in her waterfall, probably one of the anglers, and he was naked. Her first instinct was to turn her head, but her natural instinct took control and she watched. His back was turned to her, and he had his hands and face lifted up as if shouting praise to the waterfall deity.

But it was not his praising that caught her attention. He looked like a delicious carton of Neapolitan ice cream. His legs were bright red from the lower thighs down, showing huge muscles in the back of the sunburned calves. From the waist up, he was varying shades of brown, milk chocolate from waist to upper arms and rich, dark semi-sweet from the bulges in his forearms to his up-stretched fingertips. But it was the vanilla that mesmerized her. It was more than the "cute butt" from the movies. It was tight. Waves of muscle tissue cascaded from the trim waistline to the tops of his thighs. As he lifted his arms higher, he spread his legs apart, flexing the rich, creamy, good parts.

Leaving the scene never entered Betsy's mind.

Praise for Dr. Sue Clifton

In addition to her novels published at The Wild Rose Press, Inc. and elsewhere, Dr. Sue Clifton won four first-place awards at the Arkansas Writers' Conference for poems in *THE GULLY PATH*, her first novel.

Dedication

To Woody,
My fly fishing partner,
My lover,
My husband,
My best friend.
I love you.

A woman's highest calling is to lead a man to his soul,
so as to unite him with the source.
A man's highest calling is to protect woman,
so she is free to walk the earth unharmed..
~Cherokee Proverb

Prologue

Beartooth Mountains, Montana

The half-breed stood straight and tall, bare-chested, atop the boulder. His eyes closed, trancelike, hidden under long, dark hair blowing free the way his soul longed to be. Breaking through the silence, his mind pleaded, dared the lightning creeping past the mountain peaks, reminding him greater powers were in control.

With his arms stretched high, his loose moose-hide pants slipped down his hips, uncovering the pathway to the manhood once revered, even flaunted, but rendered completely useless in his present situation. He'd ceased trying to keep up with the number of days he had wandered without food, with only mountain streams to quench hunger and thirst. The uncontrollable shaking, the aftermath of the ninety-proof demons he had left in the sweat lodge, had finally stopped, but were replaced by melancholy and despair, worse torments for his soul. He cried, unashamed, leaving his body a parched desert of hopelessness. With his eyes to the mountains, he squatted, wrapping his arms around his knees and letting his thoughts consume him.

Clan Father seemed so sure the three days of sweats followed by time wandering alone in this great Bridger Wilderness of Montana would bring me a vision; some hope for the future, some reason for living.

1

"Listen to the Beartooths, nephew," he told me. "The winds will carry messages from the mountains; the spirits will whisper to your heart and fill your soul with ancient proverbs. Beware of the things your eyes see and pursue only what catches your heart." But no whispers have been heard; no vision has come, and I remain alone and destitute.

Perhaps it is due to my lack of faith in First Maker; or, more likely, to the devil trickster that has possessed me since she left, taking with her the only thing in life I treasured. I wished for death; I still wish for death. Clan Father knew this without a word being spoken between us, and insisted I try the "old ways."

The dark approached again. Maybe this night the young man would dream, something other than sleepless endurance of the frigid mountain air and the storms that always came with the late evenings, adding further punishment to his bare existence and sending him hunting for shelter in the boulders or making a quick lean-to from fallen trees in the forest.

Hypnotized by the lightning, he did not notice her as she stole through the trees, setting her aim on the human too close to her lair of babies. The half-breed sensed danger and turned, but not in time to prevent the attack. The mountain lion lunged, knocking him off the rocky pedestal, away from the path traveled by deer and moose for generations before. Both beast and man were catapulted into the raging current below. Downstream, he struggled in the white rapids before catching a tree limb caught in slippery rocks and hoisting himself onto the bank.

Minutes seemed like hours as he curled himself under the huge overhanging boulder, in a fetal position like an unborn child resisting the move into a world bent on destroying him. Hugging his broad muscular chest in an attempt to stave off pulsating pain as well as the biting chill of the mountain night air, he flexed the muscles in his arms, pressing tighter and holding his breath trying to find comfort. But comfort remained elusive.

He regretted his survival instinct had kicked in to fight off the mountain lion. Death had to be easier than enduring the torture of the deep, jagged claw punctures left in his chest. So severe was the pain he never noticed the deep cut on his right cheek, a lightning-bolt talisman that would serve in the future as a reminder of this destitute point in his life. Feeling lightheaded, he closed his eyes, trying to conjure up sleep through the shaking, not recognizing or hearing the staccato moans emanating from deep in his throat as if they belonged to someone other than himself. But sleep did not come. The most he hoped for was to pass out from the pain, but even this reprieve was not granted.

The mountain lion—could it possibly be an animal spirit sent by First Maker?

One who had strayed from spiritual concerns for so long should look upon such attention from the Great One favorably, but he wondered what kind of god or spirit would send such punishment to one of his children. Maybe his mother had been right when she insisted putting store in "Crow superstitious nonsense" would only result in more hurt and disaster.

His whimpers echoed off his boulder roof, and he gave up on both death and sleep. Crawling from under the shelter like a marmot coming out to forage in moonlight madness, he scanned the peaks, trying to get his bearings.

The mountains teased him like woolen blankets with snow-trimmed fringe, close but unwilling to warm his half-naked, pain-wracked body. His wet moccasins squished, reminding him again of the encounter with the mountain lion. As he removed the drenched pants and moccasins, the only clothes Clan Father had provided for his quest, the not-so-brave man wondered why they weren't frozen into icy shields. But June in Montana brings cold without freezing, regardless of what it felt like to his chilled body.

Gently, he placed the pants over his back with the legs draped across the deep cuts on his chest. The cold moist hide soothed his raw chest as he laced up the moccasins, the only covering for his lower body. Still shivering, he climbed over boulders and rocks, making his way to the trail above. After reaching the top, he meant to turn down the mountain trail that followed the stream to where he knew he would eventually reach his uncle's camp and the canvas-covered sweat lodge where he had sweated out some but not nearly all of his misery.

He longed for this quest to be over. No hope remained for the visions Clan Father had promised. Only more misery and suffering were offered, this time physical rather than emotional. But some unseen force now beckoned him to go farther up-trail, away from security and rescue.

Standing like Robert Frost at the juncture of two paths, he saw her. The doe stood on the trail. Beside her lay a fawn, his white spots glistening like drops of new-fallen snow on tawny earth. The moonlight flickered in the mother's soft brown eyes as she looked up at him.

For some reason, he felt embarrassed and squatted to hide his openly visible manhood. As she turned and darted up the trail, a hawk called from overhead, commanding him to pay attention. Putting all shame aside, he followed as an obedient child mesmerized by an object of intense desire. Intent on carrying out the quest, he failed to notice the pain had left his body, allowing him to move faster.

After what seemed hours, he found himself at a familiar lake. Pulling his pants from his upper body, he dressed again before climbing over boulders to reach the shadow on the other side of the water. Snowcaps, exact images of those gazing down from high, gently swayed below in the pristine, tranquil water. As he stood a few feet away and watched, the shadow moved, but it was no longer the doe.

An aura of light circled the young woman dressed in a white deerskin dress and moccasins, a play on the reflected snowcaps. Her long hair mesmerized him as it fluttered in the breeze, a mass of golden crinkles cascading behind her, the bridal veil of a ghostly being. He was reminded of a beautiful palomino mare he once saw loping gracefully through a mountain meadow with her long mane waltzing in rhythm with each hoof beat.

Unable to move, he stared until she turned and looked up at him with eyes green, the color of a summer fern. She smiled and held out her hands. Falling gently into her space, he was soothed by her soft hands brushing through his hair, pushing it away from his eyes. Pulling him closer, she traced the cut on his cheek, caressing it with the gentle touch of an angel. Kissing him, she gently directed his head into her lap and continued to comb her fingers through his hair. He hugged her knees tightly as if afraid she might escape, and a silent lullaby wafted through gentle mountain breezes, filling his heart and soul as he drifted into paralyzing contentment.

Chapter One

The South, 5 Years Later

Betsy sat incognito in her friend's borrowed beige minivan, paralyzed with dread and hopelessness. Unable to peel her hands from the steering wheel, she could only stare at the townhouse door; a townhouse in an exclusive gated community in Memphis; a townhouse kept secret by the stranger she had been married to for ten years.

Where had everything gone wrong? How long had Patrick been playing his game of musical beds without her suspecting? As she sat not wanting to move, she replayed the last few years of her marriage that led her on this path of no return.

It started with the anniversary from hell. Given her choice of places to celebrate their tenth anniversary, Betsy had chosen Jed's; it was not quiet and romantic but was her favorite place to eat. Dreamily looking out at the White River, Betsy lost count of the hushpuppies she had munched away on and had almost finished her pinto beans and green tomato relish when she looked across the table at Patrick. He stared at her with a look that did not say, "Happy Anniversary; let's hurry and get home to bed," and just shook his head.

"Your ass is already getting as broad as the paddle to that damn kayak you love so much, and you still sit there eating like a pig."

His cutting remark had crushed Betsy, ruining what should have been a happy occasion. A few days later, still devastated and unable to get the miserable anniversary out of her head, Betsy left her log home in the Arkansas Ozarks and headed for Mississippi to spend two weeks at her childhood Victorian home, Parrish Oaks, with her devoted listening-block-and-best-friend-since-birth Annie bending an ear as Betsy poured out her despair like a daytime soap queen.

But with Annie, it proved to be anything but passive listening. She always spoke her mind, especially where her friend's domineering husband was concerned. She exploded when her friend described her anniversary dinner and the cutting remark.

"He did not say that, the egotistical bastard! You're kidding, right?" Annie's face shot red, looking as if she'd hemorrhage, not believing any man could be so cruel to her beautiful friend.

"Ten years you guys have been married. Why you've stayed with him, I'll never know. I hate to even ask you this, but what wonderful tenth anniversary present did you get? I know you gave him that satellite radio for his old Corvette."

"You would have to ask. He gave me a six-month membership to a gym in Mountain Home. No 'one rose for each blissful year of marriage.' No see-through negligee. Not even a box of clear Cling Wrap, his version of a sexy outfit, like he gave me as a wonderful joke one Valentine's Day, a long time ago when we actually had a sex life. Just one month of sweaty, fat-burning sessions with a bunch of other porkers for each five pounds he says I need to lose." Betsy looked down in an attempt to hide some of the hurt she felt.

"Thirty pounds! What an asshole! Maybe fifteen, Betsy, but no more! In fact, I looked at a chart in my doctor's office the other day, and you are right in the range where you should be for your height, and so was I until I got pregnant. That's what happens, you know, if you get to looking too good, girl."

As soon as Annie made the remark, she regretted it and looked down with guilt, knowing that her friend would give anything to be pregnant. Betsy tried not to show any signs of sorrow, knowing Annie would never intentionally say anything to hurt her.

"It's okay, Annie. Besides, the only thing that could have driven Patrick farther from me, other than having a fat ass, would be if I had tried to get pregnant. He made it clear from the start he hated kids and never wanted to be a father. Remember when Patrick and I got engaged, Mom told me I needed to reconsider the marriage since she knew how much I wanted children? I was just so sure Patrick would change his mind. Guess God agreed with Patrick."

"We've had this discussion before. I don't think God gave you cancer or caused you to need a hysterectomy. It's just a sad chapter in the book of life, dear friend."

"Yeah, well, I want the book to be a fairy tale. I'm going to work to put the magic back in my marriage, Annie, if it kills me. I am a fat pig, but I'm not going to stay that way. Midge, Patrick's office manager in Little Rock, told me how she lost thirty pounds, and I'm going to try it. Starting today, I'm going to walk six miles every day and really cut back on my fats and calories. Midge said she'll be my diet buddy; I just call her if I start to fall off the wagon."

"Oh, Betsy, don't let that son-of-a-bitch make you feel unworthy. He's the one who doesn't deserve you. You are beautiful as you are. Just know I'm here for you, Betsy. Even pregnant as a porpoise and in Mississippi, I'll be there if you need me."

"Just encourage me, Annie." Betsy tried to lighten the conversation. "I know! Let's get our belly buttons pierced after I lose my weight and after you have the baby." Annie laughed at the suggestion, but vowed they would go together as soon as they could both find their belly buttons again.

Inspired by Midge, Betsy immediately clocked off a walking trail in one-mile-sections. Just to make sure she never missed a mile in her counting, she carried six rocks, changing each one to the other pocket as she completed a mile. Now here she was three weeks later and already ten pounds lighter.

Feeling more confident, she decided to surprise her husband at the condo he had bought to live in while at the Memphis office. She had not seen him since their anniversary, even though he'd been in Little Rock, where the main office for his construction company was located. Patrick was busy putting together a proposal for a large construction project in Nashville. As she headed across the Mississippi River Bridge into Memphis, Betsy plotted the surprise visit.

"What is the name of that little boutique where Patrick used to buy me gifts?" Betsy talked to herself while drumming the steering wheel with her thumbs.

It had been so long since she had gotten anything slinky or sexy from Patrick she could not come up with the name of the quaint shop, but she knew it was in

Overton Square.

In her mind, Betsy imagined the success her little escapade would bring. The romantic night would begin with Italian spaghetti, the family recipe Patrick's stepmother had taught her to make before she died.

"If Mona was alive, she'd know what I need to do to get Patrick's attention—one of those romantic little games of manipulation like she played with Mr. Wingate. If only…" Her thoughts became heavy as she remembered how Patrick's stepmother's life and Patrick's had turned out.

Betsy missed Mona terribly, much more than she missed her father-in-law, but she had never really cared for Mr. Wingate, especially after he took a swing at his son that day eight years ago, leaving Patrick heartbroken. He'd been even more devastated when his father died of a heart attack shortly after, without a reconciliation.

Mona had remarried after Mr. Wingate died, only to die in a plane crash with her new husband a few months later. Mona had been Patrick's stepmother and his confidante since he was fifteen, and he had been as crushed when she died as by his father's death. Betsy thought back to how she had consoled Patrick, smothering him with love and understanding with each loss.

"I always hurt when you hurt, Patrick," she whispered. "Why can't you feel my pain instead of making my wounds bigger?"

"There it is! Rosanna's Boutique!" Betsy spoke aloud as she turned into the parking lot, but she hesitated before getting out of the Jeep, letting her thoughts seize control again.

I know this will be pricey, but it'll be worth it if it gets the reaction I want from my husband. Besides, I have Patrick's checkbook.

Betsy held the checkbook up to reassure her thoughts before getting out of the Jeep.

Patrick may not be the most loving husband in the world, but he is generous. After all, he did buy me my log house on the Norfork River. If only that were enough.

Sighing, dismissing any more concerns, she pushed open the door to the boutique.

Rosanna's Boutique was like stepping into a shop in Tuscany with its stone floors, brightly painted walls, massive European antique pieces used to display the most elegant and expensive items, and prints of ancient Italy adorning every wall. And it was definitely not Macy's—no two alikes of any outfit. It was just the kind of place her successful though arrogant husband would shop.

"May I help you? My name is Angelique."

The young salesgirl was the most beautiful young woman Betsy had ever seen. Her name fit, although the girl looked more like a goddess than an angel with her long black hair—thick like velvet and shiny like finest silk. Her dark eyes gave her a mystical gypsy quality.

Betsy told Angelique she was looking for a red negligee, and the girl led her to a rack filled with elegant lingerie.

"How about this? Isn't it beautiful? And it is ever so red." Angelique held up a slinky red silk negligee with a tanga bottom and a split baby-doll top that was more split than top. She draped it against her own body. The size twelve would have wrapped around her twice with material left over.

"This will be fantastic with your blonde hair. Is it naturally curly? I'd kill for hair like that."

Of course Betsy took the negligee, but later she was wishing she had never entered the boutique. As she signed the check—Mrs. Patrick Wingate—the girl's whole demeanor changed and she took on a shocked, almost hostile look.

"You're Patrick Wingate's wife?" The girl stopped the checkout and stared at Betsy.

"Yes. Is there a problem?" Betsy stared back at the girl, questioning her reaction.

"Uh, no." The girl seemed to work at regaining her composure. "I'm sorry. I just didn't realize Patrick—uh, Mr. Wingate, was married."

An elegant lady with beautiful long dark hair and hazel eyes stepped up to the counter from where she had been arranging jewelry. Betsy figured the woman to be in her fifties, but she could have easily been cast on one of those exercise commercials, the ones that always caused Betsy to click the remote to the Food Network. The lady reminded Betsy of Mona but was even more stunning and shapely. Betsy tried not to show her shock at Angelique's remark, but she knew the older woman had sensed her concern. Betsy had never been good at hiding her feelings or her reactions.

"Angelique, dear, Mrs. Tatum just came in to pick up the dress she was having altered. Would you get it, please? I'll take over here."

Excusing herself, the girl left the counter and headed for the back room.

"Hello, I am Rosanna. I hope my niece was able to help you find what you wanted. She has excellent potential but is still learning. I'm afraid she has a bit of a crush on your husband, along with many other handsome clients who frequent our shop. Oh, to be that young and silly again. I do apologize for her." The owner seemed to be trying to cover up for the girl and the boutique.

"Angelique was very helpful, thank you. She's a beautiful and charming young woman. Oh, could you wrap this, please? It's for my friend, sort of an early gift for after she has her baby." Betsy refused to admit anything was wrong.

"I hope you'll come back, Mrs. Wingate. In the future, I will assist you personally." Rosanna handed the beautifully wrapped box to Betsy. "I hope your friend will be happy with your selection, but if not, please feel free to return it."

As Betsy got into the Jeep, she threw the package into the back seat, knowing she would never wear it. Glancing into the boutique as she pulled away, she could see Rosanna's hands in the air in angry animation as she reprimanded her niece. One thing Betsy had promised she would never be was the suspicious, jealous wife, but why was Patrick so well known at Rosanna's Boutique? She had not received a gift from there in years. And why was Angelique so shocked to find out there was a Mrs. Patrick Wingate? Was it just the whim of a silly salesgirl or something more serious? Was Patrick capable of having an affair? Deep down she knew it was possible. Hadn't she told Annie about their lack of a sex life and about Patrick's obsession with her weight? But still, Patrick was so good to her, at least in providing for her needs and most of her wants. Could that be out of guilt?

Confederate Park was just ahead. Betsy pulled into it, needing to think. Should she go ahead with her plans to surprise Patrick at his condo in Memphis?

"Yes, damn it! Why not? He's still my husband. There is no fairy tale without a prince, even if he's a toad." Betsy backed the Jeep out of the parking spot she'd chosen and headed toward Patrick's condo on the banks of the Mississippi River.

When she reached the condo, she laughed as she saw the key box attached to the door like the ones real estate agents used. As brilliant as Patrick was, he was always losing things, especially keys, and always excused his shortcoming with the same line, "I've got too damn many of these things to keep up with." There was a key holder at each of his residences—even at the cabin, although he was seldom there to use it.

Even though Betsy had never been to the Memphis condo, she knew what the combination to the key box would be. It was always the same number—their wedding date. She wondered if the code would last till eternity as they had promised in their vows.

The encounter with Angelique had rattled Betsy more than she would admit to herself, and she held her breath as she tried to loosen the lock, as if a new code would be proof of her husband's infidelity. As the box opened, allowing her to retrieve the key inside, she breathed again.

The décor in the condo was no surprise to Betsy. Every residence Patrick had, other than the cabin Betsy had decorated using a Southwest motif and southern primitive antique pieces, looked like a suite in an expensive hotel. Even with his lack of creativity, Patrick was a neat freak; he always criticized Betsy for her philosophy that a home should look "lived in." Patrick operated off the left side of his engineer's brain, with the kitchen counters empty and wiped clean to a shine, shoes lined up in the closet by style and color, and clothes neatly stacked and sorted in the dresser drawers. When she saw his dirty underwear folded neatly on the floor of the closet, she laughed aloud. With this in mind, Betsy walked back into the kitchen to see just how big a mess she could make preparing the spaghetti sauce.

"The magic is in the spice bag," was what Mona had taught her, and Betsy took great pains to work "the magic" for this special dinner, putting any suspicions out of her mind and concentrating on making this the perfect romantic evening. Betsy set the table, complete with candles and two antique crystal wine glasses she had brought from home. Now all she needed to do was to make her body as appealing as the dinner.

After showering, Betsy saturated with moisturizers and dabbed on a touch of the big bottle of expensive perfume Patrick had later added to the rude anniversary gift. He had even managed to put a damper on that gift by saying he chose perfume because he could indulge his flair for luxury and get the big size in that without insulting her.

Her black silk pants showed off the curves just becoming discernible again, and with the pants she wore a white silk spaghetti-strap blouse gathered slightly in the front, hanging just low enough to tease and show off the only part of her body Patrick liked and did not want smaller.

Knowing he liked her hair down and not in the French braid she usually wore, Betsy blew her hair straight and curled the ends under. The finishing touch would be the diamond tennis bracelet Patrick had given her on their fifth wedding anniversary and the dangly diamond earrings, a surprise gift from a long time ago, made even dearer by the fact there was no occasion.

"How did I let myself go from diamonds to a gym membership, Patrick?" Betsy said aloud, blaming her flaws for causing her husband's inattentiveness.

"But not too bad for a tomboy." She stared at her reflection in the mirror, turning to look at herself from every angle, beginning to be comfortable with her body again. But, deep within, she knew Patrick would still see her as imperfect.

"Okay, Prince Charming. Ready or not!" Betsy poured herself a glass of wine and sat on the sofa to wait.

****

The sun streamed through the big bay window in the condo, slapping her across the face like the fist of a violent intruder. Startled, she jumped to her feet, knocked over the remains of her third glass of wine, and winced in pain from a crick in her neck gained while sleeping on the uncomfortable sofa.

She looked at her watch. "Eight a.m. Guess Prince Charming had other plans. Maybe with the petite Angelique." Her spoken feelings tore at her heart as she headed for the kitchen to get paper towels to clean up the wine. The candles had burned to a nub in the holders before dousing themselves, and the table sat empty, beautiful but wasted, much like the ten years of marriage this handsome couple had come to endure and not treasure.

Before grabbing her bag from the bedroom and

heading for the door, Betsy quickly scribbled a note, rolled it lengthwise and placed it in the empty wine glass.

Patrick,

Thanks for a wonderful evening. The wine was delicious and your companionship was as always— nonexistent.

Betsy

Heartbroken, she pulled away from the condo as her tears caressed her cheeks like loving fingertips attempting to console. The Ozark Bluegrass music Patrick hated blasted off the canvas top as she steered the Jeep across the Mississippi River Bridge into Arkansas, back to her cabin, her river, her refuge in the Ozarks.

Sure that Patrick had returned to the condo and found the remains of her bright idea, Betsy couldn't help but wonder how he would excuse his absence or if he'd just pretend nothing had happened.

Whatever he would say didn't really matter to her at this point. It would have to be said to the answering machine. Betsy ignored the telephone rings and the messages all afternoon. Later that night, as she slid into the soft current of the Jacuzzi, she heard the phone. On the fourth ring, the answering machine picked up.

"Betsy, it's Mom. If you're there, pick up. I'll wait a minute before hanging up."

Betsy leaped from the tub and dove at the phone.

"Hi, Mom. What's up?" Betsy tried to act as if it was just a normal day in her life.

"Well, not much up here in Alaska, but I hear it's pretty hot in the Ozarks, and I don't mean the weather."

"I guess Patrick called you, huh?" Betsy sat on the

edge of the tub, ready to spill her heart to her mother, who could always sense her emotional state.

"Yep, he did. What's going on, Daughter? You think he's cheating on you?"

"I have no idea, Mom, but I know I'm tired of living like this." Betsy burst into tears and began telling the whole story to her mother, complete with Patrick's rude comments, the gym membership, six-mile walks, and the remarks of the beautiful young salesgirl.

"Well, my dear, what do you plan to do about it?"

"You're the romance novelist, Dr. Sue Ann Parish. Write me an ending and make it happy, for Pete's sake." Betsy made it sound as if she were joking, but she valued her mother's opinion. For the most part, it had always been just her and her mother.

"Well, then, since you asked, first of all, don't jump to conclusions. When Patrick called me, he seemed genuinely concerned. Said he'd been calling all day and leaving messages, but you wouldn't return his calls. He told me about your supposed surprise and was quick to explain he had worked all weekend at the office on some big deal he's cooking up. Said he accidentally fell asleep on the sofa in his office." She could tell her mom was trying to give Patrick the benefit of a doubt and not to sound suspicious.

"And Angelique, did he happen to mention a pretty young thing, obviously a new part of his life?" Betsy spoke loudly, showing her anger.

"No, he missed that one, but you're not really sure there is anything with the girl. You're not letting your suspicions get the best of you, are you?"

"I don't know, Mom. But Patrick never comes home." Betsy wiped her eyes with her towel in an attempt to ward off more tears. "I just want what you and Shade had, Mom. Is that too much to ask?" Silence followed for several seconds, and Betsy wished she had not brought up Shade, the greatest love and tragedy of her mother's life.

"My darling daughter, I wish you and Patrick could have the happiness Shade and I had, but you are not me, and Patrick is not Shade." More silence followed. "Why don't you come to Alaska, Betsy? Maybe you need some distance to think about all of this and put it in perspective."

"That's all we've had for several years now, Mom. We need contact, not distance. If I have any more distance, it will be the big 'D' and I don't mean Denver, or however that song goes."

"Just don't do anything irrational, Betsy." Sue Ann paused. "Think it through, and you know what I always tell you."

"You first!" Mother and daughter chimed the phrase together, each smiling on her end of the line.

"Don't worry, Mom. I'll figure it out."

After turning off the phone, Betsy went to bed and slept hard, physically and mentally drained. Early the next morning, she loaded the Jeep with her fly fishing gear and headed for Rim Shoals on the White River to pursue the only passion she was allowed to exercise these days.

The trout hit her fifty-sixes at practically every cast. For a good three hours, Betsy was too absorbed with cast, catch, and release to even think about her marriage, but when the trout stopped, the thoughts returned. The angler continued to wade upstream to fish even though the trout had completely stopped. Other anglers, all male, had already called it a day, but Betsy did not want to go home. For once, her cabin was not her refuge.

It was almost dark when she arrived home. As the automatic garage door opened, there sat the vintage red Corvette as if it actually belonged. When she opened the cabin door, a wonderful, familiar smell greeted her, and so did her husband, looking handsome and innocent. Betsy started to speak, primed with anger, but Patrick put his finger to her lips.

"Don't, Bets. Just let me do this." Betsy hesitated but gave in to Patrick's smile.

"Something smells good." She looked around Patrick toward the kitchen.

"It's not Mona's spaghetti sauce, but it is Italian, from a restaurant in Memphis. I kept it on ice all the way here. The table is set. Care to join me?"

Patrick pulled Betsy to him and escorted her to the dining room, where he stopped at the doorway and kissed her passionately. One end of the primitive harvest table had been set with her mother's Old Country Roses china, complete with gold-rimmed wine glasses and candles.

"I'm really sorry, honey. Can we pretend this weekend is just now starting? I love you—even if you do smell like fish." They both laughed. Anger ended, spell broken.

That night, after the spaghetti dinner that almost wasn't, Patrick ran Betsy a bath complete with bubbles, more candlelight, and wine. As Betsy lay soaking with her eyes closed, as if to savor the night, Patrick slipped his clothes off and slid in at the opposite end. No rude remarks, no mention of young salesgirls, no excuses, and no promises for tomorrow, only long-overdue passion for the moment.

Early the next morning, as he leaned to kiss his wife goodbye, she reached up and lovingly pushed back the hair that had fallen across his left eye as it always did, giving him that innocent, boyish quality she loved. Shortly after, as she heard the Corvette pull down the driveway, she smiled, hugging the pillow next to her where the smell of his aftershave lingered.

A few days later, Betsy lay flat on the bed and sucked in until she thought her lungs would explode. "Damn, another inch and a half," she groaned before exhaling a huge gush of air. Quickly she peeled off the jeans and slung them across the room. She was down another seven pounds, but still her favorite pair of Abercrombie jeans was not giving in.

Patrick had not been home since that wonderful night but had called every day to remind her that he loved her, and he'd even sent yellow roses, her favorite, two days after he went back to Little Rock. He was still working on the "million dollar project," as he referred to it, but promised a weekend soon, with no work brought with him.

Betsy was so proud she had dropped so many pounds she decided to call Midge.

"Wingate Constructors. May I help you?"

"Midge?"

"No, this is Susan. Midge is on vacation this week. Could I take a message?"

"Oh, hello. This is Betsy Wingate. It isn't important. Will she be back in the office on Monday?" Betsy had no idea who Susan was, but then, the only person she knew from Patrick's company was Midge.

Betsy knew Midge because the Little Rock office was where Patrick spent most of his time. Eddie actually ran the Memphis office, although Patrick had made some offhanded remarks lately of disapproval of how his brother was running the business.

"Oh, hello, Mrs. Wingate. I don't think we've met. I'm Susan Carson. I worked in the Memphis office until recently. I think Midge will be back Monday. Would you like her home number?"

"No, that's fine. I don't want to bother her if she's on her off time. I'll try on Monday."

It was only a few minutes later when the phone rang.

"Hi, Bets. Was just wondering if you'd like to meet me in Memphis the first of next week. I need to talk to you about something, anyway."

"Is anything wrong, Patrick?"

"No. Nothing that can't wait until next week. Will you come?"

"It's a date. I take it I won't see you until Monday?" Betsy already knew what the answer was. At least there would be no bad surprises this time when she visited his Memphis condo. She had learned her lesson.

Betsy immediately began looking through her closet to see what she could take to Memphis to show off her much smaller body. As she stretched to reach the negligee still wrapped in the back of her closet, the phone rang again.

"Hi, Betsy. It's me, Lou. Eddie said you might be in the River City next week, and I thought you might like to go shopping."

Betsy cringed when she heard the voice. It was Eddie's wife. She was about a size two, the result of "good genes" according to her. Lou was not pretty but was one of those women who flaunted her body like she was an exotic model and was somehow able to convince everyone around her of her beauty—everyone but Betsy and Patrick.

"I don't think I'll have time, Lou. I'll only be there a couple of days, and I plan to go down to Mississippi to see Annie. Her baby is due any day now."

"Oh, come on, Betsy. You're the only family I've got besides Eddie, and I never get to spend any time with you." Lou used the guilt trip that always worked with Betsy.

"Okay, Lou, but I get to choose where we eat, and I can only spare two hours for shopping."

"Will you be in your Jeep? 'Cause if you are, we can take my new BMW," came Lou's quick reply.

"I tell you what. I'll call and tell you where to meet me, and we can ride in separate cars. That way I can leave when I need to, and you can shop till you drop." Betsy followed the hated phone call with a sigh of dread.

On Monday, Betsy entered the Memphis office of Wingate Constructors and was embarrassed she had to introduce herself to the receptionist. She suddenly realized how little she knew about her husband's work.

"Mr. Wingate has been waiting for you. He's in with his brother right now but should be out in a few minutes. Would you like some coffee or a diet cola?" Betsy tried not to take offense to the receptionist's offer. After all, didn't everyone drink diet colas these days whether they were on diets or not?

The receptionist was a homely girl who looked to be in her late twenties but who wore enough makeup to fill two aisles in Walmart. As she headed to the copier on the other side of the room, Betsy had to restrain herself from laughing. Tall and bony, the girl looked like a fingernail file with feet. She had on the tightest, shortest black dress Betsy had ever seen; it gave new meaning to the word spandex, although there was very little body over which to expand. Clear plastic four-inch heels with thick, transparent soles gave the illusion she was levitating, not walking. Nor did she seem to have an abundance of personality, never even telling Betsy her name. The waiting room was comfortable, and Betsy noticed how tastefully it was decorated, obviously not by Patrick.

"This is the first time I've been in the Memphis office. I know more about the Little Rock office," offered Betsy, quick to camouflage the fact she knew little about either of the Wingate offices. "This office is decorated much nicer than the one in Little Rock, even though that one is larger."

"Mrs. Wingate, Mrs. Edward Wingate, that is, decorated it. She has impeccable taste." The receptionist continued to type and never looked up as she spoke. In fact, the only break she took from her keyboard was to push the oversized, plastic-framed glasses back up the crooked slope of a nose that went perfectly with the rest of her face. Her nose twitched as she pushed the spectacles up, and she snarled her upper lip, showing widely-spaced, pointy teeth, her thin face outlined by shaggy hair, giving her a look of something between a vampire and a ghoul.

"Are you the only secretary?" Betsy was not able to picture anyone buying the girl so much as a scarf from Rosanna's.

"Oh, goodness, no. I'm only the receptionist. There are two others who have the secretarial responsibilities." The girl never looked up as she answered.

"And then there's Susan, or is she one of the others you're counting?" asked Betsy.

This got a reaction from the girl, who stopped what she was doing and looked up at her. "She no longer works here, Mrs. Wingate."

"Oh? Why is that?" Betsy gave the girl a questioning look, knowing that Susan worked in the Little Rock office.

"I have no idea." The girl answered. "All I know is she was terminated." With this disclosure, the girl lowered her eyes and resumed typing.

As Betsy sat glancing at an architectural magazine, she suddenly heard loud voices coming from Eddie's office.

Betsy could tell the voices were Patrick and Eddie, and Patrick's voice was the louder. Only being able to detect a word every now and then, she did hear Patrick say, "No damn way will it continue, or else!" Another time, she heard Eddie yell, "Leave her out of this!"

In a few minutes, the door opened and Patrick came out. When he saw Betsy, the stern look on his face changed and he smiled like a husband happy to see his wife.

"Hi, hon. Been here long?" He gave her a quick peck on the cheek, took her hand, and led her into his office down the hall.

"I guess you heard us arguing, didn't you?" Before Betsy had a chance to answer, he added, "Eddie knows nothing about running a business. That was what I wanted to talk to you about, but I didn't plan on it being quite this quick. You got here earlier than I thought you would. It's not even lunchtime yet."

"It's not every day my husband asks me to visit him." Betsy knew this sounded ridiculous, but it was true. She had to be penciled into her husband's appointment book.

"And I am so looking forward to spending time with my wife again, and I might add she's looking very tantalizing at the moment." Pulling Betsy to him, Patrick kissed her with the passion she remembered from years back. Tingles moved up and down her body; she felt like a teenage prom queen. Patrick sat on the edge of his desk, keeping his arms around Betsy.

"I know we spend too much time apart, Betsy, and I want that to be different."

"Why the serious look, Patrick? You're beginning to scare me."

Patrick took Betsy's hand and led her to the sofa. "It's Eddie. His personal financial problems are not just eating him up but the company, as well. I've caught him dipping into construction accounts to pay off some of his debts, probably Lou's expensive habits. He's a partner in the company, but most of all he's my brother. I can't let him go, but if I don't watch what he does, he'll ruin us."

"And what does this have to do with me? I know nothing about your business, Patrick. That's how you've always wanted it. Remember? I'm not sure I want to start now and get in the middle of a family dispute." Betsy removed her hand from Patrick's and placed it in her lap.

"Our company, Betsy. It's your livelihood, too."

Patrick walked to the window before beginning again. "I'm going to shut down the Little Rock office and move the company to Memphis. All our work is this direction, and it looks like we'll get that big project in Nashville I've been working on. I may open up another office in Nashville, but not right now. I've got an auditor coming to straighten out the mess Eddie has us in, and then I want to know where every dime goes."

"What about Eddie?" Betsy spoke with concern. She had always been fond of her brother-in-law even though she was not fond of his wife.

"I'm sending Eddie to run the project in Nashville. He won't have access to any company funds until I get this mess straightened out. I'm sure his little wife won't be too thrilled about it." Patrick rejoined Betsy on the sofa. "I hear you're going shopping with her later today. Thought you better be forewarned."

"So you'll be moving to Memphis full time? Will you live in the condo and come home like you've been doing on those rare occasions?" Betsy stared into Patrick's eyes, hoping for a positive reply.

"I thought you could move here, Betsy. We can buy a nice house, if you don't want to live in the condo. It wouldn't be so bad." Patrick picked up his wife's hand again.

"Me? In the middle of Memphis, Tennessee? I don't think so." Betsy drew her head back, looking at her husband in disbelief. "How long have you been thinking about this?"

"For a couple of months, since I first suspected what Eddie was doing. I just got proof lately." Patrick put his arm around his wife. "I won't force you, Betsy. You've been through a lot with cancer, and you need to live where you can be most content and stress-free. But the Little Rock office will be officially closed by the end of the month. I've already started shutting it down and moving files and accounts here."

"So why was Susan Carson sent to Little Rock? Your receptionist said she was terminated. What about Midge? Does she know?"

"Midge knows. She was planning to quit anyway. She's going to work in her family's furniture store after she and Mick marry. I decided to transfer Susan to Little Rock rather than terminating her immediately. Midge needed help to close down the office."

"I'll miss Midge. She's been my only link with your—I mean our—company." Betsy folded her hands and took on a look of sadness.

Betsy told Patrick she had promised to have lunch with Lou. Patrick said he was glad, since he had made a last-minute appointment with the client for the Nashville project, but he promised to meet Betsy at the condo no later than seven. Betsy, figuring she might as well get it over with, called Lou.

Betsy dreaded lunch with Lou, especially knowing that Eddie was being kicked out of the Memphis office and sent to Nashville. She knew Lou would have much to say about it all, and expected her to be upset. To her surprise, Lou seemed as chipper as usual.

"I went to the Memphis office this morning. It's beautiful. I hear you were the talented young decorator, at least according to what's her name, the receptionist." Betsy started the conversation after they were seated.

"Oh, you mean Vivian. Isn't she just the most obnoxiously boring, butt-ugly person you ever met? What a frump! I love it. Hired her myself, you know.

29

She thinks I hung the moon because I gave her the job over all those pretty young skirts." Lou smiled, obviously proud of herself.

"How did you get to hire her? Wouldn't that have been Eddie's job?" Betsy asked as she looked at her menu.

"It would have been, if I hadn't found out about that slut Susan." Lou's voice became angry. "And don't you go playing like you didn't know about Eddie's little extramarital fun. Everyone in the office knew, and Patrick's the one who told Eddie to get rid of her."

"I don't have a clue what you're talking about, Lou. I make it a point to know as little about the company as possible, and I certainly don't know anything about what Eddie does." Betsy knew she was about to understand the circumstances surrounding the mysterious Susan. She figured Patrick didn't want to share another of his brother's weaknesses with her. Patrick had always been protective of Eddie.

Lou cocked her head. "I really do believe you didn't know, by that shocked expression on your face." Lou lit into the explanation like it was office gossip instead of a family affair.

"Well, evidently it had been going on for a while. I wondered why Eddie was working such late hours and had so many business trips all of a sudden, so I hired a private eye. Great guy. He's a little shady but really thorough. Name's McDonald, like the burger, in case you ever need one. I'll warn you, though. He's expensive." Lou held her head closer and looked around, giving Betsy the impression she was afraid someone might overhear her.

"He said I had three options: shame him, divorce

him for a big settlement, or go for collecting on his life insurance. Don't know if he was joking about the last one or not, but I wanted the cheapest. Anyway, the burger man found out about Susan about a month ago. Took pictures of them coming out of a hotel in Nashville. When I confronted Eddie, he denied it. Then I showed him the pictures, and what is it they say, 'a picture is worth a thousand words'? Unfortunately, Eddie couldn't come up with any words at all, just stammered and stuttered and promised he'd never do it again. How do you think I got the BMW?" Lou smiled and bobbled her head.

"I don't know how you can be so coy about it, Lou. That's terrible! So you got a BMW, got Susan fired, and all is right in your world?" Betsy gave her sister-in-law a disapproving stare.

"Oh, I don't think Eddie'll do it again. Besides, my mom always told me no man could be trusted forever."

"Well, I hope for your sake Eddie learned his lesson."

"There's one thing for sure—if there is any hiring to be done of office staff, I'll be the one to do it, and they will all look just like Vivian." Lou gave her arrogant smile again.

Lou did not seem to know Eddie would no longer be over the Memphis office, and her sister-in-law was thankful. She had a feeling Lou would not be too happy to hear she had lost her status in the decorating and hiring department.

When Betsy got to the condo for the second time, she immediately ran a bath. She was exhausted from making conversation with Lou, so she put off her visit with Annie. Betsy leaned back in the tub, but no sooner had she closed her eyes than the telephone rang. Betsy grabbed a towel and answered, expecting it to be Patrick.

"How could Patrick do this? How could he just run Eddie out like that? You knew and you didn't tell me!" Lou was screaming and crying into the phone.

"Yes, I knew, but I just found out this morning. I don't know anything about it, Lou. I told you I know very little about the company and don't want to know anything. I'm sorry if you're hurt, but this is between Patrick and Eddie, not you and me." Betsy paced as she tried to console Lou.

"Eddie said Patrick accused me of spending too much money. He accused Eddie of embezzling. It isn't true, Betsy. Eddie would never do anything to hurt Patrick. He only takes up for him. Patrick is no Mr. Perfect. You know he isn't, and if you don't know, then you've got your head too far up his butt to see. You'll be the one hiring a private investigator next, you'll see." The longer Lou talked, the louder she spoke.

"Lou, you're talking crazy, and I don't like what you're insinuating." Betsy realized she, too, was speaking loudly and tried to regain control. "Lou, you need to leave me out of this. Your financial problems are of no concern to me."

"My financial problems are caused by my husband spending too much time in the gambling casinos at Tunica. Tell that to your know-it-all husband." Betsy jumped as the phone was slammed down at the other end.

As she slid back into the tub, she was determined to put what Lou had said out of her mind. Just when things were going so great between her and Patrick, another accusation had to be thrown at her. She was determined not to believe it. Nothing was going to ruin this time with her husband, least of all her brother-in-law's pint-sized better half.

That night, Patrick took Betsy to a wonderful Italian restaurant called Villa Castrioti. He ordered stuffed cannelloni, and Betsy had the most scrumptious egg Parmesan she had ever eaten. Perhaps it was just because she had eaten so little in the past few weeks, but the first bite was a delight to her taste buds equaled only by the thrill later of getting to wear her expensive red negligee—that was at least a size too big—for a total of two minutes.

The passion was still kindled even though it had been two weeks since they'd made love in the cabin, and it was heightened possibly by Betsy's growing confidence in her own body and in her renewed belief that her husband still loved her.

She lay in Patrick's arms for a long time before finally dropping off to sleep. When she awoke, he was already dressed and on his way to the office.

"Betsy, I've loved having you here. Please think about what we talked about. I think it would be good for our marriage." With those words, he kissed her and left.

"Good for our marriage." To Betsy, the words implied Patrick felt there was something wrong with their marriage. Once again the nagging suspicions resurfaced in her mind.

Betsy stopped by the small post office in Norfork on her way back to the cabin. She had cut her stay short in Memphis because, as usual, Patrick had to make a trip out of town to check the building site of the new construction project. The box was full of the usual junk mail, credit card offers, and catalogs. At the back of the stack of mail, she found a letter addressed to Mrs. Patrick Wingate, with no return address. Her hands were full, so she waited until she got home to open the envelope.

At home, Betsy had a message from Midge with her usual encouragement and telling her she would be back in the office on Monday. The mysterious Susan had relayed her message. It was several minutes later when she realized she had not opened the letter. Betsy slit the envelope with the letter opener just like Patrick had taught her, rather than tearing it open, her preferred way.

Inside the envelope was one sheet of paper with items listed. Betsy's heart almost stopped when she realized the letterhead was Rosanna's Boutique. Someone had sent her a copy of an invoice showing every purchase made for the past year billed to Patrick Wingate, Wingate Constructors, at the Little Rock office. Collapsing on the sofa, she read aloud the list of purchases, her hands shaking.

" 'One red cocktail dress, seven hundred fifty-nine dollars and fifty-six cents; one black negligee, one hundred thirty-six dollars; three pairs black silk stockings, eighty-eight dollars and seventy-two cents; six pairs lace bikini panties, one hundred twenty dollars; one black cocktail dress, five hundred sixty-one dollars and thirty-two cents; one red negligee, one hundred ninety-eight dollars and eighty-nine cents. Paid in full.' Who the hell sent me this?" Her mind flew to the beautiful young Angelique.

Betsy wilted on the couch and began sobbing, out

of control until she forced herself to stop. Then she jerked up, wiped away the tears, and spoke aloud as if this was the only way she could comprehend her thoughts.

"Get your head out of Patrick's butt, Betsy! You know what you have to do, and you don't need a private investigator."

Betsy pulled out her cell phone and called the Little Rock office, leaving a message for Midge.

"Midge, this is Betsy. I'm coming to Little Rock tomorrow and wondered if you'd like to go to lunch; something low fat, low cal, no sugar, and tasteless, of course. If you are not going to be in the office, give me a call. Otherwise, I'll see you tomorrow."

Betsy lay on the sofa in a stupor, numb, unable to do anything but stare at the invoice. How could she have been so stupid? All the signs were there—the cut-downs, the lack of a sex life, Patrick's absence. But why would he all of a sudden go back to being the loving husband? It made no sense. Maybe he was the one jilted and couldn't stand being alone.

When Betsy reached the office in Little Rock the next day, there was a person she didn't know packing up the reception area.

"You must be Susan. I'm Betsy Wingate."

"I'm glad to meet you, Mrs. Wingate. I've heard so much about you. Midge is in Mr. Wingate's office packing up boxes. Just go on back. She's expecting you."

Susan was very pretty, and Betsy could see how Eddie could fall for her. She was small, but a normal small, with dark brown hair and bright blue eyes that lit up as she talked. She was much more attractive than

Eddie's teeny wife and, if first impressions could be trusted, was more personable and down-to-earth. Dressed in jeans, T-shirt, and flip-flops, the girl did not look like a secretary, but Betsy was sure it was because packing was dirty work, requiring work clothes. In the back office, Midge was dressed the same way and was leaning over a box while sitting on the floor.

"Looks like a grubby job to me. What happened to the heels and fancy dresses, Madame Office Manager?"

"Hi, Betsy. Hope you didn't plan on fine dining, 'cause I don't think they'd let me in. You look great, girl! Those pounds are really disappearing!" Midge got up from the floor and hugged Betsy. "Let's go to the Downtown Deli. They have the most fantastic grilled salmon salad sandwiches. Makes you forget you're eating diet food."

In the outer office, Susan was standing on a chair, reaching for a picture on the wall. Her T-shirt had hiked up, exposing a little bulge in her stomach.

"Susan, you know you shouldn't be doing that. Here, let me have it." Midge reached up and took the picture from Susan and ordered her down off the chair. "Don't you climb anymore or lift anything heavy until I get back."

"Yes, mother dearest," replied Susan with a smile. "You girls enjoy your lunch."

After they got outside the office, Betsy could not wait any longer. "So what do you think of Susan?"

"As in what respect, Miss Betsy? As a regular person, she's a dear, would do anything to help anyone. She's really a sad case, no family except for a sister who lives in New Zealand now. She never knew who her dad was, and her mother was killed in a car wreck when she was just a baby. Her sister raised her until she became too much for her sister to handle. She put Susan in Baptist Children's Home, where she lived until she graduated from high school. Susan put herself through secretarial school and then landed a job with Patrick's company."

"What a sad life. She seems a likable girl. Tell me if I'm wrong, but did I notice a bit of a bulge in the belly when she was reaching for that picture?"

"Yes. She's about four or five months, best I can figure it. She doesn't talk about her current personal life, and you know me, I let each to his or her own. I don't have to agree with their lifestyles, but I'm not going to judge them, either."

Betsy was very quiet and only picked at her food in the deli.

"Is your food okay, Betsy? You haven't said two words since we got here, and you're hardly eating at all. What's on your mind?"

"The food is wonderful. I was just thinking about Susan." Betsy paused. "I know about the affair, Midge." Betsy put her fork down, folded her hands together, and looked at Midge waiting for her response.

"You do?" Midge looked surprised and put her fork down to give Betsy her full attention.

Betsy nodded. "What's so bad is that I don't think Lou knows Susan is expecting. She thinks it was just another little fling for Eddie like she thinks all men have, sort of boys-will-be-boys crap."

"I see." Midge paused and shook her head in disagreement. "So she thinks it's in men's innate being to spread their semen around like mayonnaise just because they're men? Well, I'm sorry, but I don't see it that way. I don't believe in a double standard, and Mick damn well better not either or we won't be married long. I feel sorry for Susan, but if she hooked up with a married man, she probably got what she deserved. Unfortunately, the baby had no say-so in it." Midge picked up her fork again.

"Would you want to know if Mick was having an affair, Midge?" Betsy stared at Midge again, anxious to hear her answer. Midge was quick to respond this time.

"Yes, absolutely. And there would be no forgiveness. I figure marriage should be just like in Nicholas Sparks' novels. People should be like swans and mate for life." Midge hesitated a minute and then asked, "What about you, Betsy? Would you want to know?"

"It's not a case of wanting. It's a case of deserving to know. If you knew something, Midge, would you tell the wife?"

Midge did not look at Betsy; she put down her fork, wiped her mouth with her napkin, and dropped it on top of her unfinished sandwich, seeming to have lost her appetite, too. Then she raised her gaze to Betsy.

"I guess it would depend on how good a friend the woman was and also on what kind of a person she was. But then I'd be making a judgment call, that thing I try to steer clear of. That's a hard one, Betsy."

When they got back to the office, Midge sent Susan off for an extended lunch break. After she left, Midge looked at Betsy and smiled uneasily.

"I'll miss talking to you on the phone, Betsy. I feel like we've been friends even though I've seen little of you. I also respect Patrick as my boss. He's been good to me, and I've enjoyed working for him. That doesn't mean I approve of everything I've seen transpire here."

Midge hesitated for a minute, as if contemplating what she was about to say. "In the office down the hall lies every bill and every transaction Patrick Wingate has made in years. I don't have to tell you how organized the man is, saves everything. Since you are his wife, if you come in here and tell me you have a few things you'd like to get from his office, and he is not here to tell me otherwise, there is no way I would stop you. It is not my place. I'm going back into the other office and finish packing my boxes. The file cabinets are open. The copy machine is plugged in. When you finish, just put everything back as you found it, turn out the lights, and leave."

Midge walked to Betsy and hugged her. Both women's eyes became transparent. They both knew they would never see each other again.

Betsy closed the door to Patrick's office and began her search. Patrick was indeed organized and had every file labeled according to contents. In the second drawer, near the back, was a folder labeled "Personal and Confidential." The first thing she found was a lease for an apartment in Memphis she knew nothing about, and she copied it, placing the copy in an empty file folder. More invoices were in the file like the one she had received anonymously, but these went back as far as four years. There were also itineraries for trips—one to California, two to Florida—but only Patrick's name was listed, although they were always for two adults. There were rental car receipts, hotel receipts, even receipts for meals, mostly for two people, in places she never even knew Patrick had been, and there were numerous florist receipts.

When Betsy had found and copied enough evidence to give her heartache for the rest of her life, she put everything back as it was, turned the light out, and closed the door. She could hear Midge busily packing in the other office, but, true to her word, did not stop to say goodbye.

Betsy made an appointment with a lawyer before leaving Little Rock. She knew divorce was inevitable, but there was one more piece of information she needed before seeing her lawyer, and that information was in Memphis.

****

And now here she sat in front of the townhouse, her stomach coiled in a knot like a rattler waiting to attack an approaching enemy as the venom of suspicion spread through its circular track, head to heart, heart to head. Forcing herself from the security of the van, she headed to the familiar key box on the outside of the apartment door. The time had come, time to write the ending to the fairy-tale romance turned tragedy.

Betsy found herself putting in the code to the key box on the door. Once she had opened the door, she put the key back in the box and closed it.

Again the expensive hotel decor. Patrick needs to take a decorating course. The place seemed empty except for several bottles of wine chilling in the refrigerator. In the cabinet, she found an airtight container of expensive ground coffee, along with a nice set of china, service for four.

The bathroom was well equipped with an electric razor and expensive men's and women's toiletries, leaving no doubt this was a love nest. The first bedroom was downstairs and was of the hotel variety. Aside from a few of Patrick's clothes hanging in the closet, there was nothing to disclose any information Betsy needed. Betsy knew there had to be another bedroom upstairs, since it was a townhouse, and she expected it to be another hotel room like the first. Gingerly, she opened the door to a room as dark as a cave.

Flicking the light switch, she could only stare. The room's walls and ceiling were a deep, dark scarlet with the look and feel of velvet. The carpet, too, was red and had obviously cost a fortune, judging by the way she melted into it as she entered. The draperies were deep black velvet and were pulled tight so that not the least bit of light could sneak through.

The bed was white French provincial, king sized and round, like something out of a movie, and an elegant white satin spread covered it and draped long on the floor. The comforter was thick and fluffy, piled high with marshmallow satin pillows, giving the bed the illusion of a heavenly cloud floating in a dark red sexual abyss.

An expensive chandelier cast diamond prisms of light on the bed, bouncing off the dark ceiling in the middle like millions of fireflies gone berserk. Looking closer, she discovered a large circular mirror forming the base for the chandelier.

"What in the hell do you do in here, Patrick?" Betsy shouted the question. Her nerves were unraveling, and she was angry and more determined than ever to find out the identity of his companion who shared this elegant sex den.

Turning her attention to one of the closets, she found it difficult enough to see in the faintly lit but sparkly room and was grateful to see a light switch beside the closet. She flipped the switch on, opened the louvered doors, and began mentally checking off the list of purchases on the anonymous invoice from Rosanna's, including the red and black negligees. Betsy held each piece to her nose, recognizing the perfume as Patrick's favorite.

"Inventory accounted for," she said aloud, feeling more and more betrayed.

She was about to turn from the closet when she saw other items pushed to the back, hanging almost hidden, separate from the stock from Rosanna's. There were three dresses that did not look new. One was a bright flowered silk with spaghetti straps and a full skirt. The other two were cocktail dresses, one red and one black, both strapless and elegant but very different from the newer ones at the front. When Betsy smelled the dresses, it was the same perfume as the others but was far more pungent.

Betsy closed the closet door and headed for the other closet a few feet from the end of the bed. When she clicked the light switch, nothing happened. Either the bulb had burned out or it had been removed. Straining to see into the dark area, Betsy thought it was empty.

As she started to close the doors, her eyes traveled up to the shelf, where she could make out the shadow of something. Crossing to the window, Betsy pulled back the heavy curtain so she could get a better look.

The sunlight flowed dramatically into the scarlet pit, shooting a path of sunlight directly to the mysterious object on the shelf as if it intended for the betrayed intruder to find it. She felt wheezy, as if her legs would fall from under her. A video camera sat on the shelf, its lens aimed directly at the bed. On the shelf beside the camera was a collection of dated videotapes, with the earliest date two years prior.

"You sadistic, kinky bastard!"

Betsy crumpled to the floor, holding two of the tapes in her hands. As she sat there, she heard a car door just outside the townhouse. Carefully, she placed the tapes back on the shelf and walked to the window facing the front of the building. Her heart raced—Angelique was removing bags and hangers of clothes from the back seat of her car. Within seconds, Betsy could hear Angelique fumbling with the key box, blocking the only escape route. Retracing her steps to the bedroom, Betsy quietly closed the curtain before returning to the dark closet, where she crouched like a rat and watched through the louvered doors. Sure the girl would hear her heart and her breathing, Betsy swallowed hard and closed her eyes for a second, willing herself to relax.

A red glare filtered between the louvers as the light was turned on, and Betsy could only hope the girl's destination was the other closet. Her mind sighed silent relief when she saw the girl's high-heeled sandals stop there as hoped. Fumbling with bags and hangers, Angelique finished putting away whatever treasures she was adding to the sexy stash and quickly left the room, closing the door behind her.

Moments later, Betsy left the sex dungeon, forgetting to take the tapes. Her only thought was to put as much distance as possible between herself and the townhouse. Now the only thing left to do was to put the same amount of distance between her and the son-of-a-bitch she'd only thought she knew.

****

Betsy went to see the lawyer the next week and showed him everything she had.

"It's a lot of evidence, Mrs. Wingate, but it won't be quick. You and your husband have too many assets at stake. Your divorce will probably be nasty and will take several months."

"That is not good news," she told her lawyer. "I want to get this over with and get on with my life."

Betsy decided she wouldn't wait around until the divorce was final. She would sell her cabin and relocate, probably out west somewhere. At least now she could go back to teaching, the job she had loved. Betsy called her mother and told her everything. Her mother wanted to come and be there for her, but Betsy refused the offer.

"I need to do this on my own, Mom. I can handle it, and no, oddly enough, I'm not depressed. I think deep down I knew it was over a long time ago." Betsy sat on the sofa, clutched a cushion to her chest, and looked around at the log cabin she knew she would soon leave.

"I'm sorry your marriage didn't turn out to be the fairy tale, Betsy. You deserved better, as hard as you tried to make it work. But then, statistics are on the side of disaster, I'm afraid. You know what I always say, at least in my novels: Better a good divorce than a sorry marriage."

"I must have missed that one, Mom. But then I never read very many of your romances. Guess I better make sure I do, now that I know they have so much wisdom in them." Betsy forced a faint smile into the phone.

"Just know I'll be on the next plane out of here if you need me, my dear. And don't forget about the cabin in Montana. It's yours for as long as you want it."

"Mountains. Not the big hills of the Ozarks but real mountains, the Beartooths. I could handle that." After hanging up. Betsy decided it was time to let Patrick know. He answered on the first ring.

"Hi, sweetheart! I was just thinking about…"

"Patrick, I know." She interrupted him and spoke matter-of-factly, adding no explanation.

"Know what, Bets? What are you talking about?"

"I know everything. I know about your trips for two, your florist bills, your expensive couple's meals at fancy restaurants, and shopping trips to Rosanna's Boutique for cocktail dresses and negligees and black silk stockings. I know about your rented townhouse in Memphis, and I know about your little Italian beauty."

The phone had gone quiet on the other end for what seemed an eternity. Betsy refused to break the silence, determined to make her husband react.

"How did you find out?" he finally asked, as if uncovering the source of her information was the most important thing in this revelation.

"I have ways." Betsy paused before finishing. "I'm filing for divorce. My lawyer will be in touch with you. Until then, I don't want to see you or talk to you. Do you understand?"

"Betsy, I'm sorry. If you'd just give me some time and let me explain. I don't want this. Please! I love you."

"It's not about what you want anymore, Patrick. Goodbye." She hung up the phone as the tears flowed down her cheeks.

"The bastard! How can he say he loves me after what he's done?" She screamed the words as if there were someone in the cabin to hear her, and beat the pillow, letting the rage take hold for a few seconds before she calmed herself.

"It's over. Get a grip! Time for a new chapter to this sad book of life." Betsy stood, threw the pillow onto the sofa, and surveyed the room, preparing her mind for the packing that would soon consume her time and thoughts.

Patrick was served with divorce papers two weeks later. He had called continuously for the first week, but Betsy refused to answer until the end of the week, when she answered only to demand he leave her alone. Once again he told her he was sorry, he loved her, and he did not want a divorce. He begged her to only get a legal separation and take a few months to think about it.

"There is no chance for reconciliation, Patrick. I want this divorce over with as quickly as possible."

"No way! I'll block it every way I can. I don't want a divorce. I'll agree to a legal separation, but that's it. A few months, Betsy, that's all I'm asking. September first, if you haven't changed your mind, then I'll agree to anything you say. We'll half everything and I'll go away and leave you alone. You have my word on it. I'll turn over all the company books, all the assets, everything, on September first. Get your lawyer to draw up the separation papers, and I'll sign them. But you have to come to the meeting in person on September one. I want to hear it from your mouth that you don't still love me and you don't want to try again. Please, Betsy!"

"And you won't try to contact me in any way while

these magical months are taking place?"

"I promise. Your lawyer can put that in the contract, too. But promise me you will at least think seriously about our marriage."

Betsy's lawyer pointed out she had nothing to lose, especially if Patrick was going to try to block the divorce. It would probably take longer than that otherwise. Only the information on assets was needed before the date in question, her attorney said. In fact, it needed to be obtained as soon as possible, so the settlement could be ready for the deadline.

Surprisingly, Patrick agreed to this, and before the week was out, Betsy's lawyer had met with the accountants for Wingate Constructors and had begun the process of listing assets. The papers were signed and the legal separation was agreed to, and Betsy made it clear she never wanted to see Patrick again.

Chapter Two

Montana

"I was born in the summer of my thirty-fifth year."

John Denver, accompanied by Betsy with a few distorted lyrics, reverberated off the top of the Jeep as it neared the first view of the Beartooths. Betsy sang loudly to fake her good mood and eager anticipation of her new forced freedom. She was a single girl again—almost—but this time she had promised herself to stay a single girl.

The trail was much bumpier than she remembered, and she was glad she had her Jeep. Nothing but a four-wheel drive could have made it to the getaway. For now, she envisioned a life of hiking, fly fishing, reading, and looking at the mountains.

"There it is!" Betsy screamed the words as she caught her first glimpse.

The two-story cabin stood like a relic of the historic Northwest, almost hidden by aspen. It was just as she remembered it from fifteen years ago, a canvas of weathered, chinked logs with a backdrop of rugged mountain peaks—giant cupcakes, barely tipped with white frosting, having lost most of their snow in the early summer warmth.

Betsy laughed at the rustic sign hanging over the porch, her mother's official name for the little piece of heaven. "Castilleja Coccinea Prozactica." Indian paintbrush, the wildflower that was plentiful in this high valley, was nature's own Prozac for her mom.

This was her mom's favorite place in the whole world, except maybe for Alaska, and was where she had written many of her fifty or so romance novels. Betsy had only read a few of them but knew there was a whole library inside. Even though romance was not exactly what she thought of as entertainment at the moment, she knew she would enjoy being introduced to the characters of Dr. Sue Ann Parish's imagination.

Betsy unlocked the cabin door. It creaked from lack of use, adding to the wonderful, eerie ambiance of the spacious wood-scented interior. A huge stone fireplace, big enough to put a small barbecue grill in one end, stood on one side of the room. Several overstuffed chairs with ottomans and two sofas, perfect for afternoon naps, all in her favorite décor, American West, were placed so each focused on the fireplace.

But it was the painting in the place of honor above the stone fireplace that caused Betsy to become nostalgic. The painting was a portrait of her mother and her in Alaska, standing beneath a sky overwhelmed by the Northern Lights. Greens dominated the sky, and the fern green eye color of both Betsy and her mother played with the heavenly lights. They wore matching emerald velvet down parkas with white fox fur ruffs outlining their faces. Their long golden curls flowed from inside the hoods and cascaded down the fronts of their parkas.

The portrait was magnificent, a masterpiece, but it was the artist who made it so very special. Her mother and Shade Dubois had loved each other more than any couple Betsy had ever known, but Shade had lost his life saving Betsy and his teenage daughter Angel.

"I owe my life to you, Shade." Betsy spoke softly to the portrait. "And now, here I am, again seeking refuge in the cabin you left Mom, a place where you knew we could both heal after losing you. You chose to die so we would never have to be faced with that kind of danger again."

Betsy stood on the hearth so she could reach the corner of the portrait where Shade had signed his Alaskan code name, Raven.

"Help me, Raven." Her voice cracked with emotion. "It hurts so much. If your spirit is here in this wonderful old cabin, help me to get on with my life like you taught my mother to do." Betsy stepped down off the hearth and turned her attention back to the huge great room, smiling at the reflections of the people she loved. Shade had been the main father figure in her life, and she and her mother adored each other. It had always been Betsy and her mother against the world, and she knew her mom would be here for her again. Betsy glanced around and recognized the essence of Dr. Sue Ann Parish in every inch of the cabin.

A large primitive corner cabinet held an outdated twenty-inch TV, seldom used, with no cable or satellite. A few of her mother's favorite movies, including the entire Wilderness Family series and *Nell*, were stacked on the shelf and were all from the VHS era. And of course, there was Joan Wulff's fly fishing video and a series by Trout Unlimited on the great fly fishing streams of America.

In another corner of the great room stood a primitive pine harvest table similar to the one Betsy had left in the cabin in the Ozarks. She ran her fingers across the top of it and became homesick for one quick second before opening the draperies behind the table to unveil the most spectacular real-life "painting" imaginable.

"Sorry, Ozarks. You were awesome, but you just don't hold a candle to the Rockies, especially the Beartooth part." Betsy lifted her finger and counted the points of the nearest mountain as if she didn't know there were six giant rock peaks there.

"Six Rocks. That's what I'm going to call you. Six Rocks for the six miles I'm going to continue walking every day as long as God allows. Six miles so I can be good to me and nobody else."

As she looked at the mountains, she put her hands in her jeans pocket, the ones she could not button a short time ago but now hung low on her hips in bigness. The jeans left uncovered the diamond belly button ring she had gotten with Annie a few weeks before leaving for Montana.

"Friends forever belly button rings," Annie had called the jewels. "Guess we'll have to go for tattoos when you get back."

Betsy had not responded to Annie's suggestion that she was coming back. At the moment, all she wanted to do was get as far away from Patrick as possible.

Time will heal. Her mind assured her as she gazed again at Shade's painting. *Time will certainly heal.*

****

Betsy was unloading the boxes of groceries she had picked up in Red Lodge when she heard a familiar "Hello."

It was Custer, her mother's friend who watched

over the place and who, Betsy knew, had made sure the water-holding tanks were full and there was plenty of gas for the generator in case the power went off.

The cabin had electricity, but her mother had not made the effort to get a well dug. There was an abundance of rainwater this high in the mountains, and a stream nearby where water could be siphoned to fill the tanks if needed. The three faucets—the one in the kitchen and the ones in the bathroom—had complex water filtering systems so the water was potable.

"Welcome home, Little One!"

Betsy hugged Custer, who picked her up and twirled her around. Betsy thanked him for getting the cabin ready. His voice was a nostalgic pleasure—the familiar Native staccato, almost monotone but yet mesmerizing—the voice she had listened to for hours around the campfire, when she was a girl, as he told one Indian legend after another, with her never tiring of it.

"I see you have a big stack of wood ready for the old fireplace I love so much. Thank you, Custer. You're always taking care of me, just like when I was young and spent summers here with Mom."

"You're still my Little One, always will be. I promised Sue Ann I'd take good care of you. You need something, you let me know." It was a good two miles up the trail to his little one-room cabin, but Custer was the nearest neighbor—in fact, the only neighbor, until reaching the outskirts of Red Lodge from the Beartooth side.

Custer was a tall, broad-shouldered man in his mid-sixties, but he didn't look his age. He was still handsome and strong and wore the long braids of his ancestors, the Crows, but they were more gray now than black. Custer kept to himself, seldom even visiting his relatives. The only person he ever seemed to enjoy talking to was Betsy's mother. She understood Custer and his desire for solitude and accepted and admired him for staying true to his ancestral ways.

Custer was actually a half-breed, the son of a Crow woman and a white man. His father was abusive and, just to prove he was in control of his wife, had demanded that his firstborn son be named Custer rather than an Indian name. When Custer was ten, his father ran off with another Indian woman and left his mother to bring up Custer and his little brother, Thomas, on her own.

Custer trapped and when he was younger had worked for the forestry service as a firefighter and a ranger until he took early retirement so he could enjoy his chosen lifestyle with no pressures. The only time he went to town was to buy supplies or to sell his furs. His old Chevy truck was parked beside their cabin, since there was no forestry road to his place, and it looked like it belonged there, another relic of the past.

Custer helped Betsy take the groceries and her suitcases into the cabin, checked the water tanks, and then announced he'd be going.

"Remember, Little One, call me if you need anything."

"Uh, Custer, how exactly will I do that, since you live two miles away?"

"Have you forgotten?" Custer opened the door under the stairs and removed an old worn Indian drum and held it up. An impish grin crept across his face.

"Or you can call me on my cell phone." Custer took out an older but workable phone. "Reception is pretty good up here on the mountain. There's a new tower not far away. I don't use it much. Keep it charged by running my generator every now and then. My nephew bought it for me after I had a little problem with my heart last year."

"Now I've seen everything." Betsy laughed. "I didn't even know cell phones worked up here. Guess I didn't need that satellite phone I bought just before I left Arkansas. There's just no getting away from civilization, is there?"

"No, but we can minimize it as much as possible." With these words and another quick hug, Custer left but stopped to give Betsy a quick wave from the edge of the yard as he headed for the trail through the forest.

Betsy went upstairs to unpack her bags. As she went into the bathroom, she laughed.

"Inside outhouse. That's my mom!" she said aloud.

Betsy ran her finger over the half-moon on the door of the separate toilet chamber. There was no septic system for the cabin, but there was an energy-efficient stainless steel mechanical toilet that required electricity but no water. There was also an outhouse behind the cabin for emergency use, a relic left by the original owners before electricity or even a primitive system of running water.

Looking forward to this complex way of living simply, Betsy knew she could survive in comfort. After all, she and her mom had managed without running water most of the first year they'd lived in Alaska. Her mom had been principal of a school in the interior and had turned down the teacher housing in order to live in the remote village among the people.

"We need a real Alaskan experience, Betsy." Her

mom had easily convinced her daughter, and the two of them had thrived. Betsy had liked being a modern-day pioneer and told her mom she felt just like Laura Ingalls in *Little House on the Prairie* but with a lot more snow and mountains.

The first night in the Beartooths was everything Betsy expected and wanted—a cool, crisp summer night, just chilly enough for a fire. After a supper of tomato soup, bacon, and fried cornbread, way too southern for the Northwest, Betsy curled up on the sofa nearest the fireplace and gazed dreamily into the tawny, crackling glow. Too tired to concentrate, she had decided against diving into the shelves of her mother's novels, and, just as she'd planned, she fell asleep.

****

Morning sunlight filtered through breeze-shaken aspen leaves, playing fey shadows on Betsy's eyelids, waking her from her restful sleep. She stretched as she sat up, pulling the blanket around her. The leftover coals were still shining from last night's fire, and she added kindling and another big log to get it going again.

"It's definitely a coffee morning." Dragging the blanket, her cocoon still intact, she turned on the coffeemaker, a last-minute addition when she had loaded the Jeep. Breakfast would come later, after she walked her six miles. As she gazed up at Six Rocks, she felt her spirit lift and knew she had made the right decision coming here.

In the cupboard over the coffeepot, Betsy found her favorite mug, a slightly imbalanced piece of pottery her mom had bought in Red Lodge many years ago. It was cobalt blue and had been on the discounted seconds table. Her mom thrived on imperfection and said if the world were perfect, it would be much too boring and there would be nothing to write about.

As Betsy sat on the porch, huddled in her blanket and drinking the hot coffee, she noticed a doe at the edge of the woods. It stood looking at her with no inkling of fear for a few minutes and then, presumably, became bored with the scenario and ran back into the woods, waving its flag tail in goodbye. Just before the doe disappeared, a small fawn still in its camouflage spots trailed after its mother. On the other side of the yard, Betsy saw a hawk perched on a weathered hitching post, another relic of the past. The bird and Betsy stared at each other before it, too, became disenchanted and soared away, dipping its wings before disappearing over the mountain.

I could get used to this, she thought as she finally forced herself back into the cabin several minutes later to change into her walking clothes and tennis shoes.

After grabbing a bottle of water and a small pack, Betsy headed up the trail. It was still cool, and she wished she had grabbed a light jacket as she started up, but after only a few minutes of climbing, she was not only glad she had left the jacket but wished she had worn shorts instead of the warm-up pants. She would be better prepared next time.

When she reached Six Rocks, Betsy sat on a boulder to rest and drink water. Her long braid was wet with sweat, and she realized this was much, much harder than her trail at Norfork.

As she power-walked her way back down the trail, she heard voices—several voices in fact—filtering through the forest, backed by the sound of horses. Knowing trail etiquette, she climbed up on the rocks to the side of the trail to let the group by, realizing it was a guiding outfit, probably out of Red Lodge, with anglers set on catching high mountain cutthroat.

"Morning!" The lead cowboy tipped his hat to thank her for yielding trail to them. There were seven horses in all: the leader, who was probably the main guide; two novice horsemen, obviously the clients by the looks of agony on their faces as they shifted in their saddles trying to give each cheek a temporary reprieve; and a cowboy at the end who was also into hat-tipping and who led three pack horses tied together.

Betsy wondered which high mountain lake they were going to and hoped it was not Keyser Brown, the one closest to the cabin—perfect for a day trip and a good fishing spot. This was the lake she wanted to hike to, soon, and fish. She was seeking solitude, not rich fly fishing men with their wide-brimmed hats, white gloves, and stinky cigars. As her eyes followed the caravan before getting back on the trail, the lead cowboy turned and looked back at her, smiled, and tipped his hat again.

She blushed but did not know why. No way did she want him to think she was staring. Quickly turning away, she headed back down the trail without returning the smile. A fishing trip had been high on her list of things to do, but she'd wait a while before going to Keyser Brown.

****

Two days and three romance novels later, Betsy was packing her fishing gear into her daypack. This time she wore hiking boots, one of the short sports halters she wore for walking, and shorts, meaning her Abercrombie jeans that had gotten too loose around the waist and had been cut off just below her cheeks in order to continue life serving a different purpose. As she left the cabin, she put on her Winston Fly Rod cap, pulling her long braid through the opening in the back.

Betsy stopped at Six Rocks and drank water before heading up the steep trail to Keyser Brown. One thing she was looking forward to almost as much as the fishing was a small waterfall down a side trail not far from Six Rocks, where she planned to take advantage of the crystal clear water to get the best shower nature or mankind could possibly provide; much better than the cabin's slow trickle of a shower that left her wondering if she'd gotten all the shampoo out of her thick hair.

In her backpack was biodegradable shampoo, plus her bikini. Why she had brought the bikini, she didn't know; possibly in case the guiding outfit was close by. She had never seen anyone at the waterfall when she and her mom were there, but that was a long time ago. If Custer had a cell phone, Keyser Brown might be a tourist trap by now.

As she came to the path leading to the waterfall, she took off her big pack and dug out the small bag that held her toiletries and bikini. This would be all she would carry on the narrow, steep trail.

She rounded a curve and stopped at a dense clump of willows overlooking the waterfall.

And there he was, in her waterfall, probably one of the anglers, and he was naked. Her first instinct was to turn her head, but her natural instinct took control and she watched. His back was turned to her, and he had his hands and face lifted up as if shouting praise to the waterfall deity.

But it was not his praising that caught her attention. He looked like a delicious carton of Neapolitan ice cream. His legs were bright red from the lower thighs down, showing huge muscles in the back of the sunburned calves. From the waist up, he was varying shades of brown, milk chocolate from waist to upper arms and rich, dark semi-sweet from the bulges in his forearms to his up-stretched fingertips. But it was the vanilla that mesmerized her. It was more than the "cute butt" from the movies. It was tight. Waves of muscle tissue cascaded from the trim waistline to the tops of his thighs. As he lifted his arms higher, he spread his legs apart, flexing the rich, creamy, good parts.

Leaving the scene never entered Betsy's mind, and her eyes bugged as the Neapolitan man swung his body around to where he would have seen her, had he not been entranced, looking up, still worshiping the shower god. As he propped his hands on his hips, she saw that the ice cream delicacy was complete with an oversized, long-handled scoop.

She stared, speechless, needing to run but unable to move, completely captivated by the sight of the most gorgeous male body she had ever seen. Perhaps it was the long scar, running the full length of his chest and looking a little like a lightning bolt, that added to the intrigue and hypnotized her, giving a mighty jolt to her feminine senses.

Carelessly, she took a step back, trying to force herself to turn away before he saw her, but the loose rock of the steep trail was determined not to let her go unnoticed. Her feet slipped out from under her, and she screamed as she slid out of control on her butt down the path toward him. She made a swipe at several small bushes to the side, but the path monster would not relinquish its control until she came to an abrupt halt at the base of the waterfall.

He stood looking at her from his rock perch and made no attempt to hide his body. His clothes and his towel lay beside Betsy, who did not know whether she was dying from scrapes and bruises or embarrassment.

"You okay?" The Neapolitan man left his perch and reached to help her up. There seemed to be no shame or modesty in his demeanor, only genuine concern for her well being as he gently helped her to her feet.

"I am so sorry." Betsy wiped at the dirt on her butt and legs. "I didn't expect anyone else to know about this spot. I used to shower here when I was a kid, camped at Keyser Brown, and... Ouch!" The pain from her scraped arm brought her out of her discourse and forced her to realize she was running off at the mouth in a lame attempt to keep him from noticing she'd been watching him.

"Here, let me look at that." He still made no attempt to cover himself as he took her arm to examine it. "I've got a first-aid kit in my pack." He bent to explore the pack lying at Betsy's feet and realized the awkwardness of his nakedness.

"Sorry! Would you mind handing me that towel, and I'll try to alleviate some of that red in your cheeks? Or maybe that's more injuries from your fall."

Betsy handed him the towel without looking at him as if she would never think of staring at his naked body. When she did look up, he was smiling as he wrapped the towel around his waist, enjoying the whole fiasco. She recognized the smile.

"Aren't you going to tip your hat? Oh, yeah—you don't have one on, do you?" An impish grin sneaked across her face.

Now that the cowboy was dressed, she decided it would be appropriate to introduce herself. "I'm Betsy Wingate. Thanks for doctoring my wounds. I'm really sorry about spoiling your shower."

"No problem. Name's Hawk, Hawk Larson." He paused and then cocked his head as he stared at Betsy. "Hey, you must be Little One my Uncle Custer talks about. He told me you were coming to your mother's cabin."

"Custer is your uncle? Well, that explains the dark hair and eyes. So you're part Crow, too?"

"Actually, I'm half Crow, half white, just like Unk. My father was Thomas, Unk's brother. My mom is a half and half, too, so that makes me a full-blooded half-breed, as people call us. Actually, I prefer half-blood. Makes us sound a little more exotic and not so much like a mutt." Hawk ran his fingers through his coarse black hair, still hanging damp, almost covering his eyes. On his right cheek, Betsy could see a scar—a jagged lightning bolt that seemed to be a continuance of the scar on his chest, adding a mystical quality to his handsome, rugged face.

"So you're the culprit who introduced Custer to the cell phone. Don't you go trying to civilize him! I like him just the way he is." Betsy shook her finger at Hawk.

"No, no, not possible. Unk fights civilization like it's a rabid mountain lion. I had to make him take the phone after he had his heart attack. It was my mom's idea, but Unk wouldn't take it from anybody but me.

My dad died when I was twelve, and Custer and I have been just like this ever since." He held up his crossed fingers to show how the two were bound.

"I can't believe I never met you when I used to come up here as a kid." Betsy kept her eyes on Hawk's face as she talked.

"We lived in Great Falls back then. My mom is a nurse, and we moved there with her work after Dad died. I moved back about fourteen years ago."

"Well, it was nice meeting you, Hawk. And thanks again for patching me up." Betsy brushed off the seat of her shorts again and picked up her small pack. "Maybe I'll see you again sometime." Blushing at the slip of the tongue she had just made, she quickly back-paddled. "I mean, meet you on the trail or something."

Hawk threw back his head and laughed. "Or maybe it'll be my turn, Little One." Smiling, he put on his cowboy hat, grabbed his pack, and headed up the trail. "Well, aren't you coming? I don't want you sliding back down on your backside. I'll give you a ride up to Keyser Brown before I head on up to my clients. My horse is tied in the trees at the top."

"I'll be fine, Hawk. Really. I'm not as klutzy as it appears. Besides, I came here to get a shower. And don't get any ideas! Anyway, I brought my bikini."

"Bikini, huh? Maybe I better stand guard for you. Could be bears, you know."

"Goodbye, Hawk." Betsy put her hands on her hips and scowled.

She watched until the good-looking cowboy got to the top of the trail. Just before going out of sight, he turned, smiled, and true to his image tipped his hat. She thought this would not be the last she would see of

Hawk Larson.

He looked about her age, but she really knew nothing about him other than he was Custer's nephew and he was beautiful. Perhaps she would have thought handsome, had she not seen all his perfections, but handsome was too everyday, too worldly, too Patrick. Beautiful, the adjective used most often to describe nature, fit. Hawk Larson was by far the finest specimen of nature she had ever encountered.

Anyway, it was something she needed to get out of her head. She was still married, even though legally separated, and even though she was sure Patrick was having a ball with Angelique, she had vowed never to even look at another man after the heartache Patrick had caused her. She would put Hawk out of her head and get back to life. No more sad chapters.

An hour later, Betsy had rediscovered the joys of fly fishing the high mountain lakes. The cutthroats were hitting her yellow humpies at practically every cast when she first got to the lake, but a few minutes later, they had retreated into wherever it was fish went to hide and fool anglers into thinking it was over.

Deciding it was a good time to stop and let the fish regroup, she ate her lunch and then stretched out in the meadow grass with her head on her pack, looking up as far as she could see to the top of the mountain. A mountain goat looked down at her from high up on the side, and she wished she had remembered to bring her binoculars. The sun felt wonderful on her exposed stomach as she lay with her hands behind her head, thinking how good life had become. Before she knew it, she was asleep.

****

Hawk, on the other hand, had not forgotten his binoculars, and they were focused on her. The reflection of the sun on her diamond-studded navel had attracted his attention as he made his way up the high trail to September Morn, causing him to stop and get out the binoculars and look down at the lake below to find the source of this possible distress signal.

The cowboy sat motionless in his saddle as the sparkle blinded his senses and played on every masculine urge in his body. It was as if he were hotwired, and the charges she sent through him refused to let go until he turned his horse around and headed back down the trail, trotting when possible. Only one thought was in his head, and it was not the rich clients waiting for him at September Morn.

****

When Betsy awoke, fish were rising all over the lake, and she realized another feeding frenzy had begun, so she picked up her rod and prepared herself again for the sport she loved. Betsy was casting long and straight to each spot where she saw fish rising. Having perfected the double-haul several years ago on the White River, she challenged herself with each cast to see just how far she could get the line to take the fly.

After reaching her intended target, she stripped line in, giving short jerks to attract the trout, and almost every time was rewarded with "the dance," as her mother called it. In an attempt not to touch the fish or kill it, she let each one loose at water's edge with the quick-release tool her mom had sent her last year.

She was oblivious to everything around her when casting. In this world there was only her, the line, and the distance straight ahead where the line was laid to rest so softly not one ripple from her fly could be detected. It was as if the yellow humpy had flown in and landed naturally on the calm, turquoise water.

"Amazing!"

A voice behind her startled her. Hawk stood with one foot balanced on a rock and both arms resting on his knee, smiling down at her.

"How long have you been watching me?" came the pert reaction from the lake below him.

"Long enough to know you've missed your calling. You should be teaching at one of those high-dollar casting schools like Joan Wulff's or somewhere. I've never seen a more perfect cast, and your double haul—wow!"

"Thank you, kind sir. Go ahead and say it—for a woman, right?"

"No, for any fly fisherman, or fly fisher, however you say the politically correct thing. It's beautiful. No cutthroat could deny it. You must have caught fifteen fish in the fifteen minutes I've been watching you. I've never seen anything like it, and I've been fly fishing since I was ten, and guided every summer for the past ten years."

"Fifteen minutes! Why didn't you say something?" Betsy ignored her line and stared at Hawk.

"I couldn't—wouldn't, that is. It's like I imagine how people feel who love ballet and are spellbound watching it when it's done correctly. Always heard people say fly fishing is an art, but I never understood that saying until now."

"You're embarrassing me, Hawk. Stop it. Come on down and fish with me." Betsy motioned for him to come and join her.

"I'm almost ashamed to fish with you. But since I have my rod, I'll give it a whirl." Hawk took his fly fishing rod out of his saddlebag and rigged it. Within minutes, he was standing beside Betsy on the rock.

The two looked like a scene from *A River Runs Through It* as they tried to outdistance each other in their casting and outnumber each other in their catching.

"Does your husband fly fish?" Hawk never looked up as he asked the question. Betsy was sure he already knew she was married, since Custer was his uncle.

"No, he doesn't fish at all." Hesitant to disclose too much of her personal life, Betsy became silent. Then, for some reason, she decided to continue.

"Actually, we're legally separated. The divorce should be final around September first. But no, he doesn't like anything about the outdoors. Patrick was— is a city guy."

"Oh," he replied, asking no further questions.

"What about you? Got a Joan Wulff to go home to at the end of a week of outfitting?" Betsy stared at the far bank as she asked the question.

"No. I'm afraid she was more like Joan Crawford. She left five years ago and took little Joan with her. I haven't seen my daughter Josie since the divorce. Don't even know where they are at the moment." Hawk cast again as he answered.

"That's too bad. Must be difficult not to be able to see your child." Betsy looked at Hawk but was thinking of her own despair at not having a child.

"It was at first. Tore my heart out, but when you marry a spoiled little rich girl from the East, you can bet your sweet ass her daddy's gonna see to it his little girl has everything she wants and gets rid of everything she doesn't." Hawk tipped his head back as he glanced at Betsy. "That would be me." Hawk straightened back up and looked toward the lake. "Just had to accept it and go on."

"Guess it was hard for someone used to so much to live off an outfitter's income." Betsy commented, watching her line.

"Oh, this is not my regular job. I'm a counselor at a school on the Crow Reservation. I only guide in the summer. Of course, school pay is not much better than outfitter pay. Did you think I was a full-time cowboy?" Hawk grinned.

"You certainly tip like one, Counselor." With these words, Betsy pretended to tip her cap as she returned Hawk's smile. "Back when I had a career, I was a fourth grade teacher. Haven't taught in five years, though. Patrick hated my teaching. Said he made too much money for me to work for 'minimum wage,' as he put it. Like a dummy, I listened to him. Maybe I'll teach again now. Haven't gotten to the it's-your-life-now-live-it stage yet in my thinking."

"Well, you'll make the decision right for you. You seem pretty smart, and you're definitely independent." Hawk reeled in his line and began breaking down his rod. "I better get going." He turned to leave and then stopped. "Oh, by the way, I usually hit the waterfall late afternoons, around six or seven. This morning was just a fluke."

Betsy stopped in mid-cast, carelessly letting the line flop to the water. Pulling her sunglasses to the end of her nose, she regarded him from under her cap.

"Is that an invitation, Mr. Larson?"

"Do you want it to be, Ms. Wingate?" Hawk arched his brow.

"I believe I'll take a rain check on that, Mr. Larson." Betsy pushed her sunglasses back over her eyes but didn't smile nor take her eyes off Hawk.

"Suit yourself, Ms. Wingate. You already know what you'll be missing. All I know is, you wear a belly-button ring, and everything else I've seen so far is impressive, to say the least." The corners of Hawk's mouth hinted at a smile as he got his fill looking Betsy up and down.

Betsy pulled her sunglasses back down on her nose and glared at Hawk, not believing the conversation from this man whom she hardly knew.

"I'm joking, Betsy." Hawk leaned in, speaking in a soft voice. "Don't look like I just harassed you in the teacher's lounge. I'm not that kind of a guy. Besides, you were the one peeking, not me." The impish grin for which Hawk was becoming famous returned.

Betsy stood on the rock with her mouth open. Where had all of this come from? She would have been insulted if it had not been the truth. She had been the one watching him at the waterfall.

"I told you I was sorry about that. But I'm glad you're not serious. I don't think I'm in the mood for any man at the moment, not even one who compliments my casting. Maybe in about a million years." Betsy let her fly line dangle in the water, her casting hand resting on her hip.

"Yeah, I know how you feel. Truth is, I tend to steer clear of relationships, too. I'm not the kind of cowboy who gets right back on after being bucked off. I just walk instead. Been walking for a while now."

Hawk turned his back to Betsy as he boulder-hopped back to his horse. "Well, I'll see you around, Betsy," Hawk yelled as he mounted. "Watch out for the bears."

The strangest feeling came over Betsy as she watched Hawk head across the meadow and out of sight. This man was affecting her, and she did not know how to take it.

No way was she going to be one of those divorcees who rebounded too fast. It was much too soon to be thrown back in with a naked man, even a beautiful naked man, but somehow she knew the memories of this day would not fade without extreme effort on her part. Losing interest in fishing, she cast one more time, then packed up her fishing gear and headed home.

Chapter Three

"What in the heck do you do up there in the wilderness every day, Betsy? Don't you get bored?" The postmistress handed Betsy her mail.

"Heavens, no, Darlene. I love it. The cabin and the mountains have been a lifesaver. Mom calls it natural Prozac, and I couldn't agree with her more. Beats the heck out of moping around after Patrick. Not that I would, anyway."

Betsy always took time to visit with the postmistress. Darlene was one of her favorite people in Red Lodge, always good for a laugh. Although she was several years older than Betsy, she was one of those people eternally young, just having too much fun to grow old. Divorced a couple of times, she understood all too well where Betsy was coming from but was anything but the outdoors type. Though not a beauty by any means, the postmistress was the kind of person who would cause people to look twice just because she gave out such good vibes. Like her poofy dyed hair with the old-fashioned fly-back bangs and her overdone makeup, not to mention about fifty excess pounds, Darlene was life, the best part of it, exaggerated.

"I know just what you need. Every Saturday night there's a live band out at the Grizzly. Every available bachelor in the county'll be there. Whew! Makes me sweat just thinking about it. Either that, or I need a bigger dose of those little yellow pills. It's like a prime meat market!" Darlene picked up a cardboard document mailer and fanned herself as she talked.

Betsy frowned. "I think it's a little early for me to be meat shopping. I'm separated, not divorced—not yet anyway. Besides, the more I think about Patrick, the more I'm convinced I'll become a vegetarian."

Darlene laughed but began prodding her friend again. "Oh, come on, Betsy. It'll be fun. Come by my house and pick me up, and we'll go together. If you don't want 'em, just attract 'em to the table, and I'll take over from there." Darlene laid back her big red hair and hooted. "You got any shit-kickers? Need to get you some, if you don't. You can't go out there looking like you wandered in from New York City, you know."

How blue jeans and Tevas could be misconstrued as New York City, Betsy had no idea, but she took Darlene's word and headed downtown to see what she could find to make her blend in at the Grizzly.

"Oh, yeah! That's the pair you need." The salesgirl must have been on commission as she pushed the expensive ostrich boots on Betsy. They had a high heel that slanted—a dogging heel was what the girl called it—and Betsy could use the extra height the boots would give her.

"Oh, what the hell? If you're gonna live in Montana, you gotta have boots." Betsy wrote out the check without giving it a second thought and then asked the salesgirl about the best place to buy jeans. Since her now-too-baggy Abercrombies had taken on a different life as cutoffs, she needed new jeans, and they had to be much longer than she was accustomed to in order to scrunch just right before falling to the floor over her dogging-heeled, exotic boots.

The shop the salesgirl suggested turned out to be perfect, and Betsy left with two new pairs of size-six low-cut jeans, plus two sleeveless spandex shirts that hit her about an inch above the waist—just enough to be daring but not cheap. After all, she was Betsy Wingate, not a teenage celebrity, even though she was proud to flaunt her firm, athletic body. Betsy smiled as she looked at her new image, quite different from the size twelve her soon-to-be ex-husband had been so critical of just a few months ago.

The shirt fit snugly and showed off what she felt was her best feature, her breasts—not too big and not too small, but definitely adding to her feminine qualities. Just before leaving, she threw in a short faded blue-jean jacket she could wear with the sleeves rolled up, something to cover up with if she lost her nerve.

****

It seemed late to Betsy when the two headed to the Grizzly that Saturday night, but Darlene assured her timing was extremely important when making an entrance. Everyone who was anyone had to already be there. It had been a long time—say, college—since Betsy had been to a country western club, and she didn't know if she could remember how to dance to this kind of music if anyone did ask her.

"Redneck Woman" cut through the smoke and noise infestation as the two entered the Grizzly. The place was packed, looking like a feedlot in an early morning fog, and every bull wore a cowboy hat. Darlene led the way to her usual table, close to where the band was set up.

The band was a combination of old hippies,

cowboys, one female singer who looked like a skinny version of Darlene, and one young longhair, probably a child prodigy from the head-banger era, but somehow they were able to pull it off. The music was contagious, and before she could imagine it possible, Betsy was boot tapping and singing along with the crowd.

Darlene's friends were just like her and made Betsy feel like she'd been part of the scene for as long as they had. The group was every age that Darlene acted: some in their late twenties; some in their thirties; a couple in their forties; and one big, burly, fifty-something, long-bearded motorcycle guy with a bandana do-rag covering his shiny head, wearing enough leather to cover the outside of a family-sized teepee on the Crow Reservation. It was obvious Darlene had her eyes on Mack, even though he looked too big to line dance.

As much as Betsy was enjoying the night, she caught herself constantly looking around the room for Hawk. The club was packed, and the flock of cowboy hats bobbing in an ocean of smoke kept her from being sure he wasn't already there, perhaps camouflaged like a hidden object in one of those I Spy kids' books.

While the band took a break, Darlene began pointing out future prospects to Betsy.

"Check out the bar. Red shirt, black hat—that's Hayward Holmes. Believe it or not, he's a banker. Divorced. Good for a loan if you need one, but be wary of the collateral he wants. I don't think it'll be part of the paperwork."

"Too bad I didn't bring my notebook, but I'll just file it away in my built-in system. Hayward, negative, got it. Go on." Making a checking action to her head,

Betsy was enjoying playing along with Darlene as if she were really interested in the best Red Lodge had to offer.

"Second from the end, next to the band. That's Homer Ragon. His daddy's a big rancher and he's the only child, never been married, forty-something, not bad-looking, but questionable sexual preferences. Okay, move on down, right in the middle, black T-shirt, looks like he needs a shave. That's Buzz Littleton."

"Buzz? Sounds like a comic strip character." Betsy laughed as she gave the cowboy at the bar the once-over just to appease Darlene.

"That 'bout sums up Buzz. Good-looking guy in a rough kind of way. Probably the second-best-looking guy around Red Lodge, if you look past the scruff. He's the best dancer in the county and even teaches line dancing on the side."

"On the side of what?" Betsy scowled as she asked the question.

"On the side of drinking, which he does way too much of. Got cheated out of his wife by a pretty boy from Seattle, and let himself go. He's got a degree in business but has a hard time holding a job because of his main pastime. The women love to dance with Buzz, but he doesn't dance much. Just sits there guzzling. He's always passed out by closing time, and somebody takes him home to Mama."

"The rest of the guys at the bar are bums; especially the loud, obnoxious ones on the end with the guts that look like beer kegs."

As if on cue, one of the drinkers in question held his beer up, spilling it on everybody within ten feet of him while yelling "Yee-Haw!" He then moved close behind a young server in a short denim skirt and halter top, hunching at her every step as he sang, "Save a Horse, Ride a Cowboy" off-key. Obnoxious was an understatement. Betsy was sure this was the closest the guy ever got to real sex.

"See what I mean?" Darlene shook her head in disgust. "That's one of the Doobie twins; Ned or Ted, can't tell them apart. They're identical morons. Call themselves the Doobie brothers. Before the night's over, they'll be in at least one fight, guaranteed."

As Darlene continued with the identification and weeding-out process, Betsy became distracted as a familiar hat floated into the dance hall, conjuring up images of vanilla ice cream over tight muscles. He had on a white, long-sleeved button-down collared shirt, more Polo than Wrangler, and it served the dark, handsome god well.

His Wranglers, molded to his trim physique, fit him "real good," as Darlene would say, with heavily-starched creases that glistened under the club lights and ran the full length of his muscular legs from boots to pockets like track lights to heaven. Like the jeans of all true cowboys, they hung long over his boots, dragging the floor, accentuating the walk as only he could walk it.

But it was not the outward covering that mesmerized Betsy. She seemed to have x-ray vision, seeing three delicious flavors. Afraid Darlene could read her thoughts, she looked away.

"Okay! This is it! Here comes the prize!" Darlene rubbed her hands together in excitement. "Hawk Larson, the most sinfully good-looking man in at least three counties."

"Who does he belong to?" Betsy asked as she watched Hawk.

"Anybody he wants, honey! Anybody he wants, from eighteen to sixty, if you throw in that woman on the Bowflex commercial. He doesn't walk; he floats like he's on a cloud. Smoother than baby shit. Damnedest thing I've ever seen." Darlene shook her head as she continued to stare at Hawk and went on, "He's a counselor on the Crow Reservation when he's not outfitting, and I heard he had to request to be moved from high school to junior high 'cause those high school girls had nothing but problems requiring major counseling all the time he was there. Poor guy never even made it to the teacher's lounge, he was so busy."

"No steady girlfriend?" Betsy asked, trying not to appear too interested.

"Well, he hangs out with Amanda Saulsberry. Her daddy's a big rancher, and she's a barrel-racing champion. Movie-star good-looking girl, divorced, late twenties. Scuttlebutt is the only reason she got Hawk was 'cause she was the only woman around who didn't throw herself at him. If Hawk's here, you can bet Amanda's not far away." Darlene turned her attention away from Hawk as she took a sip of her beer.

For some unexplainable reason, Betsy felt ill. Her stomach churned, and she wondered if the one beer she had drunk was tainted. Excusing herself, she headed for the ladies' room. There was a line inside, but the ladies were taking advantage of the lack of noise to catch up on news.

One tall, stunning girl was leaning by the sinks in deep conversation. The only thing that kept her from being perfect, in the goddess sense of the word, was the cigarette she took a puff from before crushing it out in the sink. She wore her hair in a French braid like Betsy's, but it was dark brown. Her tall, high-heeled boots came to about mid-calf, exposing several inches of long, perfect legs, ending in a short leather skirt that hung low on her hips. Her flat stomach was exposed under a low-cut leather vest worn as a top. Betsy was relieved to see she did not wear a belly-button ring. A single strand of turquoise stones worn choker-style adorned her slender neck, setting off turquoise blue eyes.

"So when's Hawk popping the question, Amanda?" One of the loungers asked the question as she mimicked Amanda's actions by crushing out her cigarette in the sink.

"Don't know, but I think he'll come around. No big deal. Either he will or he won't. Just so he's with me, with or without the piece of paper." Amanda walked toward the door, dismissing the question as unimportant.

Betsy looked down at her jeans and boots and suddenly felt like a frump. It sounded like Hawk was ready to "get back on the horse," or maybe he already had and lied about it that day he fished with her at Keyser Brown.

Oh, well. At least I don't have to worry about Hawk Larson anymore.

If this thought should have made her life easier, it was not working. All of a sudden, all she wanted to do was put the Grizzly in the dust, but she couldn't leave until Darlene was ready.

When Betsy got back to the table, the band was playing again, and she was glad. Darlene was pretty perceptive and would prod her for the reason for the sudden mood change if it was obvious Betsy was not having a good time.

Just as Betsy was moving her chair farther into the shadows, BJ, one of Darlene's better-looking friends, asked her to dance. It was a two-step, something she still remembered how to do. Not wanting to hurt his feelings, Betsy followed him to the dance floor.

She tried not to look around while they were dancing, afraid of seeing Hawk with the movie-star Amanda, whom she suddenly hated, but BJ was a mover and proceeded to two-step his way full-circle around the dance floor. And there they were. Hawk was holding the young woman tight, looking like he belonged with her as she smiled at him almost eye-to-eye in his embrace, when he glanced over and saw Betsy.

Purposely, he danced over next to her, turning his partner where she could not see. Touching his hat slightly to indicate a tip, he smiled, looking like he ought to say, "Morning," although it was closer to midnight. Betsy smiled back, then turned to BJ and began talking as if she could care less that Hawk Larson was in the same state, much less the same room. As BJ led her back to the group, Betsy would not look back, and vowed not to make eye contact with Hawk again that night.

A few minutes later, as BJ was teaching her to do the electric slide, she saw Hawk sitting at the bar talking to Buzz and wondered what they had in common. Perhaps Buzz had once floated on a cloud too, until he got drunk and fell off. Amanda was sitting at a table near the band with a group of friends but kept her eye on Hawk, waiting for him to return. Hawk eventually went back to her, carrying two drinks, and sat beside his date, who cuddled up to him and put her hand on his knee.

The nauseous feeling came over Betsy again, and she was beginning to think her divorce had caused her to regress into her teens. This man was nothing to her. So what if she had seen him naked? Yeah, right!

"Something wrong, Betsy? You don't look too good." Just as she'd been afraid, Darlene noticed her somberness as she begged off dancing with BJ to "cool off a minute."

"No, nothing's wrong. I think the smoke might be getting to me a little. I'll be okay." BJ, who had happily taken over the role of escort to Betsy, took this as his cue and immediately got up to get her another drink.

"Just bottled water this time, BJ. I'm driving."

Darlene stood. "I'm going outside for a minute with Mack. You want to come with us and get some fresh air?"

"No, I'll be fine. Go ahead. Take a ride on the Harley. You don't have to babysit me."

While Betsy waited for BJ to return with her drink, she made sure she looked in any direction that didn't have Hawk Larson in it. It had really gotten warm, with all the bodies and smoke, not to mention trying to keep up with BJ, so Betsy took off her blue-jean jacket. If she came again, she'd dress a little differently, maybe get her one of those short skirts that seemed to be so popular at the Grizz'.

A few minutes later, BJ returned with drinks. As she turned to take her drink, she felt a tap on her shoulder. Wheeling around in her chair, expecting it to be Darlene returning and ready to point out another prospective loser for September, she almost spilled her drink as she stared into the dark face and eyes of Hawk Larson.

"Dance with me, Betsy?"

"Won't your girlfriend get mad?" Betsy asked, trying not to appear nervous with Hawk's close proximity.

"I don't know. Why don't we do it and find out?"

He didn't give her time to answer as he pulled her up, not letting go of her hand, holding it tight against his back as he led her to the dance floor. It was a spunky two-step, and Hawk had to lean down to hold her close enough to guide her around the floor for the fast-paced number.

As they made their second round, Betsy noticed Amanda being twirled around the dance floor by Buzz, reminding her of a music box her mother gave her one Christmas, with a Barbie-like dancer on top who spun until the winder ran out of wind. Surprisingly, Amanda seemed to be enjoying herself and not noticing her date was dancing with another woman. Betsy hoped the winder stayed wound a while longer.

"When did you come out of the high country?" Betsy felt awkward trying to make conversation.

"This morning. But I have two more clients to take up tomorrow. When are you going up again?"

"I'm planning to go up to First Rock on Monday and stay a couple of days. It's been fifteen years since I fished there with my mom and Custer, but I'm sure I can still find it. I guess the trail is pretty good, isn't it?"

"Pretty good, if you know your way, but you need to be careful. If you'll wait, I'll take you up sometime.

If you want me to, I mean."

Betsy looked questioningly up at Hawk. "Do you think you'd ever have the time with all your clients and Amanda?"

"Does that mean you'd consider letting me take you, or are you asking me how serious I am about Amanda?"

"Look, Hawk. It's none of my business what you do or who you do it with. I don't care." The music had stopped, and Betsy turned to go back to the table, but Hawk caught her hand and turned her back around as a slow song played.

"Then you won't care if I dance with you again." He accentuated the word "care" as he pulled her to him. This time, he held her tight, almost cutting off her breath as he put his cheek to hers.

"Hawk, I…"

"Don't talk, Betsy. Let the music talk."

It was a love song and, for once, Betsy did as she was told. It was more than a dance. Hawk nuzzled and kissed her ear, sending her body into shock. After one exceptionally long and suggestive kiss in which she thought she was about to feel his tongue in her ear, she shivered, causing him to envelop her in his arms even tighter. If she could have seen his face, she would have recognized the smile.

When the song ended, Hawk walked her back to her table, still holding her hand, not giving so much as a glance around for his date.

"Thank you, Betsy." He held tight to her hand as they stared at each other. Betsy let go first, but he held her gaze for a few seconds longer as if there was more he wanted to say or do. Finally, he turned and headed back to his own table, back to Amanda.

"What?" Betsy answered Darlene's questioning stare with one word and smiled.

"You've been holding out on me. You let me go on and on about Hawk Larson and never even told me you knew him. Now, come clean."

"No big deal, Darlene. I've run into him a couple of times on the trail is all."

"I know that look—yours and his—and I watched the two of you dance. Thought you were wearing the same pair of Wranglers there for a minute. This is no coincidence. I can sense these things, especially when they're that obvious."

"I'm sure Hawk Larson dances with all the women like that. You're such a romantic, Darlene, but you're calling it wrong this time. Where's Mack?" This subject was getting uncomfortable, and Betsy knew how to redirect Darlene's attention.

"Oh, yeah, Mack. That's what I came to tell you. He wants to take me home on his Harley. Is it okay with you if I ride on back with him?"

"Sure! Go ahead." Betsy gave her hand a dismissive gesture. "Let your hair blow in the wind. And, Darlene, thanks for inviting me tonight. I needed this kind of fun back in my life."

Betsy decided she'd make a departure in a little while, too, but would dance a few more rounds with BJ first, since he had catered to her all night. BJ was likable and handsome in a blonde, boyish, opposite-of-Hawk kind of way. He told her he had come to Red Lodge to work for the forestry service one summer as a college student and never left. After dropping out of college, he got his pilot's license and had been a helicopter pilot for the forestry service ever since.

Betsy had enjoyed dancing with him and talking to him, but she hoped he wasn't getting the wrong idea. BJ was getting uncomfortably cozy on the slow songs, seeming to try to imitate what he'd seen Hawk do when he danced with her. As they danced another slow song, she tried to ignore the eyes she could feel watching her. It was the cunning, hot gaze of the Hawk stalking his prey. BJ had noticed it, too, and was quick to let Betsy know.

"You and Hawk got something going on, Betsy? Maybe I better leave you alone. Hawk's got a temper like a grizzly. He may be with Amanda Saulsberry, but he's been watching every move you and I both make ever since he got here, and he's drinking again—a lot—something I haven't seen him do in years."

"No, BJ, I can assure you I have nothing going on with Hawk Larson. I barely know him. You're just imagining it. And don't you dare leave me. I'm just beginning to catch on to these dance steps. You promised to teach me to boot-scoot. Remember?"

"I'm at your beck and call, ma'am. Be here as long as you are." BJ smiled his approval and took her hand. Betsy hoped she had not given him false hope.

After BJ mentioned Hawk's drinking, Betsy began discreetly watching as he ordered beer after beer. Amanda had begun table-hopping and seemed not to be paying much attention to her boyfriend, whose mind appeared to be somewhere else.

Finally, realizing she had stayed later than she intended, Betsy told BJ and the gang she was leaving and thanked them for showing her such a good time.

"One more dance, Betsy, before you go? BJ's been

hogging you all night." This time it was Rodney. He was a nice-looking cowboy but not as good-looking as BJ. His date had left earlier, leaving him without a dance partner.

As the two danced near the bar, Rodney noticed one of the Doobie brothers eyeing Betsy, and within minutes, he began howling and following her around the dance floor. His dancing partner was a fifth of whiskey, and it looked as if he had drunk her pleasure to the bottom as he staggered, hooting.

"I want some uh that, honey!" Seeing he was right behind her doing his vulgar dance, Betsy's face registered "fury." No matter how fast Rodney tried to dance her away from him, the Doobie stayed only a couple of feet behind.

Finally, it was more than she was willing to take and she stopped, turned to face the drunk Doobie with a look like she wanted to kill, and put her hands on her hips. Her plan was to slap him when he came closer, and she knew he would.

Rodney stood behind her, looking at his dance partner, not knowing whether to go between her and the big Doobie or to run for help. Those dancing close by stopped to watch, having the feeling that Ned or Ted had messed with the wrong woman this time, even if she was less than half his size.

"That's right, baby! I knew you wanted some of Old Doob." He put his hands under his beer keg and began undoing his belt, all the while holding tight to his whiskey bottle.

Hawk shot like an arrow from the shadows before anyone even knew he was there and tackled the hustler, crashing into tables and overturning them as he hurled the man away from the dance floor and Betsy. Hawk had turned into a madman as he pulled the drunk moron to his feet and began punching him again and again, knocking him backwards until he was wedged against the bar.

Picking the big cowboy up, he threw him over his shoulder like a fifty-pound bag of horse feed and hurled him over the bar, sending glasses and bottles crashing to the floor. Placing one hand on the bar, Hawk leaped over, hitting the semi-conscious man repeatedly as if some uncontrollable force prevented him from stopping.

He beat the Doobie bloody until Jake, his outfitting partner, and some of the other cowboys pulled him off. It took several of them to prevent him from further pulverizing the downed drunk, and they continued to hold him back when they could see he was still not over whatever insanity had overcome him.

"He's just drunk, Hawk. Don't kill the son-of-a-bitch!" Jake had been sitting at the table with Hawk and Amanda and handed him his hat while trying to talk some sense back into his friend, who seemed to still be fuming.

"What the hell's got into you, man? You know the Doob don't mean nothin' he says."

Jake put his hand on Hawk's shoulder as he tried to reason with him. Knocking the hand away, Hawk whirled around to face Jake with eyes flaming and fists tight as if his friend just might be his next victim.

Jake held up his hands and backed away. Hawk glanced around at the crowd as if asking if there were any more takers. The group quickly disbanded, and Hawk slowly headed back to the table, showing no signs of regret for his actions and without glancing toward Betsy.

Betsy was flustered and embarrassed, not knowing what to do next. This was her first barroom brawl, and she didn't know whether to thank Hawk or reprimand him for almost killing this man who obviously had no clue how obnoxious and crude he was being.

The other Doobie brother helped his bleeding twin up, cursing Hawk all the while. It was the blind leading the blind, since both were "drunker than Cooter Brown," as her granddaddy Zeke in Mississippi used to say, as they stumbled their way to the exit, with one Doobie having a harder time than the other. Betsy hoped they would be off the highway by the time she got ready to leave.

"See what I mean, Betsy?" BJ was either telling Betsy there was something between her and Hawk, or that Hawk had a temper like a grizzly. Perhaps both. Either way, she chose not to acknowledge the remark.

Sitting for a few minutes to regain her composure, she noticed Hawk at his table reshaping his hat and tucking in his shirttail. His girl sat beside him with her arms folded across her chest, looking very unhappy with her date. Hawk rested his elbows on the table and began guzzling his beer again, still looking unsettled, as if he might ignite again at any second. He appeared to offer no apology or explanation to Amanda, purposely ignoring her questioning and angry stare.

A few minutes later, she left the club looking only a little less angry than her date. After finishing his beer, Hawk ordered another and walked, slightly off balance, to the door, holding the open bottle.

After giving him time to get out of the parking lot

and hopefully off the road, Betsy excused herself from the group, saying she believed she'd had enough fun for one night.

"I'll walk you to your car."

"Thanks, BJ, but I'll be fine. Finish your drink. And thanks for taking up so much time with me, teaching me those dance steps and keeping me in drinks."

"My pleasure. Maybe we can do it again sometime."

"Maybe. We'll see."

Grabbing her jacket and holding it over her shoulder rather than putting it on, Betsy headed for the door. Fumbling for her keys in the side pocket of the small shoulder pack she carried as a purse, she did not notice him standing beside her Jeep until she was right on him.

"Hawk! I thought you'd be home by now." Betsy stopped and stared at Hawk, not sure whether to continue to her Jeep or go back inside and wait for Hawk to leave.

He said nothing, as he stood propped on one leg with the other leg behind him as he leaned against the door of his Suburban. In his left hand, he held his beer bottle by the neck while taking a long drag off a cigarette in his right hand.

"Where's your girlfriend?" Betsy tried to make small talk, feeling uneasy with the way he stared at her without saying anything.

Exhaling what little smoke he allowed to escape, like someone seriously addicted to nicotine, he took his time before answering her.

"She left. Didn't wanna ride with me." His speech

was slurred.

"Smart girl. Don't you think you better get Jake or somebody to drive you home?"

Hawk only shook his head without answering as he sucked on the cigarette again.

"I didn't know you smoked. You didn't seem the type, that day at Keyser Brown. But then, I wouldn't have pegged you to be such a hothead, either."

"You got a problem with it?" Raising his voice slightly, he glared at Betsy, causing her to feel a hint of discomfort and fear.

"Yes, as a matter of fact, I do—with smoking and drinking too much, and you should, too, Counselor." Betsy wanted Hawk to see the disappointment she felt in him even though he probably wouldn't remember the conversation the next day.

"Touché." Taking another draw just to show he was in control, he continued. "I only smoke when I drink."

"And you drink when?"

"When I smoke." Setting his beer on the fender of the Suburban, Hawk took an even harder puff on the cigarette, inhaling it like it was the last cigarette of a man on death row, before dropping it to the ground and crushing it out with his boot as if to show her it was his choice when he would acknowledge his bad behavior.

"Where's your boyfriend? He not going home with you?" There was a sharp edge to his voice that caught Betsy off guard.

"I beg your pardon?"

"Thought you swore off men. 'Maybe in about a million years,' you said. From the looks of you two dancing all lovey-doveyed up, BJ must've changed your mind."

"I just met BJ tonight!" As soon as she said it, she realized Hawk had put her on the defensive, and she didn't like it one bit. "Wait a minute—that's my tumbleweed on my prairie. No concern of yours, Hawk Larson. I don't like where this conversation is heading. You're drunk. And I'm leaving."

As Betsy turned and jerked open the Jeep door, Hawk reached around her and slammed it shut, causing her to jump and drop her pack and jacket. Trying not to appear as startled as she felt, she turned toward him, finding his face only inches from hers. The scar on his cheek seemed to tighten with his seriousness as he moved closer.

"I'm not too drunk to know what I want."

Standing silent and dazed, Betsy did not know whether to scream or stay silent for fear of setting him off again. Her thoughts raced; this could not possibly be happening. Not Hawk Larson, the man she had fantasized about since that day at the waterfall. This was some monster she did not recognize.

Putting a hand on either side of her face and anchoring his fingers tight in her hair, he pulled her to him, lifting her onto her toes so he could reach her lips while pressing her body tight against the Jeep in order to hold her in the position he desired.

"You gonna crush my head now like you did the Doobie's?" Again, she tried not to show fear and to distract him from what he was intent on doing.

"Only part of it." Hawk devoured her whole mouth, forcing hers open with his lips and tongue, his tongue dancing seductively in her mouth, searching for her own. It was not the sweet kiss from her fantasies, but even with the taste of cigarette that she detested it was electrifying, igniting mixed charges of fire and fury in Betsy as her daydream turned into a sensuous nightmare.

But rage was how she reacted as she raised her hand to slap him when he finally withdrew from her for a second, allowing her to take a breath. Hawk's reflexes seemed undaunted as he caught her right hand, holding tight to her wrist with his left.

"Don't! Don't even think about it!" His warning was harsh, his glare piercing. Realizing he was scaring her, he relaxed his grip on her wrist and lowered his voice. "Be true to yourself, Betsy. You know you want me as much as I want you."

Looking him straight in the eyes, she found her courage again. No man, not even Hawk Larson, would ever tell her again what she wanted. Neither would she allow any man to take what was hers alone to give.

"You're right, Hawk. Let's just throw down right here, maybe in the back of your rig." Betsy surprised him by moving closer as she talked, causing him to take a step backward. "You're bigger and a lot stronger. You can take me, and yes, I'm a woman. I might even enjoy it. But I'll hate you when it's over, and that will be irreversible. Is that what you want, Hawk?"

Hawk's glare seemed to soften, but he kept it fastened on hers for several seconds more without saying anything and without making a move to finish what he had started.

Letting go of her wrist, he backed up, bumping into the Suburban and overturning the beer.

In a rage, he grabbed the bottle and slung it with all the force he could muster across the parking lot, where it shattered against...a pole? a curb? Preferably not a vehicle... Giving her one more look, this one full of guilt and shame, he turned away from her, stumbled to the other side of the Suburban, and jerked the door open. In seconds, he sped away.

Tension over, Betsy picked up her pack and jacket, got into the Jeep, and buried her head in her hands on the steering wheel as she cried. Was she crying because of disappointment in Hawk Larson, or was she crying out of fear? Or perhaps she was crying with the sudden realization that all men were basically bastards, regardless of how they looked on the outside.

Lesson learned. No more dreams of Hawk Larson. She headed back to her refuge.

Chapter Four

Betsy did not go to First Rock the next week. No way would she risk an encounter with the now-formidable Hawk Larson. The sense of loss she felt after the Grizzly episode was beyond her comprehension, and she tried to put it out of her mind.

On Wednesday, she went into Red Lodge to check her mail and to buy paint, having decided to do away with the dark, drab paneling that had been placed over the log walls in the bedroom upstairs in an early attempt to keep out some of the cold air that seeped through the worn-out chinking in the old logs.

Darlene looked at her in surprise. "Thought you were going up to First Rock. Figured you and the Hawk would be doing a little stargazing, and I don't mean in the heavens."

Not wanting to tell Darlene what had transpired after she left the Grizzly, Betsy just said she hadn't been feeling well and decided not to go.

"Hmm." Darlene was beginning to act like Betsy's mother and seemed to sense there was more to the story than she was telling. "Something wrong between you two?"

"Nothing was ever really right, Darlene. I'd rather not talk about it."

"You sure don't look too chipper, Betsy. Anything I can help you with?"

"No. I'll be fine. Any mail for me?" Betsy quickly changed the subject.

"Just some junk mail. Don't need a satellite dish yet, do you?" Darlene chuckled lightly but couldn't seem to make her friend laugh this time. "I know what will cheer you up. Pioneer Days is this weekend. It's a big to-do around here. Brings in good tourist bucks. I always man the soft drink stand at the rodeo. It raises money for the schools. Why don't you help me?"

"Oh, I don't know, Darlene."

"There's an even bigger dance at the Grizzly Saturday night; three different bands playing, with no breaks. BJ's planning on being there and kind of hinted he hoped you'd come. I know he's not Hawk, but you two seemed to be having a good time the other night. He's young, just turned thirty, not that age matters, but he's a good guy."

"Not being Hawk Larson is about the best thing BJ has going for him right now. Does BJ know my divorce won't be final until September? I don't want him getting any ideas there could be anything serious between us."

"Oh, yeah. He knows. He's the respectful sort; won't push you to make it more than you want it to be," Darlene answered.

"Oh, what the heck." Betsy threw up her hands. "Yeah, I'll help you. Tell BJ I'll be at the dance expecting him to teach me some more dance steps."

The next day, Betsy found herself surrounded by yellow.

"I wanted bright, and by golly, that is just what I got." She stood back to admire the coat of paint she had applied over the primer. Just as she was about to start on the final coat, she heard a knock at the door.

"BJ, What a nice surprise! Come in."

"Hi, Betsy. Hope it's okay if I came by. Looks like you've been busy." Taking his handkerchief out of his pocket, he approached her. "Here. Let me get that spot on your cheek, and maybe that one on the tip of your nose, too." BJ began dabbing at her face, laughing. "And the one on your ear. Actually, I think you've got more yellow on you than whatever you're painting."

Moving to the mirror behind the table, Betsy looked at her reflection and laughed. "Guess painting won't be my next career choice. I'm trying to cover up some old paneling in my bedroom. I need a break. How about some coffee? I just made a fresh pot."

"I'd love some."

After pouring two mugs of coffee, Betsy sat at the table where BJ was already seated. He'd removed his cap and placed it on the chair beside him.

"What brings you out to my wilderness? Must be working, since you've got your uniform on." BJ's forestry green set off his hazel eyes and blond hair, drawing Betsy's attention to his good looks. He had one lock of hair that hung over his eye, reminding her for a split second of Patrick. With tremendous effort, she restrained herself from pushing it out of his eye.

"Actually, I was hoping you'd take a ride with me. I have to fly up and check out some timber cutting over west of Cooke City and thought you might like to come along. It's the best view of the Beartooths, and I know how you love these mountains."

"Oh, gosh! I'd love to, BJ—I've never ridden in a helicopter—but I really need to get this last coat of paint on. Maybe some other time." Betsy looked at the job ahead with her hands on her hips.

BJ began rolling up his sleeves. "Nope. No rain check. Let's finish this coffee and I'll help you. Second coats are quick. I'm not in a hurry. I'll even give you time to shower your bright yellow braid when we finish." Laughing, he pulled her braid around in front to show her. It looked like it had been dipped in the paint bucket.

While they painted, BJ entertained Betsy with stories of catching poachers and fighting forest fires. His best story was running into some "gardeners," as he called them, marijuana harvesters who had tried to infiltrate the Beartooths only to find the climate and the terrain not quite as suitable as Sequoia National Forest and some of the others overrun with the crop of choice.

While BJ finished the last wall, Betsy went downstairs to get them each an iced coffee. As she passed by the window, she looked up toward Six Rocks and noticed a familiar cowboy sitting on his horse looking down toward the cabin. Hawk sat with his hands propped on the saddle horn as if trying to decide if he wanted to continue down the trail. After a few minutes, he took off his hat and ran his fingers through his hair. Then he turned his horse and headed slowly back up the trail without looking back.

****

"This is awesome!" Betsy spoke into the headset BJ had given her when she got into the co-pilot's seat. He'd also given her instructions not to remove it during the flight unless she wanted to be deafened by the horrendous roar of the helicopter.

"I thought you'd like it. Look! There's September Morn, and down below it is Keyser Brown. I bet you know all those lakes, don't you, since they're not that far from your cabin."

"Do I ever. I've been fly fishing those lakes with my mom since I was a teenager." Seeing action at Keyser Brown, she leaned forward to get a closer look.

"It's your friend Hawk, with Jake and some fishing clients. I saw Hawk's rig and horse trailer at the trailhead. They've been up here all week." BJ watched her to gauge her reaction, and Betsy pretended not to be interested as she looked in the opposite direction.

"Look! There's that same mountain goat I saw when I was fishing up here my first week this summer. He's always in the same spot. We had a staring contest."

"Who won?" BJ asked smiling.

"He did. Put me right to sleep."

As if satisfied with her lack of interest in Hawk, BJ made a sharp turn and headed over the mountain. The Cooke City side of the mountains was new territory to Betsy, and she was in awe of the scenery.

"Look at those lakes! I bet they're full of trophy cutthroat. Some way, some day, I'm going to fish those lakes." Betsy pressed her face to her window to get a closer look.

"There's an outfitter out of Cooke City who takes clients in all summer and early fall, right up to elk season. He's a friend of mine. If you want to go some time, I'll get him to take us. I'm not that good with a fly rod, but I'm willing to learn."

Betsy smiled, making no comment. Perhaps, after September first, but that was still a ways off. But September first was not the only reason she needed to wait. Even with the episode at the Grizzly, she couldn't get Hawk Larson out of her head. She almost wished he hadn't backed off that night. It would have made it easier to hate him. The whole time she was with BJ, she was thinking about why Hawk had been sitting on the trail to her cabin.

"Thanks, BJ. That was truly an awesome experience. And thanks for helping me paint." Betsy stood by BJ's truck and put her hand on his arm propped in the open window.

"Anytime." He smiled as he backed his forestry truck out of her yard and then stopped and pulled back up to where Betsy still stood.

"See you at the Grizzly Saturday night?"

"I'll be there. Save me a dance or two." Even though she was setting herself up for another night of enjoyment with BJ, she knew she'd be watching for Hawk.

****

"This is work, Darlene. What did you get me into? I'm sweating like a ranch hand."

The concession stand was so busy neither Betsy nor Darlene had time to catch any of the rodeo. The only concession busier was the one that sold ice-cold beer, something that sounded pretty tempting even to Betsy, although her real addiction was flavored bottle water.

"I believe it's the biggest crowd I've ever seen at the rodeo, but let 'em come! It's for a good cause. Our schools need the money." Darlene turned to replenish the supply of bottled water and soda pops and then stepped up beside Betsy, whispering in her ear, "I'll take over here. You can help the cowboy at the side counter."

As Betsy turned, she stopped briefly before moving to the counter.

"Aren't you at the wrong booth? The beer is over there."

"No. I'm right where I need to be..." Hawk hesitated before finishing his answer. "Want to be. I'll have a ginger ale."

As she handed the can to him, their fingers touched, and both held a couple of seconds longer than needed to exchange a can from one hand to the other. When his eyes caught hers, she felt herself blush and turned away.

"Is Amanda riding barrels today?" She began wiping the counter to keep from looking at Hawk.

"No. She's at a rodeo in Casper this weekend." Laying a dollar on the counter, he popped the top and guzzled the cold drink before ducking and leaning in to sit sideways on the counter, in no hurry to leave.

"Saw you and Jake up at Keyser Brown Thursday. Catch any fish?" Betsy asked.

"Yeah, we caught fish."

Finishing off the drink, he tossed the empty can into the garbage. Betsy was glad he didn't crush the can like some cheap Hollywood cowboys would have done.

"But I didn't see you." Hawk finished his thought and cast his eyes at her.

She took a deep breath before answering. "I flew over the lakes—in the forestry helicopter."

"Oh! BJ, huh?" Hawk dropped his eyes for a second before resuming his search for hers.

"Yeah! My first time in a helicopter. It was pretty awesome."

"I bet!" His remark sounded sarcastic, and he kept

his eyes fastened on Betsy's. As hard as she tried, she could not pry hers away from his.

"Now the event you've all been waiting for—bull riding! Clear off the rails now, fans, or you might get splattered with cowboy juice!" The announcer was loud and obnoxious, but it worked, as people left the concession booths in droves to get to their seats and feed their death instincts.

"That's my cue. I'm working the gates for this event. See you, Betsy!" Tipping his hat, Betsy watched as the intimidating Wranglers floated into the crowd and out of sight.

"What?" Again, Betsy found herself answering Darlene's questioning stare with her own one-word reply. Darlene shook her head as she continued replenishing the drink supply.

Betsy did not see Hawk again that afternoon and was glad when Pioneer Days ended. She was also glad she was going to the Grizzly that night and secretly hoped Hawk would be there, even though the prospect of a replay of the last time was cause for concern. Anyway, Betsy had promised to be there with BJ, so Hawk was no concern of hers except maybe in her fantasies.

****

"Thank goodness I had the forethought to bring my clothes with me. Thanks, Darlene, for letting me shower and change at your place. No one, not even BJ, would dance with me as sweaty as I was after working that concession stand."

"Let me look at you." Darlene looked her friend up and down as Betsy turned. "I swear, Betsy, if you keep losing weight, you'll hardly make a greasy spot. You've got to start eating more, girl. There won't be enough left for Hawk to hold on to if you two don't hurry up and get on with this romance."

"I've told you. There's nothing between us, Darlene. Besides, I told BJ I'd be dancing with him tonight. I'm not sure Hawk will even be there. Amanda is in Casper."

"If I was a bettin' woman…" Darlene did not finish what she was thinking as she took one last glance in the mirror at herself as they headed out the door.

There had been no time for Betsy to shop this week, so she looked pretty much the same as she had the Saturday night before, only with a different, tighter and shorter shirt and no blue jean jacket. The short skirt she had planned to buy would have to wait, and she'd need a smaller size. Her size-six jeans were hanging lower than she intended, exposing more stomach and giving a clearer view of her diamond belly-button ring.

The Grizzly was just the same as the week before with the exception of even more bulls in the feedlot and more fog. Mack and BJ were saving a table by the band as the two approached. Darlene planted a big kiss on Mack to thank him for the whistle he gave as he saw her in her denim skirt that hit her just above the knees, worn with short white cowboy boots. She had pulled her red, low-cut, gathered blouse off her shoulders a bit just before making her entrance. As Betsy took her place by BJ, he surprised her by planting a little kiss on her cheek.

"What'll it be tonight, Betsy?" The server was already at the table.

"Just water with lemon. I'm so tired from working that concession stand, if I drink anything with alcohol in it, I'll just fall over on this table and go to sleep." Betsy propped her chin in her hand, elbow planted on the table.

"Whoa, now! We can't have that. You've got some dancing to do tonight. You better perk up. Bring us a large order of French fries, too. This girl needs sustenance."

As the first song played after their arrival, Mack grabbed Darlene and the couple two-stepped around the dance floor like they were normal size.

"I don't know where Darlene gets all that energy. She worked even harder than I did this afternoon."

"She's got a good bit of stored energy. There's not an ounce of fat on your body. Besides, she's in love. Old Mack puts the spark in her." BJ smiled as he watched the couple.

"Now you're making me feel ashamed. Come on, BJ, let's dance." Betsy motioned for BJ to get up.

As BJ led her around the dance floor, Betsy discreetly looked around for Hawk but did not see him. Maybe he had decided not to come since his girlfriend was out of town, or maybe he didn't want to risk a replay of last Saturday night at the Grizzly. An hour later, both theories were laid to rest as he entered, looking as luscious and sure of himself as ever.

Glancing toward the dance floor where she and BJ were boot-scootin,' Hawk made eye contact with her only briefly as she turned away to keep her dance partner from seeing her looking at the man he already felt was his rival. Hawk sat in the corner at a table occupied by Jake and his date and several of their friends, the same group as before, minus the barrel racer.

A few minutes later, BJ went to the bar to get a beer. Nervously, Betsy watched as Hawk also went to the bar and stood beside BJ and ordered a beer. If there was any conversation between the two, BJ gave no hint when he returned to the table.

Seeing Hawk with the beer on the table in front of him gave Betsy a sinking feeling. The drinking Hawk was the real one, and she knew she had to put him out of her mind once and for all. At least the Doobie brothers had not shown up this night. She was grateful for that.

Hawk danced only a few times, and it was lady's choice only that drew him to the dance floor. Several pretty girls, mostly in short skirts, threw themselves in his direction, with no hint of taking on his part. He never danced with the same girl twice, regardless of how many times she might ask him.

Probably saving himself for Amanda.

Betsy tried to keep her thoughts away from Hawk and to concentrate on BJ, but it wasn't working. Even though he kept a beer in front of him, Hawk seemed to be holding it better than he had the Saturday night before. Every time Betsy stole a glance at Hawk, his eyes were on her, but he would look away or start talking to Jake or another friend, pretending it was just a coincidence he was staring at her.

Betsy was mistaken if she thought her glances at Hawk had gone unobserved. BJ had noticed.

"Why don't you go on and ask him to dance, Betsy?"

"Who? I don't know what you're talking about," she insisted.

"Yes, you do. You've been looking at him all

night, discreetly, and I thank you for that, but you have been looking, and so has he."

"You're wrong, BJ. I told you—there's nothing between Hawk Larson and me. Even if there was, he's drinking. You saw him the other night. You even warned me about his temper. I don't want to be around him or any man when they're drunk." Betsy looked down as her mind replayed their previous encounter.

"He's not drinking, Betsy."

"Of course he is. He's had a beer in front of him all night." Betsy looked toward Hawk as she made the remark.

"The same bottle. Hawk's not drinking the beer. He's outwitting it, proving to himself he can leave it alone. It's his own self-imposed test." BJ shook his head. "You've got to admire a man for showing that kind of guts. It's the same thing he did five or so years ago."

"When his wife and daughter left?" Betsy asked.

"Yeah. You know about that, then?"

"Hawk told me. Said it ripped his heart out when his wife took Josie, his daughter, away." Betsy redirected her attention to BJ.

"Hawk started drinking when they left and didn't seem able to stop. Kept it up for months. Damn near lost his job on the reservation. Don't know what happened, but he just all of a sudden stopped. He'd come to the Grizzly every Saturday night, order a beer, and sit with it all night without touching it. At the end of the night, he'd be as sober as when he walked in, and he'd throw the full beer in the garbage on his way out the door."

"That's incredible!" Betsy looked toward Hawk

103

again.

"You might as well give him another chance, Betsy."

"But, BJ…" She put her hand on top of his.

"No buts, Betsy. I wish you were looking at me like you look at him, but you're not, and I'm just farting in the wind to think otherwise. Truth is, somehow you two must have cast at the same time and got your lines tangled. You've either got to try to get your lines free or cut them loose. It's your choice, Betsy. If you see Hawk's not what you wanted and you decide to keep fishing, I'll still be around." BJ scooted his chair back from the table.

"Now, if you'll excuse me, there's a pretty little thing who's been eyeing me from across the room all night, and I believe I'll see if she wants to dance."

BJ left the table, leaving Betsy alone to think about what he had said. She sat looking at Hawk, and, once again, he looked up at her. Not seeing BJ beside her, he did not look away this time as their gazes froze in the smoke like hoar frost on a cold Montana morning.

Slowly, she left her chair and crossed the room. He had been leaning back, but as he saw her approach, he set the chair down flat on the floor and scooted back from the table to give her room to stop beside him.

"Dance with me, Hawk?" As he looked up at her, he pushed his hat back to get the full effect of her standing over him. On the table, the beer bottle stood full, and beside it was a pack of cigarettes unopened.

"Won't your boyfriend get mad?"

"I don't know. Why don't we do it and find out?"

She took his hand, holding it close to her back as she led him to the dance floor. It was a faster song than she had hoped for, but they needed the pace to lighten the tension between them. Still, it was several seconds before either of them spoke.

"Why didn't you go to First Rock? Was it because of me?" Hawk had his eyes locked on hers.

"Partially. But I had other things I needed to do, too." There was another lull in the conversation. "When are you going back up?"

"Tomorrow. Jake and I have two clients to take to Second Rock. We'll set up base camp at September Morn and hike up. How about you?"

"I'm going up Monday to First Rock. Plan to stay two or three days. Think I can find the trail?"

"If you're careful. Guess you don't want to wait and let me take you up some time."

"I'll be fine, but thanks just the same. I guess Amanda will be back soon. Guess you'll be glad."

He stopped just before the song ended and looked down at her without letting go of her hand.

"I don't care, Betsy."

"Then you won't care if I dance with you again." She accentuated the word care as she pressed her body against his. Taking her hint, he held her tight as he put his cheek to hers.

"Betsy, I…"

"Don't talk, Hawk. Let the music talk."

It was a slow song, the same one they had danced to the week before—before the night had turned ugly and violent. It was more than just a dance, but Hawk did not nuzzle or kiss her ear. He merely held her tightly, one hand firm around her waist like he was afraid she'd run away. With his other arm a little higher, he stroked her lower back and played with her braid while rubbing his face against her ear and cheek, sending her whole body into spasms. Just as before, she shivered, demanding he envelop her in his arms even tighter. This time she smiled. The daydream was back.

"Thank you, Hawk." Walking him back to his table, she was hesitant to let go as she held tight to his hand while returning his gaze.

When she finally dropped his hand, she held his gaze a while longer, backing away slowly before turning and walking back to her table. He watched as she picked up her bag and walked out the door without looking back.

By the time he got up the nerve to follow her, the yellow Jeep was pulling out of the parking lot. Hawk smiled, then reentered to discard the hot beer and the pack of cigarettes before bidding his friends goodnight.

Chapter Five

For three days, Betsy was at First Rock but saw nothing of Hawk. Now the sun was descending toward the horizon, and she had given up on the idea he would show up at her campsite. She decided to break camp and start back down, not wanting to spend another night in the tent. If she hurried, she could make it to the cabin before dark.

As she plodded along, she thought about Patrick, something she had sworn she would not do until late August. She knew for sure what her answer would be on September first. She was definitely getting over him, and no way would she consider taking him back. Patrick was damaged goods as far as she was concerned.

Wonder if Hawk's wife would tell the same story? As Lou so practically put it, "Boys will be boys and so will men, especially married men."

Lou again, another irritating thought from the Wingate history of bad memories. As she became intent upon changing these nasty thoughts, the unforgettable Hawk Larson resurfaced in her mind.

The shower scene reentered, and Betsy was trying to decide if she would want it to happen again, if given the choice. It had been a wonderful reverie, but now, after finding out about Amanda and seeing what Hawk was like when he drank, she wasn't sure.

Before she could give her answer, she was startled back into the real world by the sound of something thrashing through the trees to her right. As she turned, she saw a moose charging straight for her. The huge cow had her ears laid back, giving her prey the impression she meant business.

Suddenly, Betsy's pack felt like it weighed two hundred pounds rather than thirty or so. From her knowledge of backpacking, she knew with her new size she would have to carry less so had packed light, weighing the pack when she finished. Still, she knew her only chance for escape was to rid her body of it.

As she unfastened the belt and chest strap, she looked around, searching for cover. Dropping the pack, she ran for the biggest spruce tree she could find, darting behind the tree just in time. The moose barreled past her, snorting and pawing. Her hopes the attack was over were crushed as the cow turned, pawed the ground, and backed her ears once again.

This time Betsy had no idea where she would run. The trail was behind her, with a high hill on one side and a deep drop-off on the other. If she ran on the trail, the moose had a clear shot at her. The cow did not give her time to think of an alternative as she charged again.

Betsy ran as fast as she could, but the moose was right behind her. Her choices now were being pawed and trampled or taking her chances with the drop-off. The drop-off won. Curling into a fetal position, she dove for the other side of the trail, having no idea what lay below her. Down she rolled like a small boulder in an avalanche until an outcropping of boulders and spindly spruce trees stopped her.

****

Betsy awoke to darkness. She was terrified and thought at first she was blind. Then she found blood on her head, and realized she had been knocked unconscious. In the time since her escape from the moose, daylight had ended and night had settled in.

"Watch out for bears," Hawk had said that day at Keyser Brown. Why didn't he warn her about moose?

Her next thought was how she was going to get back to the trail. Below her, she could hear Rock Creek with its fast-flowing white water, and she knew the rocks and trees had saved her. Did she want to risk trying to climb out in the dark and possibly falling into the formidable current? Her head hurt, and she knew there was also the chance for hypothermia, since nighttime proved much colder in the mountains. She had her tent and sleeping bag in her pack, but it was somewhere up the trail where she had first encountered the angry cow. As she sat shivering, still contemplating her options, she heard a voice calling from up the trail.

"Betsy! Betsy!" It was a frantic sound like someone who sensed she was in trouble.

"I'm down here! Hawk, I'm here!" Betsy yelled up, afraid to move.

A light shone from above and scanned the ground until it found her on the rock ledge.

"Stay still, Betsy. I'll come get you."

"Find my pack. There's a rope in it."

"I've got it. Just hang on," Hawk answered.

A few minutes later, Hawk was playing doctor again, this time with the first-aid kit from Betsy's pack.

"Does it hurt?" He wet his handkerchief from her water bottle and dabbed at the gash on her forehead.

"Only like hell, but thanks for asking. Ouch!" As

Betsy winced, she began to shake uncontrollably.

"You're freezing." Without thinking about it, Hawk pulled off his shirt and wrapped it around Betsy, leaving his scarred milk chocolate exposed to the night chill.

"Now you'll be freezing. I have warm clothes in my pack. Put your shirt back on, Hawk."

Her rescuer did not do as he was told until he had opened the pack and found her jacket. Taking out her sleeping bag, he unzipped it and wrapped it snugly around her, too.

"I need to get you out of this air. It's too dark to keep going, and besides, you could have a concussion. I'll build a campfire and put up your tent."

In a matter of minutes, the tent was up and Betsy was sitting bundled in the sleeping bag and everything else Hawk could find to cover her with as he built a fire. Over the flames he heated water for the freeze-dried soup he found in her food bag.

"Here, drink this. It'll warm you." As she drank the soup, Betsy began to think of all that had transpired and wondered how the Neapolitan man happened to show up at just this opportune time in her life.

"I think my head is clearing up, and I'm wondering—just how did you know I was in trouble, Hawk? Are you psychic?"

Hawk laughed at the idea of being a psychic. It was a while before he answered, carefully contemplating what he wanted to say.

"This is hard for me to say, to talk about. I don't want you to hate me, Betsy, or to be afraid of me. I'd never hurt you regardless of how it looked that night at the Grizzly."

"What are you saying, Hawk?" Betsy gripped the cup with both hands and took a sip without taking her eyes off Hawk.

He stoked the fire, adding another log, giving himself plenty of time to phrase his words. Then he turned to face her.

"I'm an alcoholic, Betsy, just like my dad was, and Uncle Custer, and their dad before them. I thought a recovered one, but I guess I was wrong. I hadn't had anything to drink in four and a half years until the other night. Don't know why I picked that night, of all nights, to fall off the wagon. How damn dumb can a guy be?

"All I wanted to do was impress you, and what did I do? Insult you and scare the hell out of you. I'm sorry, Betsy, so very sorry. It's a hard thing for me to admit. If I could have had one more dance with you the other night, I would have apologized then."

"Is that what you were coming to tell me Thursday? I saw you on your horse on the trail above the cabin."

"Yes. But I saw the forestry truck there and figured it was BJ. I had pretty much decided it was a lost cause anyway, after watching you two at the Grizz', so I just left. I'd checked for you at First Rock all week, kept going down every night to see if you were there, but you never showed up. I figured I knew why."

"That still doesn't explain how you found me tonight."

"I didn't screw up Saturday night, and for some reason I haven't figured out yet, you asked me to dance. I figured this time you'd be at First Rock. I planned to get there on Monday but got hung up at Second Rock with my clients. Those damned cutthroat just kept hitting, and I couldn't convince the guys to leave either day early enough for me to be able to see the trail to get to your camp.

"I figured you wouldn't stay past today and told Jake he could get the guys back to camp 'cause I had business at First Rock. He knew you were supposed to be there and knew it wouldn't do him any good to argue. It was already getting dark, but I managed to stumble my way down to the lake, only to find you had already gone.

"The stones around your campfire were still warm, so I knew you hadn't left too long before, and I was afraid you didn't leave soon enough to make it home before dark. I got halfway back to Second Rock when I got worried about you and backtracked. I found your pack on the trail and knew you were in trouble. And the rest, as they say, is history."

"I can't decide if you're bringing me good luck or bad. All I know is I'm glad you decided to check on me. Who would have thought a moose could be so ornery?"

"She had a calf she was protecting. Mothers can be testy where their babies are concerned."

Motherhood was something Betsy knew nothing about, thanks to Patrick. This was the most unforgivable part of their marriage. "The ultimate bond," was how her mother explained being a mom, a bond that transcended endless miles and gave mothers a sixth sense to know when their child was hurting.

I wonder if Mom sensed what almost happened. She thought it but didn't say anything. It had happened so many times, but no time had it been as clear there was some magical power there as the time she'd had pneumonia at college and her mom called. The first thing out of her mouth had been, "Betsy, are you sick?"

"How do you feel now? Head still hurting?" Hawk brought Betsy out of her reverie.

"Not as much. What I really want is sleep, but I know I have to wait a while in case it's a concussion."

Hawk nodded. "Probably another hour, and you should be safe. I'm keeping up with the time, so don't worry."

"You should have been a doctor instead of a counselor. I wonder if I could have survived on that ledge all night. But, just like Jessica in *The Man From Snowy River*, I was rescued by a handsome horseman—but without the horse."

Hawk smiled that irresistible smile again and, before she realized what was happening, sat beside her and put his arm around her, pulling her tight against his chest.

"Don't think about it now. You're safe. I'll take care of you, Little One."

For some reason, Betsy did feel safe. The handsome cowboy had won back her trust, something even more important than her desire for him. Without any thought of how it might be interpreted now or later, Betsy laid her head on his chest as if it was the most natural thing in the world to do. They were both still and quiet except for the times Hawk added wood to the fire. Before she could stop herself, she fell asleep.

****

Sometime later in the night, she awoke and found she was inside the tent. Her clothes were still on, but her hiking boots had been removed. Trying to turn her body, she found she could not move, nor did she want to when she realized Hawk's arm was tight around her waist, his hand relaxed under her breasts.

Sharing as much of the unzipped one-person sleeping bag as possible, his left leg was between her legs with his knee pulled up, feeling extremely suggestive against her feminine parts. No way would she awaken him, choosing instead to enjoy the feeling of Hawk Larson's body molded against hers. Closing her eyes and placing her hand over his, she smiled as he snored softly into her hair.

The next morning, she awoke to the smell of coffee and dragged her much-too-big head outside, carrying the sleeping bag with her.

"Morning," he said, and tipped his fishing cap. "How's the head?"

"I think I'll live. Got enough of that for a poor, weak damsel in distress?"

"Damsel? Maybe, come September. Weak? No chance. I saw you ready to take on one of the Doobie brothers, remember?" As he handed her a cup of coffee, Betsy began thinking back to that night at the Grizzly.

"About that night, Hawk, the first night at the Grizzly?"

As she waited for his answer, she noticed he looked down as if ashamed of his actions that night. Wondering why it was taking him so long to answer, Betsy almost wished she had not brought it up. After all, he had proved himself the next time she saw him at the Grizzly, and he had just saved her life.

Hawk looked up, his eyes meeting hers. He placed his hand gently on her cheek rubbing it with the back of his fingers.

"Your green eyes are so hypnotizing, Betsy." His

gaze dove deep, but he forced himself to look away from her as he answered her question.

"I can't take it back, Betsy. I wish I could, but I can't. It happened. I just hope you can forgive me." Again, his eyes met hers as he begged for a new chance to make things right. "Can we start over? Please."

"I forgive you." Scooting closer to him, she hit his shoulder with her own and smiled. "Besides, you're obviously not a threat. I slept with you last night and nothing happened." Then she recanted, giving him a questioning look. "Did it?"

Hawk threw back his head and laughed like he had that day when he was leaving the waterfall. Pulling her to him, he placed his chin on her head as she laid it against his chest.

"No, nothing happened. But next to staring down a full bottle of beer, it's the hardest damn thing I've ever had to do."

"Thanks, Hawk."

"For what?"

"Oh, nothing much. Just saving my life last night. And for becoming my hero."

He smiled, liking the sound of his new image in her eyes as he continued to caress her hair. As hard as it was to leave her position, Betsy knew this moment had to end, since Hawk still had clients in the high country. She got up and began searching through her pack for the freeze-dried food.

"You want teriyaki chicken or chili con carne for breakfast?"

"I believe I'll settle for one of those granola bars, if it's all right with you."

Both munched on granolas and downed another

cup of coffee as they sat side by side, watching the sun squeeze its way over aspens and spruce.

Betsy sighed. "Gosh, it's beautiful here. And to think, just a few hours ago, it was trying to kill me."

"But it didn't. There will be many more sunrises in the Beartooths for you, Little One, many more."

"Are you my own personal fortuneteller, or did you see it in one of those Crow visions like Custer told me about when I was just a kid?" Betsy grinned. "Anyway, I'll trust that to be true. Now, how about we pack up here and head out. I think there might be some city slickers who will not be tipping very generously when they find their head guide has deserted them."

"I'll carry your pack. Don't think you're in any shape to carry it. I wish I had my horse, but I'm afraid we'll both have to walk this time. Think you can make it?"

As they approached the cabin, Custer was sitting on the porch. He immediately came to meet them. "Are you all right, Little One? Do you need me to drive you to see Doc Harris?"

"How did you know?" She looked at Hawk. "Did you send your uncle a smoke signal or something, Hawk?"

"Sorry to mess with the legend, Betsy, but truth is we share minutes on a cell phone plan." Hawk held up the phone he had concealed in his pants pocket. "I carry it for emergencies just like this. I called Unk last night after you went to sleep and told him to be here to watch after you. I need to head back up to see if I can salvage any of that tip." Hawk let his eyes linger on Betsy's, and without warning, he reached down and gave her a quick kiss on the lips, then turned to Custer. "Take care of her, Unk."

****

There was no convincing Custer to leave her after his nephew left, so Betsy gave in, took two aspirins, and went upstairs to bed. She slept for hours and awoke to a smell she remembered from a long time ago— moose stew. Hurriedly, she showered and headed downstairs.

"I know that smell, and there better be biscuits to go with it, Custer." Betsy headed for the kitchen.

The two old friends ate heartily and then sat by the fireplace to drink their coffee and talk. Custer would not leave until morning, and Betsy knew there was no need to even tell him she would be all right. He had given his word to her mother and to Hawk, and Custer was not one to break it.

The Indian part of Custer told her one story after another about moose attacks and Crow legends about the moose. After a lull in the moose conversation, Betsy got up the nerve to ask what she had wanted to ask all night.

"What happened to Hawk and his wife, Custer? Was he unfaithful?"

"That's Hawk's to tell, Betsy, but I will tell you this much. My nephew is a good person, an honorable man. He would never hurt anyone intentionally, especially someone he loved. I'm sure he'll be by later in the week. Ask him what you want to know."

****

True to instinct, Betsy's mom called that night on the satellite phone.

"Mom, you know my cell phone works here. Do you know how much it costs per minute to talk on this satellite phone?"

"Well, my daughter, if you would check your cell phone, you would see it isn't working. I've been trying all day. If I hadn't gotten you pretty soon, I was going to call Custer and tell him to check on you."

"Oh, gosh. I forgot to plug my phone in to charge. Sorry, Mom. But if you want to talk to Custer, I'll shake him. He's over here on the couch, snoring like a bear in hibernation as we speak." Betsy then told her mother about the camping trip, the encounter with the moose, and how Custer's nephew had become her new best friend.

"I see," her mother said in that way that always meant her mother was seeing far more than she was hearing.

Just another motherly instinct, Betsy thought. Not wanting to continue this topic, Betsy changed the subject to the novels she had read.

"Mom, your novels are great stuff! I didn't even know I liked reading romances. I don't guess I really know my mother after all."

"I bet you think I had to call in a consultant for some of those steamy scenes, don't you, not that you didn't know what was happening when Shade and I were together and you were in the house. Well, I have a few emotions and experiences I haven't shared with you, my dear. But speaking of emotions, how are you, really?"

"I feel great. This was just what I needed, even with the moose attack. I am healthier than I've been in years, walk at least six miles every day, and look forward to each sunrise and sunset with no regrets, except maybe for not doing this sooner."

"Well, I'm glad to hear you say that, Betsy. But, honey, you're vulnerable right now, so don't rush into anything. Okay?"

"What on earth are you talking about, Mother?"

"Let's see, how can I put this? I know Hawk Larson, Betsy. I tell you what. Since you're enjoying my novels so much, let me give you a title of the one I want you to read next. It's called *The Half-Breed and the Lady*. I think you'll find it pretty entertaining."

Betsy spent the next day with shoes off, feet curled under her, on the sofa on the porch, devouring the novel. Yep, her mom had definitely met Hawk. He was the half-breed hero Cutter but without the Neapolitan body. He was also totally irresistible to every woman who came in contact with him except for the wealthy Victoria Applegate who came west seeking adventure and found Cutter.

She was smart and noticed the women who threw themselves at the handsome half-breed went unnoticed by him. Playing hard-to-get was the way to win this man, and she won him, sexually at least, through shunning, cunning, and manipulation, only to lose him in the end to the beautiful Indian girl, Soft-as-Deer. Deer became his dear, and Victoria was sent packing back to the East with her heart between her legs.

It was hard for Betsy to imagine her mother writing some of these scenes, and there was no way she, as her daughter, could read the scenes without living vicariously in them with Hawk.

Don't rush, Betsy. Besides, legally you're still married. As her subconscious preached to her, Betsy noticed the thoughts of Patrick with another woman no longer hurt as they had. Was she beginning to not care about losing her husband, or was she being sidetracked by a handsome half-blood? Only time would tell.

Chapter Six

A week had gone by since Hawk rescued Betsy, and she found herself watching for him on the trail where she walked each day and constantly looking out the cabin window for him. Regardless of how hard she tried to put him out of her mind, the unforgettable Hawk Larson kept creeping back in.

As she headed into town late the next day, she stopped at the post office as always to check her mail and talk to Darlene. This time her friend found her in a good mood.

"Well, this is a nice change. And what happened to make you happy again? Been messing around with a Hawk?"

Betsy told Darlene about the moose attack and how Hawk saved her. Darlene was enthralled with the story and said it was like something out of a movie.

"I just hope you won't be hurt by Hawk, Betsy. He's carrying some baggage."

"He told me about his drinking problem, Darlene. He might prove me wrong, but right now, I trust him completely."

"Well, it was a long time ago, but the whole town's talking about his fight the other week. Why didn't you tell me?"

"I guess I was too hurt and embarrassed. But he's okay. He passed the test last Saturday night at the

Grizzly."

"We all know about Hawk's test. Told you he was smoother than baby shit, in everything he does. You know how he got back on track all those years ago?"

"No. He didn't tell me and I didn't ask."

"Custer. That man loves Hawk better than most fathers love a son. He walked in the Grizzly one night and found Hawk on the verge of passing out like usual, grabbed him by the scruff of the neck just like he was a kid, and drug him home.

"Nobody saw either of them for weeks, but when Hawk showed up again, he was his old self; thin as a young pine tree, but sober. Had this staring contest going on with a beer bottle and continued it for months before finally being able to come and go to the Grizzly without drinking anything and without wasting a perfectly good beer. Quit smoking, too.

"The whole town admired him for it. We were all disappointed to hear he backslid the other night, especially the Doobie brothers. Now you know what you're up against."

Betsy shook her head, grinning. "I should have known Custer had something to do with setting Hawk straight."

"What about Amanda, Betsy? Is she still in the picture?"

The smile faded. "I don't know. We didn't get that far in the conversation."

As Betsy left the post office, she got the answer to Darlene's question, but it was not the answer she wanted. Spotting Hawk's Suburban outside a restaurant on Main Street, Betsy slowed down. Through the window, she could see Hawk sitting at a table with

Amanda.

Now she knew who had kept him from checking on her. There had been no interest in her on his part, and he had been fooling her all along.

Refusing to be hurt again, she decided to put an end to this pretend relationship. She'd tell him once and for all that she had no interest in him except maybe as a friend.

As she got out of the shower after her walk the next morning, she stood in front of the antique oak mirror in the bedroom and looked at herself. Patrick would not recognize her now. Even a size-six red negligee would hang off her small-but-healthy frame. But she was getting too thin and would either have to start eating more or walking less. Even her new jeans were getting baggy, and she would have to make a shopping trip to Billings soon or pull out the L.L. Bean catalog she had tucked in one of her boxes when she left.

Muffins were the answer that immediately came to her mind, wild raspberry muffins, actually. Custer had brought her several jars of canned berries.

Soon the cabin was filled with the wonderful aroma of oversized whole-wheat, raspberry muffins, and after devouring two of them with her mug of coffee, Betsy decided she would take some to Custer. Besides, it was July fourth, and she didn't want to celebrate it alone. It had been too long since she had visited her old friend at his cabin, and it was time she did something for him.

Custer's cabin stood just off the path, a few yards from the small creek that was his water source. It was just as she remembered it—a small log cabin with a low roof and a door its owner had to duck to get through.

Inside, she knew she'd feel she had stepped back fifteen years. Nothing would be changed.

Several moose racks hung on the outside of the cabin, with one especially huge one over the door. The small porch was just big enough for the couple of straight chairs Custer had made out of willow and spruce. Their patina was a brownish-gold earth tone showing the chairs had been on the same porch for many years. Just as she was about to knock on the door, she heard voices coming from behind the cabin.

"Hello! Custer!" As she stepped off the porch to make her way to the voices, Custer came around the cabin.

"Little One, you came to visit your old friend. I was just talking about you."

Behind Custer stood Hawk, cowboy hat, smile, and all. His horse was tied to a tree at the side of the cabin.

"Hello, Betsy. How's the head?"

"Just like normal. It's been a week, you know. Not that it matters. I'm perfectly capable of taking care of myself." As soon as Betsy made the remark, she wished she could take it back. It sounded like a reprimand for Hawk's not checking on her. Why did he do this to her? It was like "open mouth, insert heart," every time he came around.

"I knew Unk would check on you. I've been busy with two different sets of clients. Besides, I was going to head that way when I left here." Hawk, obviously not accustomed to being put on the defensive, did not play the role well.

Custer stood staring at the two before finally speaking. "Heard from Sue Ann lately? I keep expecting her to walk up that path. Don't seem right for her Little One to be here without her."

"Oh, she'd like to be, but I won't let her. I know she's busy writing a new novel, and besides, I like being by myself." Betsy kept her eyes on Custer and refused to look in Hawk's direction.

"Is that a hint?" Hawk cut in. "I won't stop by if you want your privacy." Propping his boot on the edge of the porch, the cowboy stared at her.

"No, not at all, Hawk. Feel free to come by for coffee any time you want. Anyone who saves my hide is a friend forever. But don't feel you have to come on my account." Betsy walked over to stand by Custer, as far away from Hawk as possible. "You don't owe me anything, Hawk. I know Amanda keeps you busy when you're not working. As a matter of fact, how is she? Did she win in Casper? Saw you with her yesterday in town." More digs. She just couldn't stop herself.

"Had a few things I needed to explain to her, Betsy. I owed it to her." He made the last statement emphatically as if he had to speak in a loud and succinct voice in order to make his point. Betsy felt disheartened, hearing Hawk admit to owing Amanda.

Custer's eyes darted between the two as if he were watching a tennis match with each player trying to see who could hit harder. Seeing his nephew's anger, he gave him a disapproving scowl and changed the subject.

"Come in, Betsy, come in. I've got something for you. Been meaning to bring it but couldn't ever remember it till I was halfway there. Must be gettin' old."

As Betsy started through the cabin door, she noticed Hawk holding back.

125

"You comin', Hawk?" she asked over her shoulder.

"No. I'm heading down. I'm free this weekend, and I'm thinking about taking my drift boat to the Big Horn. I have a client coming in a few weeks who wants to do some fishing there. It's been a while, so I need to refresh my memory on where the good runs are." He turned to his uncle. "I'll see you soon, Unk. Keep that phone charged. Betsy, maybe I'll see you around." His last statement was filled with sarcasm and irritation.

Betsy watched him get on his horse and head down the trail. No backwards glance, no hat tipping, no unforgettable smile. He just left.

Her look said it all, and Custer caught the disappointment in her.

"Hawk's a good man. Likes you. Said so. Told me what a good fly fisherman you are and said he wanted to take you out in his drift boat. Don't know why he didn't go on and ask you."

"I blew it, Custer. But he just makes me so mad! One minute I think he's interested in me, and the next minute he's with Amanda. Damn it! I've never been in a drift boat. Me and my big mouth!"

****

Custer smiled as his Little One stormed into the cabin and flopped down in a chair at the table. It was like she was that young teenager again, the one he had grown to love years ago. He sensed there was some magic between Hawk and Betsy, but he also knew the timing was not just right; there was obvious tension between the two.

"Remember this?" He held up an aged wicker creel with moose hide straps and a latch made out of a piece of a large porcupine quill.

"Your creel! It's still as beautiful as ever. I put a load of fish in that when I was a kid. Mom and I practically lived off trout when we were here. That was before catch and release, of course. Boy, does this bring back memories."

"I want you to have it. You always liked it, and I don't have any need for it. Besides, I'm downsizing."

Betsy laughed at his remark and held the creel to her chest. Custer knew she had accepted the gift proudly. Then came the hug he had joyfully anticipated.

Little One always made him reflect on his chosen lifestyle. Maybe he had been wrong not to marry and have children.

He had been in love only once, but nothing had come of it. His nephew was the son he never had, and part of the reason he had let himself become so close to Hawk was what he'd seen in Betsy and Sue Ann when they were together.

Custer sighed inwardly. It had been too long since Little One had been in the mountains. Much sadness had come her way in her other world, and he hoped she would be content and stay here.

Custer devoured two of the muffins as he and Betsy drank coffee and enjoyed each other's company.

****

Betsy couldn't help but notice how much Custer and Hawk looked alike, with the exception of the braids. Hawk's hair hung to his collar and was all one length. If he were blonde and lived in California, he'd look like a surfer.

Betsy thought of how Hawk had looked on that unforgettable day as his coarse black hair hung wet in his eyes. As she watched Custer devour the muffins, she wondered if Hawk would look like this when he was older. She hoped so. Not that she would be around to notice.

****

Custer watched his Little One as she moved out of sight on the path still clutching her treasure to her breast.

"If it's meant to be, it will be," Custer said to himself, trying to put Hawk and Betsy into proper perspective. "But it wouldn't hurt to help a little." The old friend smiled as he pulled his cell phone from the fringed moose-hide pouch.

****

The trail down to the cabin was full of natural splendor that could change even the worst of moods to a happy one, but Betsy meandered along watching her feet, oblivious to the glory of her surroundings. If only she had thought more carefully about what she wanted to say to Hawk. He was more than a friend, and she might as well admit it, and she hated the thought of him being with Amanda or any other woman. There was something about Hawk and her, something exciting, but she had killed it with her stupid "friend" remark and her jealous mention of Amanda.

With her head down, she did not notice she wasn't alone on the path until she practically ran into him. She screamed, dropped the creel and grabbed her chest as if having a heart attack.

"You scared me to death, Hawk! I thought you were miles from here."

"I was. I backtracked."

He said it loudly as if irritated she didn't already know. Standing in front of her, only inches away, the irate cowboy glared down into her face. She tried to turn away from his stare, but he grabbed her chin with his left hand and brought it back around, holding on until she repositioned her eyes to look directly into his. Dropping his hands and hooking his fingertips in his pockets, he began.

"Why are you always doing this to me?" His voice was angry and scary, like the night outside the Grizzly. "Making me turn around and retrace my steps? It's time we had a heart-to-heart, little lady, and got some things out in the open. No mealy-mouthed 'friend' shit, either."

Betsy kept her eyes locked on Hawk's, wondering where he was going with his reprimand.

"I feel something when I'm with you—something I can't let go of—and I think you feel it, too. Unk taught me to be myself, tell the truth, and don't play games with life or life'll come back and kick you in the ass. I tried to play the game when I was married, and look where that got me. And maybe that was a good thing, 'cause I'm more careful now. And now there's you."

"But Hawk…"

"Be quiet, Betsy! I'm not through. I don't give a damn about Patrick or September first, or what your life was before, and I don't give a damn about Amanda. You're here and I'm here, and this moment is what counts, nothing else. Do you understand what I'm saying?

"Now, if you don't want to be part of this, part of me, then now's your chance to get rid of me forever. Just go around me and hike on down this trail. But listen good, Little One, 'cause I ain't saying this but once. If you think there's a chance in hell there could be something wonderful to come out of all this, then get your pretty little butt up on this horse and let me take you home. And I won't leave until morning—or maybe not then. Do I make myself clear?"

"I, uh…"

"And another thing. Do you want to go with me to the Big Horn on Saturday?"

Betsy walked around Hawk like she was going on down the trail but stopped by his horse. Putting her foot in the stirrup and holding on to the horn, she swung into the saddle and then lifted herself to take her place behind where she knew the handsome horseman would sit.

"Yes," came her pert answer as she gave the same impish grin she had given him that first day at the waterfall.

He tipped his hat and smiled. Balancing himself in the stirrup with his left foot, he swung his right leg over the front of the saddle horn, taking his position in front of the woman he obviously cared for and wanted.

"Hold on, ma'am. Tight! As they say in the movies, 'we're burnin' daylight.' And we've got a detour to take before we get home." With these words, he spurred the horse into almost a run up the steep trail, causing Betsy to hold even tighter if she was to stay on behind the determined cowboy.

She could hardly contain her desire as she felt Hawk's hard stomach. Every inch of her body was aching from the closeness, and she sensed this was the shortest friendship in history. They rode in silence, and instead of turning in the direction of the cabin, the cowboy reined his horse toward Six Rocks. Not wanting to break the spell of the moment, Betsy held on and asked no questions.

"What are we doing here?" Betsy asked when they stopped, arching her eyebrows and smiling at Hawk, indicating she had an idea what was on his mind.

Swinging his leg back over the front of the saddle without dismounting, he took his hat off, placing it over his propped knee. As he turned to answer her, he took her chin in his left hand and pulled her face to his.

"This, for starters."

There was never a kiss to compare with this one between the half-blood and his woman, and she thought there could never be another one quite as wonderful. After dismounting, he reached up and took her from the horse, lifting her as if she were a child, holding her tightly to him, lowering her body slowly so he could feel her slide against the full length of his body, pausing to kiss her again as her feet dangled a few inches from the ground. With her arms tight around his neck, she melted into his embrace.

They shared the sensation of being one body on fire as the warm parts touched, and she could feel his anticipation of what was to come. He picked her up and carried her to the waterfall.

"My turn."

Gingerly, he laid her on the flat rock, where he sought her mouth, softly caressing her tongue with his own. Leaving her lips, he moved down her body to start with her hiking boots. She had never thought of shoelaces as being seductive until Hawk Larson untied them and removed her boots and socks, rubbing and kissing her feet as he moved up.

After unbuttoning her shirt and removing it, he unfastened her bra and slipped it off her body. His hands found her breasts first, but soon lips followed hands, giving equal attention until both stood firm, begging him to continue. She lay still with her eyes closed as if afraid moving might cause him to stop.

As he unzipped her shorts, her navel began to sparkle, beckoning him to hurry, for his own cravings were overpowering him. His hand stopped as he gently fingered the diamond he now claimed as his own, sending spasms of electricity below it. Moving his mouth to his new treasure, he fondled the jewel with his tongue and lips as she arched her back and moaned in what could only be the prelude to ecstasy.

She lay naked on the boulder, unashamed, and watched, propped on one elbow, as her beautiful lover undressed and exposed for her again—this time knowingly—the beauty of his exquisite stature. Leaning over her, he kissed her again even more sensually than before, his tongue searching until it found a partner and began its erotic dance in her mouth.

"You're beautiful, Betsy, just like I knew you would be from that first day here."

Running his rough cowboy hands the full length of her body, he absorbed every inch, every hidden detail, savoring the hidden wet spots he uncovered. As he moved lower, he continued kissing her in all the secret places his hands had discovered. Just as she thought she would explode with wanting him, he stood and pulled her up. Standing together, they kissed again, looking like a statue of the Greek god and goddess of love.

Picking her up, he carried her to the soft meadow grass, where he gently laid her as he once again began his stroking and kissing ritual. This time, gentleness grew to a ravenous devouring of her mouth first before moving to her breasts. She held his face to her chest, encouraging his intense attack as she moved in ravenous harmony beneath him before taking his face in her hands and redirecting his passion to her navel and below.

When neither could stand the craving for fulfillment any longer, he entered her, gently at first, blazing a passage in her small body, and then building momentum, thrusting harder at the urging of her fingernails digging into his back, driving until each lover reached the pinnacle of pleasure.

Hawk held tight as she moaned and writhed in hot, painful pleasure, compressing his body into hers, overflowing it with the liquid passion pent up for weeks. Waves of exhilaration rippled through their bodies, leaving the lovers drained and exhausted, the rapture temporarily over, the ecstasy complete.

They lay without speaking for several minutes, both trying to regain their strength. Propping on one elbow, Hawk looked down at her as she lay still with her eyes closed, one hand over her head.

"Damn! That was incredible, just like I knew it would be." Still she did not speak or open her eyes, and he become concerned.

"Are you okay, Betsy? I didn't hurt you, did I?"

Opening her eyes, she smiled up at him. Threading her fingers through his long hair, holding it out of his face, she pulled his lips to hers, casting her tongue into his mouth. Their tongues played like trout fingerlings in a wild current until she pulled back, holding his face close to hers while tracing his scar with her soft touch.

"Do I look like I'm in pain?" Her eyes twinkled. "I'll admit you did scratch my throat a little—from the back side."

He laughed, pleased with her reference to his male endowment as she continued, "Actually, I was just thinking. At this very moment, life is so awesome, I believe I could write cowboy poetry."

"Am I your first cowboy?" Picking a piece of Indian paintbrush peeking from behind a rock beside her head, Hawk ran the flower across her cheek and down between her breasts.

"First cowboy, first Indian. How lucky can a girl get to have the Lone Ranger and Tonto in one beautiful package?"

"I want to be your last cowboy and Indian."

As he moved the red petals to her belly button ring, Betsy gave her elfish grin and pushed him over on his back. Lying on top of him, she kissed him again, a quick kiss as if announcing closure to the seriousness of the moment, and then jumped to her feet, pausing to look down at her surprised lover.

"Race you to the waterfall!"

Without giving him time to respond, she ran across the rocky path as surefooted as a deer and took her position on the perch where she had first seen him naked. Gasping to catch her breath as the icy water hit her, she laughed as the tough cowboy grimaced each time he stepped on a rock as he tiptoed to the perch.

"For a cowboy, you sure are a tenderfoot." Taking the hand she held out to him, he leapt onto the rock to join her.

"That's what boots are for, darling."

Loosening her braid, Hawk wrapped her hair around his hand and pulled her to him for a long, hard kiss, and together they gave praise to the waterfall god.

Chapter Seven

After a dinner of trout almandine that Hawk cooked, Betsy sat and watched him clean up the kitchen as he insisted. When he turned away from the sink, he had a serious look on his face.

"Betsy, we need to talk about something we should have already discussed. My mother would be so pissed at me if she knew I hadn't talked to you about this before, considering we've made love already."

"What, Hawk?" Looking at him questioningly, she suddenly realized where he was going. "Oh, I think I know what you're thinking about. Protection."

"I'm sorry, sweetheart. I was so obsessed with you for so many weeks, it just wasn't a priority, but it should have been. For God's sake, Betsy, I'm a counselor! How many times have I preached it to kids?"

"Well, if you're worried about getting me pregnant, you can be at ease. Cancer took care of that five years ago."

"That's too bad. It may be a little premature, but I sense I would have loved getting you pregnant at some point. But it's the other I was thinking more about. I had a physical a couple of weeks ago and had all the extra tests to make sure, just for my own peace of mind, and maybe I was hoping something would happen between you and me after that first encounter with you at the waterfall. I've never thought much about it before, but now I know I'm clean, so don't worry." Seeing the questioning look on her face, he continued. "And no, I haven't had sex with anyone except you since the physical, so don't even go there."

"You don't have to worry either. The first thing I did after I found out about Patrick's affair, or perhaps affairs, was to have tests run. I'm clean, too."

"So I don't have to use that case of condoms my mother, the nurse, has made sure I have?"

"Not unless you're planning on sleeping around." She paused watching to gauge his reaction closely. "Are you?"

Throwing the dishcloth down, he pulled her from her chair and lifted her, placing her on the counter where he could reach her mouth as he repeated the same delicious kisses he had shared with her earlier on this lucky July fourth.

"Does that answer your question?"

"Maybe, but you might have to convince me again in a few minutes." She smiled at him and then started her questioning again. "You won't go back to Amanda? I did take you away from her, didn't I?"

Holding her to him, Hawk nuzzled her ear like he did the first time he danced with her. "How can you even think about that? No, I only want you, Betsy."

"But she is so beautiful, and the two of you looked so...so intimate and connected that first night at the Grizzly." He took her down and led her by the hand to the sofa before squatting to stoke the fire.

"Be wary of looks, Betsy. Things are not always as they seem. All I could do that night was look at you. I wanted you beside me, not Amanda. She sensed it right from the start, but somehow you didn't. You were driving me crazy, and you didn't even know it. I think that's why I drank that night. Not that I blame anyone or anything but myself. I damn near killed a Doobie in the process."

"I guess I just couldn't believe it, Hawk. Good thing Buzz asked Amanda to dance, or I certainly wouldn't have had a hint you thought anything at all about me, not even a two-step around the dance floor."

Stopping, still holding the poker, Hawk turned, half scowling at her. "Betsy, do you honestly think that was a coincidence that Buzz asked Amanda to dance?"

"Well, wasn't it?"

"Buzz drinks. He doesn't go to the Grizzly to dance. I went to the bar and gave him an offer I knew he wouldn't refuse. All he had to do was dance with my date through two songs back to back and I'd pay his tab for the night. Do you have any idea what that two-step around the dance floor cost me? Buzz is a fish!"

"Gosh! I wish I'd known. I left there feeling pretty dejected."

"And as for Amanda being beautiful? Yeah, she's a good-looking woman, but she doesn't hold a candle to you, babe. Doesn't come close." Moving to the sofa, he sat on the edge, clasping his hands together with his elbows propped on his knees, watching to gauge her reaction.

She sat still, as if in deep thought, looking at him. Then she stood, knocked his hands apart, and took her place between his legs, grabbing his hair with both hands and locking her eyes with his before she kissed him. Sensing she had something more on her mind, he awaited her next move.

Placing her hands on his shoulders, she pushed him down flat on the sofa and landed on top of him, lacing her fingers in his hair again and holding tight as if to prevent an improbable escape. Diving into his mouth, parting his lips with her own smaller ones, she met his tongue with hers in the dance of passion each already expected. The cowboy lay motionless and obedient, feigning helplessness.

Leaving him, she moved to his boots, tugging to get them loose. Never had horseshit been so arousing. Once his socks and boots were off, she straddled him, moving erotically, though fully clothed, until she felt him bulging beneath her and saw him close his eyes, taking deep breaths in anticipation.

Leaning over him, she began her long, wanton kiss again, all the while unbuttoning his shirt. As she stroked his chest, she stopped to kiss each spot where her hands lingered, beginning with each nipple and stopping just above his navel, making a declaration after each.

"I claim this…and this…and this…" She continued to move down until her hands reached his big silver buckle. Hawk sucked in his stomach, bidding her safe passage to the space below, and sighed as her hands worked at releasing the buckle and zipper, unleashing the part of him she wanted most.

"And this." His Little One gave him pleasure he had only dreamed of until this moment, a woman in control, and he liked it. Not wanting to break the spell she had cast, he helped her little with her efforts to finish undressing him.

Hurriedly, she tugged at jeans and boxers, anxious to complete the ritual so foreign to her until this moment. With her lover lying naked and eager, she undressed and climbed on for the long-anticipated ride.

****

They spent most of the night just enjoying each other's embrace as they stared into the fire. It would be a Fourth of July not to be forgotten, and although she wasn't sure she had made the right decision to move on her feelings, Betsy had no regrets.

"Are you happy, Little One?" He lay behind her on the sofa, propped on one elbow, with his other arm around her, his fingers gently twirling her belly button ring.

"Mm. Ecstatic. And you, my handsome hero?"

"Never happier. Promise me this will last, Betsy. After today, I don't think I could live without you."

Turning to face him, she took in the serious look on his face. Stroking his face, she returned the seriousness. "You don't think promising is premature?"

"Not if you know what you want."

"Do you realize how long it took for us to get from that first day at the waterfall to today? A month, Hawk. How do I know you won't change your mind? I've watched you. Everywhere you go, women—beautiful women—lift their skirts and click the heels of their boots to get your attention."

"It's your fault it took so long." Hawk smiled at her. "You had me with that first look you gave me when I tipped my hat to you on the trail. Make me yours, and those women will leave me alone."

"Do you think I didn't think about you after that day? You got to me. I just wouldn't acknowledge it. Remember, I had just come from a world of hurt. You've had five years since yours. I'm afraid mine is still too fresh. I want to trust again, Hawk, and right now I think I do, but you'll have to give me some time. I've never felt or shown this kind of passion for any man, not even Patrick. I will promise you this—at this moment, I would do anything to make sure you and I are forever."

"Then that'll have to do for now." Taking her face in his hands like he had done that night outside the Grizzly, he kissed her again, but with the gentle passion she associated with this man she was sure she loved even though she would not admit it to him; it was too early.

Some time after midnight, they slept, choosing not to move to the bedroom but to remain surrounded by the warm glow of the fire.

They were awakened the next morning by the ringing of her cell phone. Betsy frowned when she saw the caller ID.

"Lou? How did you get this number?" Betsy moved away from the sofa and Hawk as she held the phone away from her ear because the woman was screaming angrily into the phone, just as she had the last time Betsy talked to her.

"Calm down, Lou! I can't understand you when you're screaming like that."

"It's that bastard husband of yours! He told Eddie he's no longer a partner and he needs to find another job as soon as the Nashville project is over. It's your fault, Betsy—you and your holier-than-thou attitude! If you'd stuck it out with Patrick, this wouldn't be happening!" Lou continued to rave on the other end, and Betsy was furious to have to listen to it.

"What do you mean it's my fault? I'm in Montana!

I don't give a shit about you, or Eddie, or Patrick for that matter. Wingate Constructors is none of my business, and this is none of yours."

Hawk was awake now as he watched Betsy pace the room with the phone held away from her ear. Wearing only his shirt, she was gorgeous even in her present state of anger. Her hair hung almost to her waist and in its disheveled state renewed the sensations of the day before.

"Oh, it's your business all right. That's the problem. Your damn divorce is going to clean us right out of Wingate Constructors. Patrick is putting the business in both your name and his as part of the divorce settlement. He says there won't be enough profit for a three-way partnership, and who gets thrown to the dogs? We do. It's not fair, Betsy. You can stop this. Come home and act like a wife ought to and stop this insanity!"

"You're crazy, Lou! I'm not coming back. The divorce will go through, and I don't give a rip what happens to any of you, you least of all. And don't you call me again. If you do, I'll get this number changed."

"You'll be sorry, Betsy! You will damn well be sorry if you don't do something about this. I didn't marry your creep of a brother-in-law for his looks, and I refuse to live like a pauper. I've been there and I'm not going back. You just go to hell!" With this the phone was slammed down.

"The nerve of that little bitch," Betsy fumed. "How did she get this number? And why does she always have to bash the phone at the end of her screeching?"

Hawk crossed the room after pulling on his boxers and took the cell phone from Betsy. "You're really sexy when you're mad. Wanna take a shower?" His hands reached under the shirt and began massaging her cheeks as he pulled her to him.

"Do you think you can wait till we get to the waterfall?" Betsy's eyes twinkled.

"I was thinking more of the trickle upstairs. I'll just sweep you off your feet like yesterday, and we'll be there in no time." With that, he picked her up and ran up the stairs, taking two at a time.

"Hey, cowboy, did you get those muscles from carrying women up stairs?"

"No. I work out at school every day with some of my students. Teaches self-discipline. It's an old counselor's trick. Concentrate on the outside in order to get to the inside."

"And I, for one, can see the amazing benefits, Counselor. Isn't that the same method you use in seducing your women?"

He stopped on the stairs, propping her on one knee, and stared at her without smiling, making sure he had her full attention for what he was about to say.

"Woman, Betsy. I have only one woman." He continued looking at her, refusing to move or smile until she acknowledged she understood what he had said.

"I got it." Betsy stared back at him and then kissed him, tightening her hold. They held the kiss as he carried her the rest of the way to the bathroom, where he undressed himself and then her after turning on the shower.

As they lay in bed later, he held her and began twisting her curls around his fingers. With the other hand, he softly stroked her skin, coming to a standstill at her breasts.

"Your skin is so soft, like a deer."

"Soft-as-Deer," she whispered. "If I were your Indian lover, my name would be Soft-as-Deer."

"Soft-as-Deer. I like that." And Hawk and Soft-as-Deer made love again.

****

"This is so amazing! I can't believe how many fish I've caught." Betsy could not contain her excitement with her new adventure. "Are you sure you don't want to teach me how to use those oars so you can fish? It looks so easy when you do it, except for when you backtrack upstream to go back through a run."

"No, ma'am. I'm enjoying being your guide. Besides, I'm hoping for a really nice tip later." Hawk smiled as he rowed the drift boat backwards through the run.

"I think you've had plenty of advance tips. Good thing you're doing the thirteen-mile run, or you might have to refund. Oh, darn, I lost that one. Stop distracting me."

Betsy reeled in her line to check her flies and discovered the big rainbow had made off with her dropper. She had to strain to see the tiny, size-twenty pheasant-tail flashback that could somehow attract huge rainbows and browns.

"Let's pull over, and I'll tie that fly on for you. Besides, I need to put some more sunscreen on my legs. I just stopped peeling from getting burned the last time I fished in shorts. I owe the pale part of me that burns so damn bad to my Caucasian ancestry."

As he rowed to shore, he noticed Betsy laughing.

"What?"

"Oh, it's nothing, Neapolitan Man." Betsy snickered.

"What are you talking about?" Hawk let the boat drift, anxious to hear Betsy's explanation.

"The three shades of your body—chocolate, strawberry, and vanilla—that first day at the waterfall. Now I know where the strawberry came from."

"And now that you've tasted me, what's your favorite flavor?"

"Luscious vanilla, definitely. It was that day, too, but only in my mind. I have to admit, the scoop ain't bad either. Funny, I don't think I'll ever eat Neapolitan ice cream again without getting aroused."

"Great! I'll make sure your freezer's full of it." Betsy was still trying to tie the fly on, and Hawk took it away from her.

"Are your eyes getting old or something? Give me that. See how easy this is?" In a matter of seconds, he had tied on the fly and handed the line back to her.

"I'm thirty-five, if that was a hint. Am I robbing the cradle?"

"Yes, ma'am, as a matter of fact you are. I just turned thirty-four in March. It's okay, though. I like older women; especially the ones with belly button rings." After kissing her as if reassurance was needed, he took his place at the oars again.

The enjoyment Hawk got out of rowing the drift boat and guiding on the Big Horn was contagious, and Betsy didn't know when she had enjoyed fishing more. It was a different kind of fly fishing. Some day she'd row one of these, maybe even this one, and become a guide herself.

She had heard of a school in Jackson Hole,

Wyoming. It was called Reel Women, and it taught female anglers how to control a drift boat and to guide. She thought she would pursue that next summer.

Next summer, I'll be free of Patrick and all the heartaches he's caused. Her only hope was that Hawk would still be around.

****

Hawk watched, hypnotized, as Betsy stood in the lock-in, casting and looking as beautiful as he had ever seen her, wearing one of his way-too-big fishing shirts with the sleeves bulkily rolled up. The tail was tied in a knot high above the waist over zip-off fly fishing shorts pulled low intentionally to expose the belly button ring he craved.

Every time she turned toward him, the ring sparkled, grabbing his attention and making him very uncomfortable sitting on the hard rowing seat, as his shorts kept getting tighter. Her Tevas had been removed as soon as she got into the boat, in an attempt to let her feet catch up with her legs with their tan.

He had hit the jackpot this time. Betsy was nothing like Diane, his ex, and he couldn't be happier. Nor was she like Amanda. Here was a woman he could share his passions with—fly fishing, cowboying, and his love affair with the mountains, not to mention the synergy they created in the lovemaking department.

If only it will last.

Hawk smiled at her, thinking again of how they had met only a month earlier. Still, there was the divorce she had to go through, and he was afraid it would not be easy despite Patrick's promise it would be. Hawk wished he knew him, just to know what Betsy was up against, but he had remained ignorant by choice about their marriage and their problems. Hawk and Betsy knew each other, and they were alike. Hawk Larson was in love for the last time in his life and could only hope she felt the same.

Betsy went to sleep on the way back to Red Lodge, exhausted from a day of fishing. Her head was on Hawk's driving leg, and, regardless of how cramped he felt, he refused to move her. He thought about how much his uncle loved Betsy and her mother and wondered what he would think if he knew his nephew was in love with his Little One.

Surely Unk would approve. The only true friends Custer had ever had were Betsy and her mom. But then, his uncle was very perceptive where he was concerned and probably already knew how he felt.

"I'll take care of you, Little One," he whispered as he twisted a curl around his finger.

Chapter Eight

Hawk was a permanent fixture in Betsy's life, and she couldn't imagine life without him. True, he was gone for days at a time, but he would usually sneak down from the outfitter's camp and spend a few hours with her.

Now it was mid-July, and she was getting nervous. She had been uneasy ever since Lou had made the hysterical phone call. The fact she and Hawk were an item was common knowledge around Red Lodge, but this was not information she wanted to get back to Patrick, when the divorce was so near.

All of a sudden, she had friends coming out of the woodwork. Everywhere she went, people asked about Hawk, and she was pleased to tell them where he was guiding just to let them know he was still in her life, but she couldn't help but be wary.

Betsy went to Red Lodge at least once a week to check her mail and pick up supplies. She was also expecting a package from L.L. Bean with new size-four jeans as well as a letter from Annie, who wrote weekly and kept her informed about her newest godchild, Michael.

Betsy wrote often but had not told Annie about Hawk. This information would be saved for their next porch visit at Parrish Oaks, her mom's old home place in Mississippi, probably around September first, when she would have to make a personal appearance to tell Patrick she no longer wanted him in her life. This was not something she was looking forward to but was something she wanted over with as soon as possible. There was a new reason for wanting it over, a reason she thought she was entitled to after her disappointing marriage.

****

"Hi, Darlene. How's Mack?"

"I call him Mack the Knife. Cuts right to my heart, that one; that big, bad, burly, bald babe of mine. We're thinking about moving in together. And how's the Hawk? Still can't believe you pulled such a fast one on me that night at the Grizzly, but you couldn't keep it from me. One look at you two and anybody with half an ounce of sense could see what was destined to happen."

"Got any mail for me or Hawk, Darlene?"

"Yep, got a package and a letter, besides the usual garbage. See you got something from L.L. Bean. Don't tell me you're still losing weight. Can't you get that man of yours to feed you? The next time I see him, I'm giving him a talking to about how he's not taking care of you."

"Please don't do that, Darlene. He already stays after me. I have to eat steak every time he's home, and I'm not fond of red meat. Besides, my weight has leveled off. I think I'm where I'm going to stay now."

"Well, I hope so. One of these days I'm gonna start that walking business myself, but right now Mack likes me just the way I am. That's the good thing about having a big man in your life." Darlene gave her famous headshake and hoot that always made Betsy laugh. "What you up to today?"

"I'm going to do a little shopping. Hawk won't be in for a couple of days, and I've been meaning to get me one of those short skirts that are so popular at the Grizzly. I think we're going Saturday night, and I'm pretty excited. For once, I won't have to look for Hawk. He'll be right beside me. We've been together three weeks now. He says it'll be a little anniversary celebration."

"Are you sure he's ready, Betsy? I'd hate for him to get back on the bottle."

"Oh, yeah. I'm not worried, Darlene."

Later, Betsy was working her way through racks of short leather skirts at her favorite shop downtown. Two of the young sales girls were helping her. A four was a perfect fit, and she had just about decided on a low-cut, short brown leather skirt but was foregoing the vest that matched, not wanting to look like a carbon copy of Amanda.

The salesgirls were having as much fun as Betsy trying to find the perfect top for the skirt. Since her ostrich boots were gray, the skirt meant buying another pair of boots, as well. She chose shorter brown leather ones with the same heel as her others, needing the height to prevent her dance partner from having to strain to get to her.

Patty, the younger of the two, found an off-white, silky, low-cut blouse with spaghetti straps that hit her just above the belly button, leaving the jewel exposed like Hawk wanted it.

"Try this, Betsy. I think it's perfect. Man, I wish my mom would let me get my belly button pierced. That is so cool!"

****

Hawk let Jake out at his house and took the trailer-load of horses as fast as the Suburban would pull it to town. He knew Betsy wasn't at home because the Jeep was gone when he and his entourage of clients and pack animals had reached Six Rocks, where he could see the cabin in the distance below. Coming to a fast stop at the post office, he left the door open as he hurried in.

"Hi, Darlene. Seen Betsy?"

"Cute little thing? Comes just below your chin? Yes, I have seen her. Pretty as a puppy but way too thin. She needs a man that'll feed her. Can you find her one?"

"Come on, Darlene. Where is she?"

"What are you doing in town? She said you weren't due in for two days."

"One of our clients got sick and we had to cut it short. Where'd she go?"

"Shopping, downtown. Getting her something to wear to the Grizz' Saturday night." Hawk turned and rushed out the door. "And you better behave yourself, Hawk Larson, or I'll sic Mack on you!" Darlene was yelling at him as the door swung closed.

As he spotted the Jeep, Hawk pulled the big rig over, taking up several parking spaces in the process. He knew which shop she'd be in, and he wasted no time. Even though he looked pretty scruffy with a two-day beard and wearing a dusty black T-shirt and smelling more like a horse than a man, he was still a cowboy who could stop traffic.

"Anybody seen my girl? About this tall?" He held up his hand to the upper part of his chest. "Long blonde braid, belly button ring?"

The girls laughed to see the famous Hawk Larson

in a ladies' clothing store looking like it was an everyday occurrence. Patty pointed to the fitting room, and Hawk headed in that direction.

"She's in the one on the end, but you can't go in there. Besides, the door's locked.

He held up his hand and made the gesture of a key turning, and Patty shook her head. "No." Hawk pulled out a twenty-dollar bill and handed it to the girl, who looked at the older salesgirl as if asking if she should or not.

"Go ahead. This could be better than reality TV."

As the girl turned the key in the dressing room door, she jumped back as Hawk bolted in, looking back to smile and wink at her, giving her a thrill that would last several days.

"Hawk, what are you doing in here?" Betsy stood barefooted, dressed in her new outfit.

"Wow! I like it! Is this for me?"

"Well, I don't know who else it would be for. What are you doing here? You're not supposed to be in for two days."

"Is that all you've got to say?"

The next sounds the salesgirls heard were moans of happiness, the obvious result of some heavy-duty kissing. Both girls smiled, and the older one tiptoed away. She then retraced her steps to pull the younger one out of hearing range even though they both found the scene pretty entertaining.

"Now there's a sight you don't see every day." Betsy stood with her hands on her hips, looking down at her guy, giving him the twinkle. "A six-foot-three cowboy bowed up trying to fit on a three-foot bench in the fitting room of a ladies' boutique."

Hawk had one boot propped against the wall of the small space with his knee practically to his chest while balancing himself with the other boot on the floor. Still he managed to pull Betsy to him, plopping her on his chest and pulling her mouth to his.

"Damn, I've missed you. You 'bout done here? I'm ready to get you home."

"Could you take a little interest in this shopping trip, please?"

Hawk reached under the short skirt and began rubbing her upper thighs, moving higher quickly, tugging at her bikini panties.

"Hawk, stop it!" Betsy was trying to whisper, but her order was going unheeded. Finally, she pulled herself off him and put her hands on her hips.

"Okay, let me get changed and we'll go home."

Hawk sat with his arms crossed, looking at her.

"I said, let me get changed and we'll go home."

Hawk held his hands up and gave a smirk she interpreted to mean "so what's stopping you" as he smiled and crossed his arms, making no effort to leave the dressing room.

"You are impossible, Hawk Larson!" She faked disapproval as he watched her take off the skirt and blouse and then began rearranging his jeans as they ceased being the comfortable fit they had been when he walked into the shop.

Standing in her bra and panties, she had reached for her jeans when he quickly swung his leg off the bench and grabbed her, pulling her onto his lap, kissing her neck, all the time moving lower. This time, she just sat still, knowing a reprimand would go unheeded. His hands were already working to release her bra.

"This is not couth, Hawk! What if some little old lady goes into the dressing room next door? We could make her have a stroke."

"Oh, yeah! That's what I came to tell you!" Stopping his actions, he put his hands around her waist as she pulled her bra straps back in place.

"That a little old lady is stroking out in the dressing room next door?"

"No, the little old lady reminded me. I've got the next two days off, plus the weekend. I want to take you to the reservation and introduce you to my mom and grandmother. Mom is there from Great Falls, visiting with Nana."

"But, Hawk, what will they think when they find out I'm not divorced yet? Won't they think I'm some kind of terrible person?"

"Mom already knows. She doesn't care as long as I'm happy. And I am very happy. They'll love you, Betsy, just like I do." Betsy put her arms around Hawk's neck and kissed him.

"Do you think we can get out of this cubbyhole now, Hawk?"

As the two left the dressing room, the salesgirls were all smiles. Two elderly women, obviously tourists with their Red Lodge T-shirts, Yellowstone sun visors, khaki pants, and white Keds, had been looking through the sale rack but now stood with their mouths open as Hawk walked out of the fitting room behind Betsy. He pretended to ignore them, but Betsy saw the twinkle in his eye and the faint smile on his lips and knew he was enjoying the whole scenario.

"Well, that was certainly a first." The older salesgirl began ringing up the skirt, blouse, and boots, still smiling. Hawk was looking at dresses, ignoring the stares of the two older women, who were more interested in the cowboy than the sale.

"Sorry. Hawk doesn't exactly play by the rules," Betsy whispered as she dug her checkbook out of her pack.

"It's okay, Betsy. It was just another boring day of shopkeeping till Hawk came in." They both laughed.

"Betsy, I like this dress. What are you, a six?" Hawk was holding up an emerald-green dress, low-cut and sleeveless, of tight-fitting spandex.

"Let's see. Yeah, that's pretty, but I wear a four."

"Darlene was right. You are getting too little. We'll stop and get some steaks to cook tonight." Putting the dress back, he pulled out a smaller one and put it on the counter as he reached for his wallet and pulled out his credit card.

"I've got it, Hawk."

"Put that away. I'm getting this."

"Thank you, generous sir." Knowing better than to argue, she picked up the bag containing the purchases, including the dress, as she walked ahead of Hawk to the door. Just before leaving, Hawk turned to the salesgirls and the two women who were still staring and tipped his hat.

"Ladies."

Even the older women smiled as the handsome cowboy put his arm around his girl's shoulder to escort her out. Betsy gave Hawk a pretend scowl and shook her head.

"What?" Hawk smiled at Betsy as he opened the Jeep door for her.

"You loved that, didn't you?" Betsy asked as she

slid into the Jeep seat.

"I don't have to be predictable all the time, do I?"

"Oh, believe me, Hawk Larson. You are anything but predictable."

"Oh, yeah? I bet you can read my mind, Little One. What do I want to do right now?" Hawk propped his foot on the Jeep running board and leaned in.

"Oh, give me another one. That's too easy." Their game was interrupted by the sound of horses pawing and nickering in the trailer.

"Damn horses! You distracted me and made me forget about 'em, Betsy. Let's stay at my place tonight. It's closer." Getting the kiss of approval, he moved away from the Jeep and headed across the street to his rig.

As Hawk stepped up on the running board of the trailer to look in at the horses, he heard someone say, "Smile, cowboy!" Turning, he saw the two elderly ladies from the shop grinning, holding digital cameras.

Leaving one foot propped on the trailer running board, he tipped his hat and smiled as they clicked away. Betsy watched from the Jeep, shaking her head and laughing.

Anybody he wants, honey, from eighteen to sixty.

Darlene's statement that first night at the Grizzly was all she could think about as she watched the two giddy women comparing shots as she pulled away, following the newest tourist attraction to Red Lodge. She'd have to tell Darlene to up that age limit to about eighty.

****

Hawk's cabin was an older one and small, basically two big rooms with a loft. It was a few miles out of Red

Lodge toward Roscoe and sat in the middle of a hundred acres surrounded by another side of the Beartooths.

Though it definitely looked like a normal man full of testosterone lived in it, the cabin was not dirty, and Betsy smiled as Hawk's personality and passions radiated from every stick of furniture and piece of décor. The cabin was filled with Native American artwork, both prints and originals, with Hawk's favorite artist being Kevin Red Star, a Crow artist who lived near Red Lodge. Several Russell and Remington prints completed the art collection. Happily, she noticed there were no beer empties sitting around.

Betsy helped Hawk feed and water the horses before settling in for the evening. Taking her hand, he led her through the bedroom.

"Now for the bath I've been thinking about sharing with you ever since we left that boutique of yours."

There was no shower in the cabin, but there was a bathtub, a big old antique one with claw feet. Hawk started the water running as he turned to Betsy and kissed her, eager to begin a romantic first night at his place. He dreamed of sharing this place with her permanently some day.

"I don't have any clothes or anything with me, Hawk, not even a toothbrush."

Reaching into the drawer in the bathroom cabinet, he pulled out a new toothbrush, still in its package. "As for clothes, who needs 'em?" Smiling, he pulled Betsy close, kissing her as he began the undressing ritual he loved.

"Now let's get rid of the smell of horse manure." Hawk peeled off his T-shirt, exposing his scarred milk chocolate and bulky semi-sweet.

"I don't know, cowboy. Horse shit's pretty arousing. Kind of like when I was a cheerleader in high school my senior year, when I went back to Mississippi from Alaska, and we'd go into the football players' locker room and smell that pungent male sweat we girls thrive on."

"Does that mean you want to make love before the bath?" Starting to kiss her again, he pulled back, giving her a pretend frown. "Wait a minute! What were you doing in the boys' locker room?"

"On second thought…" Quickly, Betsy slid into the tub. A few seconds later, her handsome lover was sliding in at the opposite end, causing a flashback to a similar episode only a few months earlier.

"What's wrong, Betsy? Why the serious look? Did I do something wrong?"

Leaving her end of the tub, she nestled into his arms, hugging him, laying her head on his wet chest.

"No, Hawk. You've done everything just right."

They never made it from the tub to the bed, choosing instead to add to the warmth of the water the completeness they always found in each other.

Later, after he forced her to eat half a steak almost as big as she was, she sat on the sofa holding his head in her lap. As she combed her fingers through his hair, she looked down at him and smiled as he slept.

Some day, my love, you will be mine forever.
****

"What are you in such deep thought about, Betsy? You're not nervous about meeting my folks, are you?" They had finally entered the Crow reservation after driving for a couple of hours.

"A little. I just wish I could be as sure as you are that they'll like me."

Pulling her across the seat of the Suburban, he put his arm around her and twisted her braid.

"Okay. Worst case scenario? They hate you. Do you think it would make any difference in the way I feel about you, Betsy?"

"Well, I'm at a disadvantage here. My mom already knows you. In fact, she warned me about you, handsome devil that you are. Somehow she knew you were going to sweep me off my feet, so to speak."

"That was a long time ago when I met Sue Ann. I hope you look just like her when you're that age. She's a beautiful lady."

"When did you meet her, exactly? She never mentioned you until I told her about the moose attack."

"About five years ago. I was staying at Custer's. It was a pretty dark time in my life."

"Oh. I think I know this story. You don't have to tell me, Hawk." Betsy reached over and took Hawk's hand.

"No. You have a right to know. My skeletons are your skeletons now. We're one, Betsy, whether you're ready to admit it or not."

"Darlene told me Custer walked into the Grizzly one night and literally dragged you out and took you home with him."

"That's pretty much what happened. I've never told this to anyone else, not even Jake." Hawk paused for a few seconds.

"I was drunk. Had been for days—or, really, more like months. I don't actually know. Somebody told Custer, and he came to get me. I don't think I'd be here if he hadn't come, but I didn't appreciate it at the time.

"I missed the last two months of school that year. Just quit going to work. One of the board members, an old friend of my dad's, came looking for me, and when he found me, he told me to get my act together or be fired. Offered me treatment. Alcoholism is pretty rampant among my people, among Native Americans in general, so they always offer treatment. You got any idea how embarrassing it is for a counselor to need treatment, Betsy?"

"Hawk, you don't have to tell me all of this. You were hurt. I know what it's like to be hurt. A person can get pretty desperate." Betsy squeezed Hawk's hand again to reassure him she understood.

"Not because Diane left me. Our marriage was over long before she decided to leave. I read an email she had sent to an old boyfriend from back east and knew it was just a matter of time. It was losing Josie that killed me."

Pulling down the visor on his side of the Suburban, Hawk took down a small snapshot worn with age. It was Hawk holding a little girl about three years old in front of him on his horse. The girl was a smaller image of her dad, with long, dark braids, dark eyes, and a big smile.

"She's beautiful, Hawk. No wonder you were crushed."

"Yeah. She's somebody else's beautiful little girl now, and I can't blame that on Diane. Judges don't award children or even visitation to alcoholic parents. She'll probably never know I exist. I stayed so drunk after they left, I don't even remember signing the papers giving up my rights to Josie."

"How did Custer bring you back to reality? If you want to tell me, that is."

"The old ways. Custer believes in spiritualism—sweat lodges to rid your body and your spirit of poisoning, and all of that. Nana, my grandmother you'll be meeting, is Custer's and my dad's mother. She's full-blooded Crow. Her dad was a spiritualist, kind of a medicine man, and he taught Custer the rituals. Believe me, I did some major sweating those weeks I spent with Custer."

"I've heard of sweat lodges, but I'm afraid I'm not up on Crow culture. You'll have to teach me."

"This one was small and rounded, made from birch limbs and covered with canvas and some deer hides. Custer built it up by Second Rock. Drug my hung-over butt up there the day after he pulled me out of the Grizzly, tortured the hell out of me. It took us ten hours to get to Second Rock. Wouldn't let me ride a horse. Made me walk and carry a heavy pack till we got to Keyser Brown. If I fell, he'd kick me in the ass and make me get up. I'm not ashamed to admit I cried like a baby a couple of times and begged him to let up. At the time, I was sure I'd die before we got there."

"When we got to Keyser Brown, I passed out, wringing wet with sweat, probably about ninety-proof. When I came to, he was dabbing my head with his handkerchief, which he'd wet with cold lake water. He let me sleep for about an hour and then started on me again, but he did carry the pack the rest of the way."

"Custer did all that? I can't believe it." Betsy shook her head.

"Oh, believe it. I know you think he's a big teddy bear, but he can be a grizzly when he wants to be. I learned a long time ago not to buck him when he means business, and he meant business.

"When we got to Second Rock, he built the sweat lodge. Took my clothes and made me 'live in the elements' as he called it. I damn near froze to death at night. Several times a day, he'd drag me into the sweat lodge, more than is customary. When he did finally let me come out, he'd throw me in the lake.

"Do you know how cold those high mountain lakes are? When I got out, he'd start all over again. Wouldn't let me have anything to eat, just water, and he limited that. I got where I tried to hide it when I'd get the shakes 'cause I knew he'd throw me in the sweat lodge again."

"So you finally got the impurities out. Then what?" Knowing this was something Hawk had shared with few people, Betsy gave him her full attention.

"He sent me on a vision quest. Scared the shit out of me when he took me into that wilderness and turned to leave. I told him I'd die. He looked at me and, in that profound way he has with words, he said, 'Better to die trying to live than to die trying to die.'

"I still don't know how long I was up there in those mountains by myself, but I had no food and no water except what was in the streams, and no water filter, either. Somehow I survived without getting giardia. Unk knew if I had a filter I'd drink more than I needed to survive, so he wouldn't let me have one. I was surprised when he gave me clothes—a pair of moose-hide pants and moccasins, no shirt. I thought he was going to make me cut off a finger like they did in the old days, but thank goodness he drew the line somewhere. It was while I was on my quest I got this scar on my cheek and the one on my chest—a little run-in with a mountain lion."

"A vision quest. Wow!"

"Yes, really. You think it's a bunch of mumbo-jumbo, don't you?"

"I don't think anything, Hawk, except it must have worked. You stayed sober for almost five years. You never backslid? Not one time?"

"No. Not until that night I thought you'd found somebody else, but I'm okay now, Betsy. You have to believe me. It won't happen again. As long as I have you with me, I know I'll be okay."

"Hawk, please don't depend on me like that. You have to have faith in yourself. I came close to dying once already when I had cancer. Fate can be nasty."

"I'm sorry, baby. I didn't mean for it to sound like I was putting this burden on you. I know my drinking is my problem, and I'll be in control, with or without you. It will just be so much easier with you." Pulling her to him, she laid her head on his chest as he rubbed his face against her head.

****

Hawk's grandmother's house was an older doublewide. The yard had beds of flowers everywhere, and interspersed in the flowers were cattle skulls, rock sculptures, and wooden carvings of animal figures. To Betsy, it was like looking at a still life in a Georgia O'Keefe painting, a beautiful reflection of the Native American West.

Hawk's mother didn't wait for her son to come to the door. She greeted him on the porch with outstretched arms. She was taller than Betsy, but not nearly as tall as Betsy had anticipated, given that Hawk was over six feet tall, and even though she had the dark hair and eyes of a half-blood, she looked and sounded more non-native. Her hair, cut shoulder-length and turned under, had streaks of gray in it that only added to its natural beauty.

"Mom, this is Betsy. Betsy, this is my mother, Isabel."

"It's so nice to meet you, Betsy." Isabel gave Betsy a hug. "I've heard so much about you from my son and from Custer. Come in, please, and meet Nana. She's been looking out the window every five minutes all day."

As Hawk and Betsy entered the house, Hawk's grandmother reached for Hawk and pointed to her cheek.

"How's my Nana?" Hawk took her hands and kissed her on the cheek. "Nana, this is Betsy." He smiled as he took Betsy's hand and led her to his grandmother's chair. She immediately reached for Betsy's hand and held it, smiling up at her, seeming to try to absorb everything about her in this first meeting.

"She's beautiful, Hawk, just like you said."

Betsy's cheeks flushed. "Thank you, Mrs. Larson. I'm so pleased to meet both of you."

"Call me Nana, please."

"And call me Isabel, Betsy. We both feel like we know you since you're all Hawk talks about when he calls. Come and sit down."

"Don't give her the big head, Mom." Hawk took Betsy's hand and led her to the sofa covered with a brightly colored Native American blanket.

"How's Sue Ann, Betsy? I haven't seen her in so long."

"Busy. She's always writing. I hope she'll come to Montana soon. She says she will when she finishes this novel."

"I've read every one of her books. They're wonderful. Tell her to keep them coming. I look forward to hearing from her because when she does take time to write me, there's always a new book in the puffy envelope with her letter."

"I didn't know you liked romances, Mom."

"There's a lot you don't know about me, son."

"Now you sound like my mother, Isabel. She's always telling me that, but the more I read her novels, the more I'm learning about her. Lots of surprises there."

Later, as the four sat at the dining room table eating the lunch Hawk's mother had prepared, Betsy noticed the wall was covered in family pictures, mostly of Hawk from childhood to college graduation. Also proudly displayed were his high school diploma, his bachelor's degree, and his master's degree in counseling.

On the end on the bottom row was a family portrait of Hawk, Diane, and Josie. Josie was just a baby and was seated in her dad's lap. Behind him with her hand on her husband's shoulder stood Diane. Betsy couldn't help but stare.

Diane was pretty, with dark brown hair and blue eyes. To Betsy, she had the same features as Amanda but with shorter hair, and looked to be average height in the picture. Hawk caught her gaze and became apologetic.

"I'm sorry, Betsy. I've tried to get Nana to take that picture down, but she won't."

"And she shouldn't." Betsy was quick to answer. "It's part of your family history, Hawk. Besides, if Josie is as headstrong as her daddy, some day she'll walk through that door as a grown-up young woman demanding to know her other family. Seeing that picture might be just what she needs to see she belongs."

"See why I love her, Nana? She always thinks positively, and most of the time logically." Hawk moved his chair next to Betsy's and put his arm around her.

"What do you mean, 'most of the time'?" Punching Hawk, she looked at his grandmother, who was smiling at them both. Betsy helped clear the table when they were finished eating and set the coffeepot up at Isabel's request. As she was getting cups out of the cabinet, she overheard Nana talking to Hawk in the living room. Isabel stopped rinsing dishes, obviously listening to the conversation in the living room. The scowl on her face showed she did not approve of what she was hearing.

"She's the one, isn't she, Hawk?" Nana tried unsuccessfully to whisper.

"Yes, Nana. She is, but there's part of it that doesn't fit. I'll have to wait and see."

"The Great Spirit will work it out. Have faith, Grandson."

Betsy followed Isabel into the living room with the tray of coffee mugs and a plate of cookies Nana had made earlier.

"Nana, you're not filling Hawk's head full of Native superstition again, are you? Hawk, you know how I feel about that. If you have a question or a problem, you get on your knees and pray about it."

Isabel reprimanded her son and his grandmother.

"Mom and Nana have differing beliefs when it comes to religion, even though they both believe in the same Great Spirit: Crow First Maker, white God or Heavenly Father—just different names for the same Great Being. It's kind of a sore subject around here. Mom prides herself in being more white than Native."

"I can't help the way I was raised, and I raised you white, too, my dear son, and don't forget it. It's your Nana and Custer that feed you Crow supernatural nonsense."

"Tell me about Custer when he was a boy, Nana. He's pretty special to me and to Mom." Betsy wanted to change the subject and hear about her friend.

"To know Custer as a boy and as a man, all you have to do is look beside you. Hawk is more like his uncle than like his own dad, Thomas. Thomas was a quiet boy, but Custer and Hawk were scrappers as boys and sometimes as men, not afraid to fight. It's hard to believe Hawk is a counselor now, as much trouble as he stayed in when he was in school. Right, Isabel?"

"I'm afraid we agree on that one. And Custer was even worse. Now look at him, living up there in the woods like an old Crow elder. I have to admit he did help my son when he was in crisis, and I'll always be grateful to him for that, even if we do disagree on methodology." Isabel sipped her coffee to signal the end of her discussion of Custer.

"Custer is a good man." Betsy smiled at Nana, who nodded in agreement. "He's always been there for Mom and me."

****

The afternoon passed fast and included looking at

166

picture albums and scrapbooks of Hawk's growing up. Nana could hardly keep her hands off Hawk and made him sit right beside her.

"Mom, Betsy and I'll have to go in a few minutes. We're stopping in Billings. I haven't taken her anywhere nice to eat, and I think it's about time I did. Besides, I've been given strict orders by one of her friends to start feeding her more before she dries up to nothing."

"Please don't make me eat another steak tonight, Hawk!"

"Actually, the Windmill is pretty famous for its seafood, especially shrimp, as well as its prime rib, so you're off the hook tonight."

Betsy excused herself to the bathroom and freshened up, changing into the green dress Hawk had bought her. With it she wore black heels with delicate straps across the toes and around the heels. The dress fit snugly, as it was supposed to, and was shorter than she was sure Isabel and Nana were accustomed to seeing, but Hawk had insisted she wear it.

Hawk had changed into a light blue monogrammed button-down shirt, worn open at the top, exposing his magnificent chest. Over it, he wore a khaki western sports jacket with his starched jeans and dress boots. As she entered, he rose, staring and whistling.

"Now, that's my girl!" Planting a kiss on her cheek, he took her hand and led her to the sofa.

"My, what a handsome couple you two make!"

"Hawk picked out this dress. It feels a little different from my jeans and boots, but kind of nice for a change. You look wonderful, Hawk."

"My beautiful son! Don't you think he's beautiful,

Betsy?"

"Handsome, Mom. Men are handsome, not beautiful."

"I thought you were beautiful the first time I got a good look at you." Betsy smiled at Hawk and winked when no one was looking.

As they headed out the door, Nana called Hawk back. "She's the one, Hawk. I know she's the one." Her grandson smiled and kissed her again before heading for the Suburban.

As they drove away, Betsy looked at Hawk questioningly.

"What did she mean, Hawk? I'm the one what?"

"You probably wouldn't believe me if I told you. I'll tell you when the time's right. But right now, I want you to bring your pretty little butt over here as close as you can so I can look at you and feel you next to me where you belong." Placing his hand between her knees, he began to rub her thighs and give her those looks that she understood all too well. "I kind of wish we were going straight home instead of out to eat."

"You know, cowboy, if you keep exchanging lovemaking for food, you'll be the one losing weight, and I'll have to push steak on you."

"I'll take my chances." Hawk lifted his eyebrows and smiled at Betsy.

After parking at the restaurant, Hawk sat looking at Betsy, making no attempt to get out.

"If this is carryout, why'd we get all dressed up? Aren't we going in?"

"In just a minute. But first, I've got something for you." Reaching into the back seat, Hawk pulled up a small jeweler's bag with a long box inside. "You need this to go with the dress."

"What did you do, Hawk? Stop spoiling me." Inside the box, Betsy found an expensive emerald necklace. "Hawk, this is too much. You don't need to spend this kind of money on me."

"Don't you like it?"

"It's the most beautiful necklace I've ever seen, and emeralds are my favorite. Now I know why you wanted this green dress. How long have you had this?" Betsy began taking the necklace out of the box.

"Since last week. I saw it when I was in Billings one day buying supplies for a trip. All I could see when I looked at it were your emerald eyes, and I knew I had to get it. The dress just happened along at the right time. Here, I'll help you put it on."

Betsy lifted her hair so Hawk could fasten the necklace around her neck.

"Thank you, Hawk, for this and for loving me." Taking his face in her hands, she kissed him like he had kissed her at the waterfall, and he held her tight, hoping time would stand still a few minutes longer.

****

As they sat eating muffins and drinking coffee the next morning, Hawk made a proposal.

"Okay, sweetheart. Here's the deal. We've got three days, counting today. You get two, today and tomorrow, but I get Sunday so I can rest up before I have to pack in for the next set of clients on Monday. Deal?"

"You mean I get to choose what we do for two days, and you won't complain?"

"Scout's honor."

"Were you a Boy Scout?"

Hawk almost choked on a sip of coffee. "Yeah, right. You heard what Nana said. I was trouble, nothin' but." Hawk put his coffee cup down. "So, do you still want to go to the Grizzly Saturday night?"

"I do." Betsy paused and smiled at Hawk. "But I want to do something else more. We might do both if we're not too tired."

"Anything you want, baby. If we can't do both, we can go to the Grizzly next Saturday. I'll be coming down early. In fact, I'll be home every weekend till I have to start school again. What's on your mind?"

"I want to go to Second Rock and fish and do anything else we can fit in."

"All right. That sounds good to me, especially the 'anything else we can fit in.' I can handle sleeping with you in a tent now that I don't have to act like I'm celibate. We'll take two sleeping bags and zip them together this time. I 'bout froze my ass off that night you had your run-in with Mrs. Moose."

"Great! We better get our packs ready so we can leave, if we want to get some fishing in today."

"You don't want to take the horses as far as Keyser Brown and hike up from there? It's a long way." Hawk watched for Betsy's answer.

"No way! Unless you think you can't make it, that is?" Betsy smiled, knowing she would get a rise out of Hawk.

Dropping his muffin, he looked up at her and scowled.

"You think I'm gettin' soft, huh? Can't make it? I'll show you who's fit." Leaving his chair, he headed for Betsy, who had already taken off running. He tackled her as she ran by the sofa, scooped her up, and headed for the stairs like he had done three weeks earlier.

****

The day could not have been any more perfect, and Betsy made the hike easily, helped by the fact Hawk made her take out most of what she usually carried, including her extra clothes, to lighten her pack to twenty pounds.

"You don't need to carry more than that, Betsy. We're just going for one night. I'll carry the heavy stuff." When he was in his protector role, she knew better than to argue.

They stopped at Keyser Brown to eat lunch and to fish a while before going on up. Standing on the rock where they had first fished together, Hawk began to smile as he cast.

"What are you smiling about, Hawk, or do I want to know?" Hawk reeled in his line and laid his rod down as he sat watching her.

"I was thinking about that day I watched you fish here. I never told you how I knew you were here, did I?"

"No, you didn't. I thought it was just coincidence. Do I want to hear this?"

"Well, you sent me the signal." Hawk looked straight ahead at the lake.

"What?" Betsy let her line fall to the water and looked at Hawk.

"Your belly button ring. I was way up there on the trail to September Morn, and I saw this bright, shiny light like someone was signaling for help from down below. I got out my binoculars, and there you were, stretched out with your hands behind your head. There was nothing I could do but turn around and come back down the trail. Jake was madder than hell when I did get to camp. He had the clients fed and geared up and already fishing."

"Did you tell him what took you so long?"

"Not then, but I did later that day."

"And he said?"

"He asked me if you were the one we saw on the trail. When I told him you were, he just said, 'Well, that explains it. I would've done the same thing.'"

"And I thought that goat was the only one staring at me. I better keep my pants higher from now on."

"Yeah." Hawk stood and picked up his rod. "When you're not with me."

"Gettin' a little possessive, aren't you?"

"Just protecting what's mine, babe." As he cast, he pretended not to notice her looking at him over her sunglasses like she had done the other time at Keyser Brown. Finally, he gave in and smiled at her, giving her his usual reply.

"What?"

"Nothing." Betsy began stripping in her line. "Let's head up. Best I can remember, it's a good two hours on up to Second Rock."

As she climbed over the huge boulder field, Betsy was glad Hawk had made her take out the extra pounds from her pack. Hawk must have been carrying fifty or sixty pounds but made it look easy.

"You okay, Betsy? Need to stop and rest?"

"I'm fine, Hawk. I just don't have the stride you do. You know I take about four steps to your one, so I'm walking four times as far. And a boulder to you is a mountain to me, but I promise you I'll make it."

"I have no doubt you will. You're the fittest and the most determined woman I've ever known. I just want you to have some energy left when you get there."

"I swear, Hawk, you have a one-track mind."

"Maybe I meant for fishing. Did you consider that?" Hawk cast a sideways glance at Betsy, waiting for her comeback.

"Yeah, right."

An hour and half later, Betsy unfastened her waist strap and let her pack fall as she sat overlooking Second Rock.

"I had forgotten how beautiful it is here. Worth every sore muscle."

Hawk took his pack off and sat beside her, massaging her back and shoulders.

"Where does it hurt most?"

"Everywhere. That feels so good."

Laying her head across his lap, she hugged his knees and moaned as he hit all the right spots. In no time, her eyes closed. Fifteen minutes later, he was still massaging her when she awoke.

"I can't believe you let me go to sleep. I should be massaging you. You carried all the weight."

"I'll take a rain check on that. I get mine on Sunday."

"I've got a feeling I'll be paying for this backrub for a while. You never told me what you want to do Sunday."

"I'll tell you then. Come on and help me make camp so we can start fishing. I thought we'd pretend we're not catch-and-release people and poach some trout to go with those potatoes I threw in at the last minute. Sound good?"

"I can't wait."

After they set up the tent, the fishing competition began. It was ten to eight, and Betsy was in the lead. When the fish stopped hitting, the casting competition began, but Hawk beat on this one. He had the sneaking suspicion she let him win but didn't admit it.

"So tell me where the sweat lodge was, and where did you go on your vision quest from here?"

"The sweat lodge was back in those trees over there, and across the razorback up by Hell's Canyon and another two or three hours into the Beartooths was where Custer took me and left me. Pure wilderness. I doubt very many people have been in there."

"How did you find your way out?"

"I don't know, but I did. Unk told me I'd make my way back to Second Rock when it was over. He was right. When I got here, he asked me nothing at all about what I'd seen, heard, or felt. I'd dropped about fifteen pounds in the days I was here and was about starved, could hardly keep my pants up, not to mention being scarred for life by that mountain lion. I walked up to Unk from behind, and he held out a plateful of fish and potatoes like he was expecting me at that exact moment. But that wasn't the strangest thing he did. He had a bottle of beer chilling in the lake. He walked to the edge of the water, retrieved it, and handed it to me."

"What did you do?"

"Well, I can tell you I wanted to suck the bottom out of it, but I just shook my head, refusing it. That's when he told me about the test. Said I had months ahead of me before I passed. I ate every meal the rest of the time we were there staring at that damn bottle of beer, and I finally got where it didn't bother me quite so bad." Hawk became quiet for a few seconds and then looked at Betsy.

"I'm a little anxious about going to the Grizzly tomorrow night, but I know I can do it, Betsy. Just don't get worried if I buy a bottle. I won't drink it."

"Hawk, will you ever tell me about it, what you experienced on your vision quest?"

"Some day, but not yet."

After they ate their meal that night, Hawk asked her if she was ready to take the plunge.

"The plunge?" Betsy cocked her head as she asked.

"The lake, Betsy. I want you to see how cold it is, and we better do it before the sun goes completely down or you'll freeze to death. It's deep, so you can jump in and get it over with quickly."

Before giving herself time to think about it, she began taking her hiking boots off, quickly undressed, and jumped from the boulder where they were sitting. She came up gasping as the cold water took her breath.

"Aren't…you…coming?" As she wheezed out her challenge, gasping for breath between each frozen word, Hawk already had his hiking boots off and was peeling off his clothes. Diving in, he swam to her, with both of them laughing as they treaded fast in the freezing water.

"That's what I like about you second most, Betsy. When somebody offers you a challenge, you take it without giving it a second thought."

When they got out, Hawk grabbed a towel from his pack and wrapped it around her as she sat on the boulder, too cold to move, with her chin quivering out of control. Then he helped her loosen her braid and towel dry her hair.

"And you did this after being in a sweat lodge?" she asked through chattering teeth.

Betsy found another towel in the pack and made Hawk wrap up in it as he began to shake.

"Oh, yeah. You just think that water is cold now. Come on. Let's get in the sleeping bag and warm up."

"Gladly! I'm freezing!" Hurriedly, Betsy plunged ahead of Hawk toward the tent.

****

The stranger followed, always keeping the same distance, stealthy, trained to stalk undetected. Dressed in khaki shorts, T-shirt, and baseball cap, he looked like an ordinary tourist hiker with his new Northface pack.

But as the sun sank below the mountains, he positioned himself behind a boulder high above Second Rock. With his high-powered binoculars focused, he unzipped his pants to give himself temporary relief as he watched the naked lovers below. After Hawk closed the tent flap, the watcher laughed sadistically.

"Enjoy, Hawk. But it'll be me that gives your little beauty her last pleasure, at least in this world."

****

When Betsy came out of the tent later that night, the moon was shining and the mountains had doubled their beauty as they reflected in the water. The couple had indeed warmed up in the sleeping bag after their swim in the icy water, and before either could help themselves, they had fallen asleep.

Betsy sat on the boulder dressed in Hawk's white thermal top that hung past her knees. She had tiptoed out of the tent, trying not to wake Hawk. Pulling the long sleeves over her cold fingertips, she drew her knees up under the top, staring awestruck at the panoramic view.

The magnificence of the mountains surrounding her gave her a feeling of being immensely small but deeply satisfied and complete. But the mountains didn't compare to the wonderful twist her life had taken now that Hawk was in it.

****

Hawk stood several yards away, looking at her as she sat on the boulder. The wind whispered to him through her golden curls, glistening in the moonlight like spun silk, and he remembered the words of Custer, his Clan Father, as he left him to begin his vision quest. *"Certain things will catch your eye, but pursue only those that capture your heart."*

He could see her profile as she sat swaddled in his white shirt, and he knew he had seen her here before, just as she was now but wearing white deerskin. She'd had wildflowers in her hair then, and when he approached her she had turned and smiled. Afraid of making the illusion disappear, he hesitated in going to her but finally could hold back no longer. As he came nearer, he stopped and picked two stalks of Indian paintbrush growing at the edge of the rocks.

Looking up, she smiled just as he had seen her do before—before he met her that day on the trail. Pushing her hair behind her ear on one side, he placed the wildflowers in her hair and pulled her to him. They sat looking at the lake and the mountains for a long time, Soft-as-Deer in the arms of the Hawk. She had captured his heart, and he would never be able to live without her.

When the moon went behind the clouds, Hawk felt Betsy shiver. Taking her hand, he led her to the tent, anxious to warm her with lovemaking and to hold her tight the rest of the night.

****

Just as the sun was peeking over the mountain, Betsy woke up to answer the call of nature. Gingerly, she tiptoed out, trying not to wake Hawk, shivering as the cold morning air penetrated her bare body. As she made her way back to the tent, she saw a doe drinking from the lake. It looked just like the one she had seen her first morning at the cabin.

"Hawk! Hawk! Wake up. There's a deer out here!"

Drowsily, he sat up and looked out the tent flap. Seeing how excited Betsy was to see the animal made him smile.

"There was a deer in my vision."

"Really?"

"Yep. When you're lucky enough to encounter a spirit, it usually comes in animal form, but it can change into human form, as well. I had two different animal spirits, and one was a deer."

"What was the other?"

"What else? A hawk. Funny, ever since my quest, I rarely see one without the other."

"That is so strange. My first morning at the cabin, I was sitting on the porch drinking my coffee and I saw a doe. She just stared at me for the longest time before she ran away. Her fawn, still in spots, jumped up at the edge of the woods and followed her as she ran by. And believe it or not, a hawk sat on that old hitching post at the end of the yard at the same time. Maybe I was on a vision quest and didn't know it."

"Maybe." As they continued watching the doe, Hawk moved to his knees, putting his hand on Betsy's back as he stretched to look up. "There he is, Betsy! There, in the tallest tree. I told you I never see one without the other."

"You're right. I see him." Betsy pointed to the tree limb. "He's just sitting there looking at the doe. That is spooky but really beautiful. Do you think they're your animal spirits?"

"I'd like to think so. I'd also like to think they're the same ones you saw. It would mean something wonderful is happening with you and me, that 'forever' you talk about."

"Something wonderful is happening, my love." Betsy put her hand on Hawk's cheek and kissed him.

"My love? Does that mean you love me, Betsy?" Hawk sat in the entrance to the tent, propped on one hand, looking longingly at Betsy.

"I'll say the words when I know forever is possible, Hawk. I've told you before. I will only love one more time in my life." Leaning into him, she stroked his face and kissed him again.

As they kissed, the hawk flew away, calling his departure. When they looked again, the doe, too, had retreated into the woods.

"Boy, the timing is way off, and I hate to break the spell, but I've got to go see a man about a horse."

"In Mississippi, the saying is, 'I gotta go see a man about a dog.' "

"Well, you're in Montana now, sweetheart. We do horses here, not dawgs." Betsy laughed at Hawk's poor attempt at a southern accent as he rushed out of the tent and into the woods.

****

The sun was high, but neither Hawk nor Betsy

wanted to move from the warm sleeping bag or from the comfort of each other's embrace. Their bodies were just waking up the second time and had begun to respond to their closeness when they heard someone outside the tent.

"Anybody home?" As she heard the voice, Betsy panicked and dove deeper into the sleeping bag, knowing their clothes were still lying by the lake where they had left them the night before.

"Jake! You better have a damn good reason for being outside this tent, or I swear I'll kill you!" Hawk threw back the sleeping bag and opened the tent flap while Betsy quickly grabbed the covers, pulling them to her chin again.

"Just thought I'd come tell you two lovebirds a Boy Scout troop is headed this way. They're about ten minutes down trail."

"You're shittin' me!" Hawk plunged out of the tent naked, heading to retrieve their clothes. "Ouch! Damn pine cones! How the hell do people from the South walk barefooted, Betsy?"

"Good grief, Hawk! You could at least have grabbed a towel!" yelled Betsy from the tent, not about to budge until Hawk brought her clothes.

"It's just Jake, Betsy. He's seen me in the buff plenty of times."

"Don't worry, Betsy. I'm not looking at his scraggly butt. I'm waiting for you to come out." Jake smiled, waiting for Hawk's reaction, which he knew would come.

"Watch it, Jake! You'll be looking like a bloody Doobie 'fore you know what hit you." Hawk handed in Betsy's clothes as he began dressing outside the tent.

"You're serious? Boy Scouts?"

"Yep. My nephew's troop, ten of 'em. My sister suckered me into this at the last minute. I came ahead and noticed your tent and figured I better warn you. I don't think there's a badge for what you two might teach those little boys if they got here too soon, especially with your clothes out here."

"Good morning, Jake. Thanks for the warning." Sheepishly, Betsy left the tent, picked up her hiking boots, and carried them to sit by Hawk on the log used by many campers before for seating. Her long hair hung in her face, and she caught it, pulling it all over to one side so she could see to tie her boots.

"How the hell do you do it, Hawk?"

"What?"

"Get a gorgeous woman like that to rough it up here with you? Damn! Do you always look this good first thing in the morning, Betsy?" Jake was staring, smiling, all the while knowing his remarks would get a rise out of his partner.

"Well, just check it out the next time I run by naked, and you'll know how I got her—Shorty!"

Betsy's cheeks flushed. "Oh, please, you two! Can we change the subject?"

Hawk and Jake burst out laughing.

"Really, Jake. How far are they?"

"Actually, I told them to stop and fish at the other end till I come back for them. And really—it's just my nephew and his dad. I just wanted to see your ass get in a hurry for once, Hawk."

Hawk tackled Jake, knocking him off the other log as the two wrestled on the ground like two little boys, with Jake laughing and pleading for mercy.

****

"Are you ready for our debut as a couple, darling?"

Hawk and Betsy stood outside the Grizzly. They were later than they meant to be, but both had died of fatigue after getting back from Second Rock and napped longer than they meant to. Betsy could tell Hawk was nervous and wondered if he would have to do the test tonight.

"By the way, you look gorgeous, sweetheart. I like the skirt, especially the way it hangs below my belly button ring. Just make sure you don't dance with anybody but me tonight."

"Hawk, are you telling me if BJ asks me to dance you're gonna pitch a fit? 'Cause if you are, I'd just as soon leave now." Betsy stood with her hands on her hips.

"I'm kidding, Betsy. You can dance with him—once."

"Oh, I see! And if Amanda is here?"

"She won't be. I know she's at a rodeo."

"And how do you know?"

"She's at one every weekend in the summer. Jealous?"

"Do I have a reason to be?" Betsy put her hands back on her hips.

"If you don't know by now, darling, you're not as smart as I thought." Noticing she was not smiling, Hawk pulled her to him.

"I love you, Betsy. My forever is in front of me." As they kissed, they heard someone clear their throat.

"Could you two move it out of the doorway? My lord, every time I see the two of you, you're lip-locked. Are you joined at the hip already?"

"Close." Hawk took Betsy's hand and led her through the door as she turned to speak to her friends.

"Hey, Darlene, Mack. You guys are late, too."

"Yeah, Mack's been working on the Harley all afternoon. If you two aren't sitting with Hawk's usual crowd, come on over and sit with us."

"We promised we'd save Jake a spot, but we'll be over later," Betsy answered.

By the time they were seated, the server was already there.

"Beer, Hawk?" she asked.

"No, not tonight. Just a ginger ale for me. What do you want, babe?"

"Water with lemon is fine." After the server left, Hawk turned to Betsy.

"You can have a beer if you want it, Betsy. You don't have to hold out on account of me. I can handle it."

"Don't want it, Hawk. Always preferred lemon water. Besides, I've got what I want beside me."

"You two sure cleaned up good. Well, you did, Hawk. Betsy always looks good regardless."

Jake and his date sat down, and Jake introduced Cindy to Betsy. Betsy liked her right off. Between Jake and Hawk picking at each other and Cindy's wholesome laugh, it was destined to be a fun night.

"Betsy, I need to go talk to Wayne. I've got to finish paying for all that stuff I broke the other week. I'll be right back."

Betsy watched Hawk and wondered how she had gotten so lucky this time. He stopped to talk to the Doobie brothers, who for some unexplainable reason were not drunk yet. When he first approached them, the

Doobie closest to him left his bar stool and backed up until Hawk assured him everything was okay. Hawk lingered, talking to the brothers a while longer. Ned or Ted, whichever one it was, turned and looked over at Betsy and continued talking to Hawk. Before leaving the bar, Hawk and the Doobie shook hands.

Taking out his wallet, he gave some money to Wayne, who shook his hand before going back to serve his customers. Betsy was proud of Hawk for taking responsibility for his bad behavior.

"What was that all about, with the Doobie brothers?" As Hawk sat by Betsy, he put his hand around her exposed upper leg.

"I needed to get it off my chest. I apologized to Doobie for beating the hell out of him that night and asked him if he was all right. He told me to apologize to you. Said he didn't even remember what started the fight till people refreshed his memory. Now, how about you and me dance?"

As they danced, Hawk held her tight and was back to ear nuzzling. Betsy noticed everyone staring at them and began to feel uneasy.

"Hawk, why is everyone staring at us?"

"They'll get used to it. They just can't believe I finally found someone to love."

"What about Amanda?"

"We were never a couple, Betsy. We didn't live together. Red Lodge is small, and everybody knows I'm never at my place anymore. Does it bother you?"

"Just makes me a little uneasy, but I want everyone to know you're mine. I don't want those women kicking up their skirts at you anymore." Betsy put her head on Hawk's chest.

"I don't think you have to worry about that. I believe it's pretty obvious who my girl is. Just concentrate on me and forget the stares." Hawk put his head on top of Betsy's as he held her tight.

As the night wore on, the staring ended except for a man sitting in the shadows in the back corner. Betsy didn't notice, but Hawk's keen senses, reacting like radar where Betsy was concerned, tuned into him immediately.

"Betsy, do you know the guy sitting at the back table by himself? Black hat. Long hair and a mustache."

Betsy glanced over at the man, who never took his eyes off her.

"No. I've never seen him before. Why?"

"That guy has been staring at you for at least half an hour, ever since he got here. I'm about ready to go beat the hell out of him."

"Please, Hawk! No more fights! He's probably just another drunk. If he keeps staring, let's just leave."

"Well, I don't think he's going to stop. He sees me looking at him and he just keeps staring, looks right past me at you."

"I'm beat anyway. Let's go home, Hawk. But first let's go sit with Darlene and Mack a few minutes, so she won't think I'm ignoring her."

Darlene greeted them with, "Well, I can't say you two are wearing the same jeans this time. I like the outfit, Betsy. But I believe that's about as close as I've ever seen two people dance. Pull up a chair. Oops! There's not but one empty."

Hawk pulled the chair to the table and sat down, pulling Betsy into his lap. With her arm around his neck, she played with the hair hanging past his collar under his hat.

"Hawk Larson, you never cease to amaze me! If you had to fall for somebody—and it was bound to happen sooner or later—I'm glad it was Betsy."

"Me too. I don't know what I did before I found her, but I bet it wasn't pretty. Do you think she loves me, Darlene?" Hawk looked at Betsy, waiting for Darlene's answer.

"Well, if looks can be trusted, I'd say your chances are good. Have you asked her?" Darlene leaned into Mack, who put his arm around her and squeezed her.

"Yes, he has, and he knows the answer to that one already." Kissing him, she noticed he had become distracted, looking in the direction of the stranger again.

"Darlene, do you or Mack know the guy in the black hat sitting back at the corner table? He's been staring a hole through Betsy, and I'm about to have to kick the son-of-a-bitch's ass."

"No. I've never seen him before. Have you, Mack?"

"Nope. Probably just some drifter with too much to drink."

"Hawk, let's go home. I'm tired." Betsy stood beside Hawk.

"Are you sure, babe, or are you just trying to keep me out of trouble?"

"Both."

As Betsy headed toward the door, holding Hawk's hand, she felt him pulling back. He had stopped at the door and was having a staring contest with the stranger. Finally, the man looked away.

"Let's get out of here, Hawk. Now!" Betsy gave Hawk a tug.

"Okay, okay!" Hawk opened the door and followed Betsy out. As they headed down the road from the Grizzly, Hawk watched in the rearview mirror as a car pulled out and stayed a distance behind them.

"I think he's following us, Betsy. I'll make a loop up here and see if he is."

After Hawk turned, he watched, and the car made the same turn. Backtracking, he pulled back into the Grizzly parking lot. The car continued past.

"I'm going in and see if he's in there. If he's not, I'll know it was him."

"No, Hawk. I just want to go home." Betsy reached across and rubbed Hawk's leg.

"Okay, but when you see Darlene, ask her if the guy left when we did." Hawk paused and then glanced at Betsy. "Do you think Patrick would have you followed?"

"I don't think so, but then I don't really know Patrick, do I? It doesn't really matter. Even if he did have someone following me, it won't change anything. I'm not giving you up, Hawk, ever." This was the closest Betsy had come to "forever," and Hawk smiled.

"Come here, you." He stopped as they pulled onto the forestry road to the cabin and pulled her over to him. With his arms around her holding her tight, he kissed her.

****

Betsy awoke first the next morning and slipped out of bed, choosing not to wake her sleeping lover. The first thing on her agenda was to take a long shower and get the smell of smoke out of her hair from the night before. Afterwards, she wrapped a towel around her and sat on the bed beside Hawk, who was just beginning to wake up as she played with his hair.

"Good morning. That's the first time I've been able to sneak out of bed without waking you. You must be worn out, my strong, handsome hero." She continued playing with his hair, moving it out of his eyes.

Throwing the covers back, he pulled her in beside him after unwrapping her towel and discarding it on the floor.

"You smell good." He nuzzled her neck and scrunched down, laying his head on her breasts and closing his eyes again.

"It's something special called soap and shampoo. You like it?" As she stroked his hair, he began snoring again.

"Well, this is certainly a first. Am I losing my charm?"

Opening one eye, he jumped up, pulling her deeper under the covers as he began kissing her, then moving down her body to grab the belly button ring with his lips, twirling it with his tongue.

"You devil! You were faking it! Stop for a second. I want to talk to you."

"Talk? You want to talk? Maybe I'm the one losing my charm?" Moving back up on the pillow, he put his arm around her, moving her head to his chest.

"Okay. Talk," Hawk said.

"It's Sunday, your day. What's your pleasure, besides the obvious?" Betsy smiled up at Hawk.

"Oh, yeah! Gentleman's pleasure! What are my choices?"

"Anything you want. To start with, what do you want for breakfast?"

"Besides you? That T-bone in the fridge you

refused to eat last night for dinner, three eggs over easy, and toast—slightly burned, two pieces for starters, with butter."

"I hate to even think what your arteries look like, but I guess I can handle that. Then what?"

"Depends." Hawk looked sheepishly at Betsy.

"On what?" Betsy sat up, anxious to see what Hawk was up to.

"Do I get you before or after breakfast?"

"You're giving me a choice?" Betsy cocked her head.

"Only one you get for the day."

"After. You get a shower while I fix your breakfast. You still smell like the Grizzly." As she got out of bed and headed for the closet to get dressed, Hawk stopped her.

"Wait a minute. I get to pick what you wear today." Hawk stopped beside Betsy.

"Oh, Hawk! Not my green dress! I hate those heels."

"No. This." He reached in the closet and pulled out his shirt, the one she had worn on the first morning they woke up together. "Nothing else but this."

"Anything else, Master?" Betsy curtsied as she took the shirt from Hawk.

"Yeah. Brush your hair out and leave it long. Let your curls crinkle down that amazing back of yours." He pulled her to him, tracing a trail with his fingers from her neck to below her butt.

"No braid and no makeup," he added, letting his hands linger on her cheeks while he kissed her deep, a prelude to passion.

****

As Hawk devoured the steak and eggs, Betsy sat eating her dry toast and drinking her coffee, her fingers laced through the handle and holding tight to the blue mug, drinking from the side opposite the handle as she enjoyed the sight of her guy sitting in his boxers and T-shirt and looking very content. When he looked up and saw her watching him, he smiled and winked. Betsy was surprised at how something as simple as a wink from this man could arouse her, especially after all the extreme passion they had shared.

"Delicious!" Hawk took his empty dishes and put them in the sink. "Thank you, darling." He leaned down and kissed her and then picked her up like he always did and headed for the stairs.

"Now for the main course."

****

"Okay, Hawk. Are you checking off your wishes? What's next?"

Leaving the bed, he pulled his boxers back on but left his T-shirt off. Then he held up the shirt he had picked out for her, and she put her arms in as he turned her to face him while he buttoned the middle buttons, leaving two unbuttoned at the top and bottom for easy access. Grabbing a pillow off the bed with one hand, he took her hand with the other and led her back down the stairs.

"Sit here." When she was seated on the sofa, Hawk placed the pillow on her lap and headed for the bookshelves holding Sue Ann's novels. "Which one has Cutter and Soft-as-Deer in it?"

"*The Half-Breed and the Lady*. It's on the end. I've read it three times—at least parts of it."

"Good. You should be able to make it very

dramatic as you read it to me, then."

"Are you serious?" Sue Ann arched her eyebrows, questioning Hawk's wish.

"As serious as I am when I tell you I love you. Get started. I want to hear the whole book before this day is over. If there's a part that bogs down, just ad lib and move to the juicy parts. If I yell, 'Stop,' it means—well, I bet you'll already have a clue what I want. Oh, yeah. Whatever you do, don't mention to Jake I spent the day listening to chick lit. He'd never let me live it down."

Putting his head on the pillow in her lap, he pulled her face down to kiss her and then took her right hand and placed it on his head. On cue, Betsy began reading while combing her fingertips through his hair.

Betsy took few breaks while reading the book. When she wanted coffee, Hawk would make it and tell her to keep going. As she role-played each part, they were both entranced, transported back to Montana in the late 1800s as they relived the parts of Cutter and Soft-as-Deer vicariously.

When reading the scene where Victoria first manipulated Cutter into making love to her in a mountain stream, Betsy noticed Hawk getting a little antsy, turning on his side and pulling at his boxers. As he put his hands between his knees, drawing them up, he noticed Betsy had stopped reading. Lifting his head and looking up at her, he recognized the grin.

"What?"

"Need a little relief? Is it gettin' to you, my darling?"

"It's that damn sexy drawl of yours that's killing me. But I'm holding out for Soft-as-Deer. You just watch out, sweetheart! When Cutter takes Deer, I'm taking you. I'll have the king of hard-ons by then."

"Lookin' forward to it, darlin'. Lookin' forward to it." Betsy smiled, knowing how the book ended and wondering what Hawk's reaction would be.

As she got to the last page, Betsy began to smile, making the words extra sexy and dramatic, something she knew would be pure torture, given the ending.

They sat on Cutter's horse at the top of the ridge, gazing down as the cloud of dust from the stagecoach moved across the desolate valley below, carrying Victoria back East, away from the man she had only thought she owned.

"Are you sad to see her go?" Soft-as-Deer asked.

"No, all I've ever really wanted was here all the time."

"But what will you do without her, Cutter?"

Turning to face the beautiful Indian girl who sat behind him, he swung his right leg over the saddle horn, placing his hat on his propped knee. Taking her chin in his left hand, he dove into the black canyons of Soft-as-Deer's eyes, determined to erase her look of despair.

"This, for starters."

He engulfed her small lips, his kiss deep, filled with fire and love she would realize once and for all were for her only. As he released her mouth, she smiled, giving him the consent he needed to turn his horse toward the cabin. The End

Jerking himself to a sitting position, Hawk stared at Betsy almost in a rage.

"That's it? It ends before he gets her to the cabin?"

"Yep. Guess you'll have to use your imagination." Betsy did not try to withhold her grin.

Bolting from the sofa, Hawk headed for the bookcase, where he turned his head sideways trying to read the titles.

"Damn! That can't be the end! Where the hell's the sequel, Betsy?" Hawk thumbed through the rows of books.

As Betsy moved toward Hawk, she began unbuttoning her shirt—his shirt—stopping by the primitive table across from the bookcase, the table her mother had used to write many romances, including *The Half-Breed and the Lady*.

"It's here, Hawk." As he turned to face her, she smiled letting the shirt drop to the floor.

Throwing the book he had in his hand over his shoulder haphazardly, the half-blood returned an even bigger grin as he stared at her before making his way to the table.

She was the essence of seduction as she posed, leaning against the table with her weight on one foot, one knee relaxed in front of the other, anticipating what he had promised. Stopping before reaching her, he stepped out of his boxers to show her his status as monarch.

The lovers never made it past the table as he picked her up and placed her on the edge, where his body could enter hers perfectly. There was little foreplay except for the kneading of her breasts with his lips as she leaned back on her elbows, beckoning him to enter his domain. After one long, deep suck on her breasts, the king of all erections moved into his queen's realm, giving her pleasure unequaled in her life with the exception of making love the first time at the waterfall.

"Keep your eyes open, Betsy. I want to look in

them while I make love to you."

Moving in perfect synchronization, the lovers moaned as Hawk shifted his weight from leg to leg, moving his hips in circular motion to heighten her pleasure.

Just before they reached the moment of exaltation, he picked her up without withdrawing from her. As she locked her legs and arms around him, holding tight, he pressed his hands firmly, with one hand on each hip, and entered into the unfathomable depths of her desire. She gasped, breathless as he carried her to the bearskin rug stretched out on the floor in front of the bookcase.

With the soft fur beneath her, he continued his forcefulness, becoming almost violent at her urging as he plunged them both to a peak of unrestrained satisfaction unequaled in either of their lives. After spilling into her, he collapsed in pleasant exhaustion, rolling onto his back and pulling her on top of him.

He kissed her and then moved her head to his chest as he coddled her, stroking her hair and back. Neither of them moved from their position even after he released naturally from her, not wanting to ruin the contentment they felt. Before either could prevent it, they slept, absorbed in the warmth of the old grizzly and in the contentment of their embrace.

Chapter Nine

"You know, I'm glad you came in today, Betsy. There's something I've been meaning to tell you and never could think of it. There was a man in last week asking about you, wanted to know where you lived, that sort of thing. He said he was a friend of your mom's from Alaska and was just passing through. Hope it was okay. I told him where your cabin was. Did he find you?"

"No. I don't know anything about it, Darlene."

"He seemed like a pleasant sort. I probably told him more than I should. He asked if you had a guy, and I told him about Hawk. I can't believe that handsome hunk finally gave in to someone, and I'm so proud it's you that hooked him. Never did like that Diane. She was a real corker, that one. Can't say as I care much for Amanda, either, but I don't think she was ever in the picture as much as she liked for folks to think." Darlene babbled on as usual while gathering Betsy and Hawk's mail.

"I don't have a clue who it could be, but don't worry about it. I'll ask Mom the next time I talk to her. Did he tell you his name?"

"Let's see. I wrote it down somewhere so I could tell you after he left." Darlene turned everything over on the counter until she finally came up with a yellow note. "Here it is: Jim Smithers. There was a woman sitting in the car, but he didn't tell me her name."

As Betsy left the post office, she opened her letter from Annie. A folded newspaper clipping fell out and landed in her lap.

"I saw this in the Sunday edition of the *Memphis Commercial Appeal* and thought you might need it for your lawyer." Annie ended the letter with the usual hugs and kisses and said she was looking forward to seeing her in September. The clipping was an ad for a new boutique, Angelique's. There was a picture of Angelique with her aunt and two more people standing in the background outside the new store.

Guess this is where some of Wingate Constructor's money is going. Maybe it was Angelique who caused Eddie to be "thrown to the dogs."

Betsy immediately put the clipping in her wallet and out of her mind as she looked at the rest of her mail.

There was an update from her lawyer telling her everything was on schedule, assuring her she would have a nice settlement. The divorce would be finalized on September first just as Patrick had promised. This was good news, but she knew she could not be totally relieved until the divorce papers were in her hands.

When Betsy drove up at the cabin, she was surprised to see Hawk's horse in the small corral he had built in the front yard. The saddle was off and the horse had been fed and watered. It looked as if Hawk was planning on staying for a while.

"Hawk!"

"Up here! Just got out of the shower."

"What? No invitation?" Betsy bolted up the stairs as she called to him, but he was already dressing when she entered the bedroom.

"Sorry, baby, but I've got to pick up some new clients in Billings. They'll be at the airport at six-thirty. Do you mind taking me in? I've got a proposition for you."

"What's the proposition? You've got my curiosity up."

"Strangest thing. Call it fate, but there's a guy and a woman coming up, just booked with us this morning. They want to fish high mountain lakes, but they're both novices. They requested two guides, and one needs to be a woman. I guess the wife doesn't think a man can teach her to fly fish. Well, you said you wanted to learn to guide. Now's your chance."

"Oh, I don't think I'm ready, Hawk."

"Come on, Betsy. You're a pro at casting, and you're already a teacher. What better combination to teach a fellow wannabe fly-fisher woman? Besides, get this—the guy is some bigwig businessman from California or some damn place and is paying us triple if we can get a female instructor for his wife. What do you say, Betsy?"

"Well, it is tempting." Betsy put her finger to her chin as if thinking.

"I'll take a tent just for the two of us. We can finish what Jake interrupted the last time we were in the high country." His shirt was open and he pulled her to him, making the offer much more tantalizing.

"Now you're making me an offer I can't refuse." Outlining the scar on his chest as she always did, she kissed him. "When do we leave?"

"Tomorrow morning. Early. I've got a room for them at Red Lodge, so I'll probably have to stay at my place tonight. Stay with me?"

"If I'm going to guide, I've got to pack. I better let you pick me up at the cabin. What horse will I be riding?"

"How about Smoke? He's a little too spirited for the city slickers, but you can handle him. Besides, he already loves you. I'll ride one of the young horses we're training."

"And who will do the cooking?" Betsy frowned, showing Hawk he'd better give her the right answer.

"Jake's going. He just won't be guiding this time. You know him. He'd rather cook and sleep than fish. That's why we're such a good team."

The couple was waiting outside the terminal and was easily distinguishable, looking like they'd stepped out of an expensive fly fishing catalog. Even their luggage was readily identified by the famous logo. Their names were Bob and Linda McIntyre, they appeared to be in their early forties, and if first impressions were right, they would have no trouble making the trip into the mountains: both looked quite fit.

"You two been married long?" Bob asked the question as Hawk drove toward the hotel, and Hawk and Betsy just looked at each other, each waiting for the other one to answer.

"Bob, what kind of question is that? You know not everybody believes in vows these days. Just ignore him. He's a little old-fashioned."

"Have you ever fly-fished, Mrs. McIntyre?" Quick to change the subject, Betsy looked into the back seat, waiting for a reply.

"Please call me Linda. Actually, I tried it once but

couldn't get the hang of it. I told Bob the instructor didn't have a clue how to teach a woman. The only way I'd come on this trip with him was if he could find me a female instructor. Bob has had several lessons, so he's much further along than I am. You've got your work cut out for you, Betsy. I know it takes practice, but if I could just catch one fish, I'd be happy."

"Oh, I can assure you you'll catch more than one fish, Linda. The lake where Hawk is taking you is full of cutthroat trout. There's another lake higher up, a little harder to get to, but if you're game, you'll each catch more than you know what to do with."

"You two look pretty fit. Do you work out?" Hawk had noticed the large biceps on Bob and figured he was into weightlifting.

"We belong to a gym, devoted exercisers. The usual yuppie stuff, if you know what I mean. We try to eat healthy, too. Want the old ticker to last as long as possible. Right, honey?"

Linda nodded her head in agreement with her husband. They seemed amiable enough to Betsy, but she was not sure how enjoyable this trip would be. Linda just did not seem like the fly fishing type to her. Her nails were long and polished, every hair was in place, and she seemed a little prissy for the outdoors.

Bob, on the other hand, looked like he could bench press five hundred pounds, and even though he tried to put on the city slicker façade, he seemed rugged underneath, giving Betsy an impression of something she could not quite put her finger on but felt didn't fit the outward demeanor.

"Well, here we are. It's not the Hilton, but it's comfortable. Your room should be ready." Hawk helped Bob unload the suitcases and took them to the hotel office. "You can leave your gear bags if you want. I'll rig up your rods for you tonight."

"No!" Bob almost shouted as he quickly grabbed the two bags from the back of the Suburban. "My rod is pretty special to me, anniversary present from Linda this year." He hugged his wife, who looked at him adoringly. "There's no rush. You can rig us both up when we're at the camp."

As Betsy and Hawk pulled away from the hotel, Betsy waved at Darlene, who was across the street in the parking lot of one of the local burger places, sitting on the back of Mack's parked Harley. Darlene waved, proud to be seen with Mack the Knife.

"Bob and Linda, now there's a strange pair. What do you think, Betsy? Will you be able to teach Miss High Society without getting her hands dirty?"

"Oh, I think I can handle it. Once she starts catching fish, she'll be just like the rest of us—hooked."

****

It was hard for Betsy to leave Hawk that night. She hadn't spent any real time with him in a few days, and he almost convinced her to stay. But if she was going to play guide for three days, she had to be ready.

As she headed up the forestry road to the cabin, a deer jumped out in front of the Jeep, causing her to cut a donut in the road in order to miss it. As she stopped to gather her nerves before straightening the Jeep, she noticed a dark SUV parked behind a clump of trees several yards off the road. It looked as if the driver had attempted to hide it. She would never have noticed it if it hadn't been for the deer.

Betsy thought it was strange—she had never seen any vehicles out on this road other than hers, Custer's old truck, and Hawk's, plus the occasional forestry truck—but she didn't really think anything about it. After all, it was hard to find a spot where there wasn't an invasion of outdoors enthusiasts anymore, especially in the mountains. Her main hope was that it would never happen in her mountains in her lifetime, but she knew eventually the best-kept secret in Montana would be out. Still, no locals wanted this area to become like other parts of the Northwest, where urbanites were moving in and driving up prices of land to build their huge mansions for holiday houses. The secret was safe for a while.

It took an hour for Betsy to pack her fishing gear, and she still had not started on clothing and camp gear. She was so tired she decided to take a nap on the sofa before finishing. Turning the lights down, Betsy crawled under one of her mom's cozy family quilts, kept on the back of the sofa.

She had not been asleep long when she thought she heard a creak on the front porch like someone walking. Immediately, she thought it must be Hawk, hoped it was Hawk. Crossing the room, she never thought twice about opening the door. It was never locked, anyway, and she thought sure she'd open it to discover a posed cowboy waiting to make his entry.

As she got closer, she heard footsteps on the porch again, but it sounded like someone running. Yanking open the door, she was surprised to find the porch empty.

"Hawk, is that you?"

There was no answer, but she could hear something

running through the woods at the side of the cabin. Instantly, she thought about the doe that visited her often and decided the deer must have gotten overly brave and stepped up on the porch, maybe to eat the petunias Betsy had planted in the windowbox.

Nonetheless, as she closed the door, she did something she had never done since coming to the cabin. She locked the deadbolt and then went to the back door and did the same. Betsy had never felt uneasy here and couldn't explain why she was feeling this way now, but she was not going to take any chances. She vowed to herself not to let it become a habit. It had taken over a decade for her to become brave after she was kidnapped in Alaska as a teen, especially after Shade lost his life saving her, and she had vowed never to go back to being afraid after she finally won her bravery back.

"This is my home, and I will not be frightened out of it." She whispered the words to the portrait, Shade's artwork in the cabin he had given her mother, a place of solitude—a place of healing.

****

True to his word, Hawk and the convoy of horses and anglers showed up at eight the next morning. Betsy was ready and waiting and had even made a fresh batch of raspberry muffins and two thermoses of coffee for their first rest stop.

Before going out the door to help load her gear, Betsy made a quick call to Custer. He did not answer, and she assumed he was probably charging his cell phone and didn't have it with him, so she left him a message.

"I'm going with Hawk for a few days, Custer. He's

taking a couple up, Bob and Linda McIntyre from California, and they've requested a female fly fishing instructor for Mrs. McIntyre. The Jeep keys are in the drawer by the refrigerator. Why don't you use it and pick up those truck parts you said you needed? I'll call when I get back. Love ya."

"Did you stay up all night, Betsy? Smells wonderful."

Betsy slapped Hawk's hand as he reached into the container for a muffin.

"Not now, Hawk. This is for our first stop on the trail." Hawk gave a pretend pout, then hugged Betsy and gave her a big kiss in front of the McIntyres and Jake.

"Won't work. You still have to wait until we stop." Betsy put the container in her saddlebag, knowing that was the only way to keep Hawk out of it.

The McIntyres were not novices to horseback riding, but Linda kept trying to rise in the western saddle like an English rider. When she wasn't looking, Hawk winked at Betsy and motioned for her to look. Betsy had to restrain herself from laughing out loud.

The first fly fishing lesson went well for teacher and student, and Linda was actually able to catch a few fish that day without scaring them to death. Screaming each time she managed to get one to the bank, Linda McIntyre became more irritating as the fishing continued. Bob looked like a pro after only a little instruction, and Hawk began to wonder if he didn't know more than he claimed.

Jake's cooking went over extremely well, and even though steak and fried potatoes was the main course, Bob and Linda ate as if they had forgotten their "healthy eating" lifestyle.

As they sat around the campfire after dinner, Hawk began to notice the way Bob stared at Betsy every time she moved. Every time he realized Hawk was watching him, he would fidget nervously, poke the fire, go for another cup of coffee, or direct some pretentious, lovey-dovey remark to his wife, who seemed totally uninterested in her husband.

After about an hour had passed, Linda asked where she might wash up, and Betsy offered to show her where the outdoor bathroom had been set up, well away from the stream as camping regulations required. No way would she be sharing her and Hawk's waterfall with this city woman who was becoming more unlikable as the trip wore on.

When the women left, Bob decided to try to make amends for the staring.

"That's one beautiful woman you've got there, Hawk. You're a lucky man. Of course, no woman is as beautiful as my wife to me, but it's hard not to stare at Betsy. I hope you don't take offense."

"Yes, she is beautiful, and yes, I am lucky. Do I care if any man stares at her? Damn right I do. Wouldn't you?"

"Yeah, guess I would. I'll try to restrain myself. Sorry." With this apology, he excused himself to his tent, saying he was tired.

Later, when everyone was in tents for the night, Hawk held Betsy to him and decided to play the protector role fate had so graciously cast his way.

"There's something about Bob I just don't trust, Betsy. I don't like the way he looks at you, and his little romantic remarks to his wife sound forced and fake. I want you to be careful around him. Promise?"

"I think you are getting a little too protective, Mr. Guardian Angel. I don't think he means any harm."

"Just the same, I don't want you alone with him."

Betsy shook her head and gave a look of total disbelief and lack of concern that immediately irritated Hawk.

"Damn it, Betsy! Listen to me!" Taking her arm more forcefully than he meant to, his remark came across more like an order than a concern, and he spoke more gruffly than he intended.

Betsy jerked her arm free as she sat up, staring at him, casting daggers of anger.

"Hawk, protecting me is one thing, but don't start getting possessive! I've lived with one control freak, and I won't replicate it. I can take care of myself. Don't ever forget—I came to these mountains alone."

"Sorry!" The sarcasm in his voice told Betsy he did not understand or approve of her taking his warning so defensively.

"I need some fresh air."

Huffing, she threw the sleeping bag back and stumbled out of the tent. Slipping her hiking boots on without tying them, she grabbed the flashlight and stomped toward the path leading to the lake.

Hawk turned away from where she had been lying, angry at her for taking his warning so lightly. He lay there for a few minutes not knowing whether to go after her or to let her stew on her own for a while. Besides, he had no intention of taking back what he'd said.

Damn it! She needs to listen to me.

In his thinking, he was looking after her interest, not just his. Just when he had decided to let her stew, he heard someone moving around the campsite. Quietly, he unsnapped the flap and looked out to see Bob slipping around the side of his tent.

Where the hell is he going?

Not giving his mind time to answer, he threw on his shorts and hiking boots and left the tent. Something told him Bob was going in the same direction as Betsy.

Hawk knew Betsy would be sitting on the rocks looking at the reflection of the moonlit mountains in the lake. Bob must have seen her when she left the tent and followed her. As Hawk reached the boulders overlooking the lake, he saw the man he was coming to despise squatting by a tree, watching Betsy.

"Anything wrong, Bob?"

"Oh, Hawk, you scared me." He jumped to his feet. "No, I'm just having trouble sleeping. Too quiet out here. Who would think a person could miss the sounds of sirens and traffic. I see Betsy is having the same problem."

"She has no problem at all sleeping. Just likes to look at the lake and the mountains. You need to be careful leaving the campsite. There are bears in these mountains." He paused and looked toward Betsy and then glared at Bob. "And other things that can hurt you." Hawk meant for Bob to hear the anger in his voice and to take it as a warning.

"Well, I'll be getting back to the tent. Linda will wonder where I am if she wakes up."

As Hawk made his way over the boulders, Betsy turned to him and smiled, letting him know her anger had subsided.

"I'm sorry, baby. I didn't mean to be a jerk. Forgive me?" As he sat by her, he held his arms open, beckoning to her.

In the moon-glow dancing across her face, her emerald eyes sparkled as if gold had been added to them just for this moment. Taking her into his arms, he kissed her while holding her gently as if she were a delicate treasure to be protected at all costs. In reverent silence, they gazed at the mountains, she with her head on his chest and he with his arm around her, twisting her hair just like he always did at these moments.

Not wanting to risk starting the argument over, Hawk chose not to tell her that Bob had followed her. But he vowed to himself to be overly vigilant where this guy was concerned. He had convinced Betsy to come on this trip, and he was not about to let anything happen to her.

****

Custer drove the Jeep to Red Lodge and picked up what he needed at the local auto parts store, then headed to the post office on the odd chance he would have any mail. Usually, his box was filled with junk mail like satellite TV offers and credit card applications, both of which amused him greatly. He had about as much need for one as the other, but he always left the post office with them rather than throwing them in the trash before leaving. There was something about leaving a post office empty-handed that always looked sad when he witnessed it in others.

"Hey, Custer? See you cleaned out that box finally. About time! If you don't start coming in more often, you're going to have to rent a drawer instead of a box."

"Maybe I'll just let you stop loading all that junk in there one of these days, Darlene. Never even look at any of it anyway. Don't have much need for Pay-Per-

View or Mastercard."

"I saw Betsy found that friend of Sue Ann's from Alaska who was looking for her last week."

"What friend? She never said nothin' to me about it."

"Uh, Smithers was his name, Jim Smithers. Asked all about her, where she lived, if she had a guy. I wouldn't a told him anything, but he seemed genuine enough, and he knew her mother. I saw Betsy and Hawk let him and the woman who was with him out over at the Rainbow Inn night before last."

"No, that was some couple, the McIntyres, they picked up at the airport. Betsy and Hawk took them up to the high country on a guided fishing trip yesterday morning. They're from California. Must've just looked like...what was his name?"

"Jim Smithers. No, it was him all right. Good-looking, muscular guy. A single girl like me would remember something that handsome. He did have a woman in the car waiting on him, always my luck. That was the first of last week when he came in the post office to mail some postcards. I know they didn't fly in the day I saw Betsy and Hawk with them, least not unless they left and came back."

"Huh! That's strange. I'll call Sue Ann and see if she knows this guy."

"Smithers, Jim Smithers. If you catch up with him and he's single, send him my way, just in case Mack takes off on me." Darlene's double chin and her big hair shook as she laughed.

As Custer headed out of Red Lodge, he drove faster than usual, worried about what Darlene had told him, and he listened to Betsy's message again.

Confirming the names she gave him for the couple made him uneasy, and he sped up again. Before reaching the dead-signal area in the valley ahead, he pulled out his phone and dialed Sue Ann's number.

"Custer, you old brute! What are you up to? Taking care of my little girl?"

Custer wasted no time in telling Sue Ann what Darlene had said and about the couple Hawk and Betsy had taken to the high country.

"I've never heard of a Jim Smithers or any McIntyres. Something is wrong, Custer. I don't like it. You know me and my intuition where Betsy is concerned. I've had that same nagging feeling I get that something was not right with my daughter for several days now. Betsy would just laugh at me if I said anything, but this scares me to death. People can do crazy things when there's a divorce, especially when the ex has a big bank account. Can you get to her, Custer?"

"Don't worry, Sue Ann. I'm on my way. But Hawk'll take care of her or die trying. I'll call you when I have her back safe at the cabin."

Custer sped up, taking the sharp mountain curves almost on two wheels as he rushed to get back to his cabin and head up to the high country. He took no time to close the Jeep door as he jumped from it and ran up the front steps of Betsy's cabin. Never stopping, he took the stairs two steps at a time as he headed for the bedroom.

After a few minutes of digging in the back corner of the closet, he pulled out a high-powered rifle. Then he reached on the top shelf and felt around until he found a box of cartridges. Reaching into another corner of the closet, he pulled out a pair of moose-hide moccasins. Quickly he took off his boots and put on the moccasins, lacing them tightly up his calves.

Custer ran up the trail, oblivious to the weight of the rifle hung by a shoulder strap across his back. As surefooted as a young brave, driven by his adrenaline and fear for his Little One, he settled into a slow but steady jog for the hours it would take him to get to the outfitter's camp.

There was no time to grab food or water. He would take his chances as in the old days and drink from the streams as needed. Custer hoped Darlene was wrong and this was all unnecessary, but his senses told him otherwise, and he was determined to get to Betsy and Hawk and ward off anything bad that could happen.

****

"How far is it to Second Rock? I'd like to tackle it. Reckon you could make it, Linda?"

"I can do anything you can do, dear. What about it, Hawk? I'd like to catch some of those prize cutthroat and take some pictures."

Jake prepared lunch for the foursome to take with them and couldn't wait for them to get out of sight so he could get back into the collection of western novels he had brought with him. This was just the kind of outfitting he liked.

Hawk offered to take the heavy camera pack for Linda, but she said Bob would carry it.

"He needs to work out. He's had vacation enough with you here taking up all the slack, Hawk." Bob looked at his wife and smiled as he placed the pack on his back.

The group stopped two hours into the hike and ate

some of what Jake had prepared for them. Hawk warned the couple, "The trail is pretty rugged from this point on. Are you sure you want to try it? I'm warning you, it's one boulder patch after another."

"We're game. Right, honey?" Bob reached over and put his hand on Linda's shoulder.

"Sure. Let's get going. Those trout are calling my name." Linda reached for her pack.

After an hour of sifting through thick brush and briars and crawling over rock pile after rock pile, it became obvious Linda was slowing the group down. Hawk had been watching her, and it looked almost intentional to him. Somehow he felt Linda McIntyre had a lot more stamina than she was showing.

"Whoa! I need to stop and rest for a minute." Linda flopped down on a big rock overlooking a ravine filled with hundreds of huge boulders as Hawk moved lower to give the group room to spread out.

"This is a good place to stop, anyway. The two trails meet at the top of this ravine, and one of them goes to Second Rock. Bob, how are you holding up with that pack? Want me to carry it for a while?"

"Are you trying to make me look like a wimp? I'm fine. So is that where we're heading, up there in that opening?"

Hawk covered his eyes to block the sun and looked up where Bob was pointing. "No, the lake is down the trail going to the east. The north trail goes to Hell's Canyon, on the other side of that opening, a sheer drop-off. You don't want to go there."

"How far is it to this Hell's Canyon?"

"Why?" asked Hawk, knowing there was no way he was taking anyone to the slippery and potentially deadly spot.

"Just trying to get my bearings and figure out distances from one point to another. It all looks so close when you're looking at it from this level. But when you start hiking to it, it's a different story."

"If you're an avid mountain trekker and exceptionally fit, you can probably make it in a couple of hours, maybe less. For a novice, more like three or four. Betsy, how are you doing? You're pretty quiet."

"Couldn't be better. I was just wandering through my childhood, remembering back when Mom and I stood up on that razorback and spit down into Hell's Canyon. It was awesome but scary."

"Yeah, there's been a fair amount of my spit, plus a hundred or so rocks, let loose up there when I was a kid, too. Uncle Custer took me there every time we ever came to Second Rock to fish. I'd make a wish and then spit as far as the wind would let me."

"Bob, I think it's time to get that camera out, don't you? Looks like a perfect shot to me."

"You know, I think you're right, honey." Bob took the pack off and began searching through it before pulling out a smaller bag and handing it to his wife. "Here, you get this part out while I…"

As he was fumbling through the pack, he picked it up and moved behind Betsy who was resting on a boulder several yards above Hawk.

"What the hell are you doing?" yelled Hawk as he boulder-hopped toward Betsy.

Just as Betsy turned to see what Hawk was yelling about, she was jerked to a standing position. Bob held her close with one arm around her neck as he put a gun to her head with his other hand. Hawk stopped dead still, staring up at the two as if afraid he would set the gun off if he came any closer.

"Show's over, pretty boy! I'll be the guide from here." Bob tightened his grip on Betsy.

"You son-of-a-bitch, are you crazy?" Hawk made another move toward Betsy.

Bob cocked the revolver.

Hawk stopped and held up his hands. "Don't...don't hurt her! Please! I don't know what the hell you want, but I'll do anything. Just don't hurt her."

Betsy struggled to free herself from Bob's clutches, kneeing him in the groin and almost getting away. He grabbed her by the hair as she stepped to a lower rock trying to get to Hawk, yanking her backwards while knotting her braid around his hand as she inhaled a scream.

Again Hawk attempted to get to her, leaping to another boulder, looking like a mountain lion on its final attack. At this point, Linda stood, using both hands to hold a high-powered revolver aimed at Hawk.

"What a loss!" Linda declared as she smiled the deceitful smile of a killer.

A shot echoed through the mountains as Linda fired the gun, hitting Hawk in the side, knocking him off the boulder. His body ricocheted off the large boulders until reaching a final resting spot at the bottom of the ravine, where he lay motionless and silent.

"Hawk!" Betsy screamed as she looked down at his inert body and tried to go to him. Bob pulled her back again by her braid. As her knees buckled, Bob let her fall to the rock, knowing she was no threat to him or his supposed wife.

"I've got to get to him! Please!" But her cries and

pleading were useless against her cruel, callous captors.

"You've got bigger problems than your dead boyfriend, my little beauty. The buzzards can take care of him. Are you ready, Julia?"

His partner, Linda or Julia or whoever she was, leapt to her feet, grabbing her pack. All of a sudden she was a surefooted professional outdoorswoman—a heartless one ready for anything, including murder.

Betsy could do nothing to help Hawk now and felt her world had ended. Even if by some miracle he survived the gunshot, he wouldn't be able to come after her. The only thing she could do at this point was try to survive long enough to escape from her captors and come back to him.

****

Custer stopped at the camp only long enough to ask Jake which way Hawk and Betsy had gone before continuing his jog up the even steeper trail. A horse would be faster, but it was impossible to use a horse on a trail thick with brush and boulders.

He had been on the high trail for about an hour when the gunshot echoed through the canyon. Once again his adrenaline surged, and the man's will to watch over these two young people he loved pushed him onward.

****

At the base of the ravine, Hawk regained consciousness as a wicked pain shot through his side. When he attempted to right himself, he saw a puddle of blood where he had lain and remembered he had been shot. Pulling his shirt off, he tied it securely around his waist in an attempt to stop the bleeding. It appeared to be a clean wound, the bullet having gone all the way through. He could survive that, and no bones were broken that he could tell, but he knew he was badly bruised from the fall, probably with some broken ribs in addition to the gunshot wound.

"Betsy! I have to get to Betsy!"

He steadied himself at the bottom of the ravine, letting his head clear for a second, and then began his climb up, trying to ignore the stabbing pain in his body and the widening splotch of blood on his shirt. His only thought was to get to Betsy. He knew where the murderers were taking her—Hell's Canyon.

As he climbed, holding his side, Hawk mentally beat himself up for not seeing through this hoax. It was his fault Betsy had been caught in this trap, and he wouldn't be able to live with the knowledge of that if anything happened to her.

As he reached the top of the ravine, he turned in a different direction from the path he knew the others would have taken. It was a shortcut his uncle had showed him, and though not easy to decipher in all the overgrown brush, he knew it was his best chance—his only chance—to save her.

****

Custer was breathing hard and knew he should be worried about his heart, but he couldn't think about it now. His mission was much more important than his own life. He had lived his life. Maybe he'd not had everything he wanted and done some things he was not proud of, but it was a good life. Betsy and Hawk deserved a good life, too, and he had to make sure they had a chance to live it.

As he reached the ravine he had always called Boulder Junction, he stopped to see if he could hear anything. The huge rocks lay piled as if they'd been propelled out of a giant volcano. Two paths lay at the junction, one to Second Rock and the other to Hell's Canyon.

Debating which way to go, he noticed drops of blood on the rock and on the ground where he was standing. The blood had dried to a soft gel, but it was fresh. Searching for more blood, he realized someone who was hurt had headed in a different direction, not choosing either trail. Only one person knew the shortcut to Hell's Canyon, and that was the path his uncle would follow.

****

Betsy tried to slow her captors down as much as possible, hoping and praying that Hawk somehow had survived the shot and the fall. She knew if he had breath left in him and could drag himself, he would come after her.

"Why are we going this way? If you're going to kill me, why don't you just shoot me like you did Hawk and be done with it?" Betsy asked the question as soon as she realized where they were going.

"Somebody wants you dead, pretty woman, but the contract says it has to look like an accident. Hawk wasn't in the deal and was just added fun."

"Would you knock off the 'pretty woman' shit? I'm sick of it. She won't look so pretty after she hits bottom." The woman pushed Betsy hard with the butt of her gun, causing her to fall.

"Hurry up! I know you can go faster than this. I've seen you boulder-hop and everything else when you're showing off for your Indian boyfriend, but he's making his trip to the happy hunting ground now, and I'm ready to get this over with and get the hell out of Deliverance."

"My, my, aren't we the jealous one? You might as well get ready for it, Julia. Before she takes her little fall, I'm going to give her a little pleasure to take with her to the afterworld. I've had a hard-on since I first laid eyes on her that night at the Grizzly."

"Oh, please! You're not that good. Besides, you always have a hard-on. That's why you spent all those years in the slammer. The few brain cells you have are all behind your zipper and make you careless as hell."

Betsy looked terrified as she realized this had been planned for a while.

"That was you that night, with the long hair and the mustache."

"Nice disguise, huh? Thought your man was going to blow my cover there for a while." Bob smirked, enjoying the success of his plan.

Hawk had been right that night at the Grizzly. Betsy vowed to herself never to question Hawk's suspicions or protectiveness again if they were allowed to live through this nightmare and be reunited. Tears stung her eyes.

You'll make it, Hawk! We will be together again. I refuse to believe otherwise.

****

Hawk stopped at a stream and untied his shirt. It was soaked with blood, but when he examined his wound, it had stopped bleeding for the moment. As he bent to drink from the stream, his head began to spin, and he knew he was about to black out again. Collapsing on the ground by the stream, he cried out, "Please, Great Spirit! Heavenly Father! Let me get to her in time! Help me like you did before, when I was lost on my quest. I'll never drink or have to test myself again if you just help me. Even if she's not meant to be mine, Great One, I won't complain. Just help me to save her! Send my animal spirits to help me!"

As his head cleared, he quickly immersed his shirt in the cold water, wrung it out, and tied it tightly again across the wound at his waist. Heading back onto the steep, wooded trail, he heard a hawk calling overhead.

"Hold on, Little One! I'm on my way!"

His belief that his animal spirit was leading him pumped strength into him, and once again he rushed toward Hell's Canyon, battling and defeating the pain trying to overcome him, aiming to save the one person he loved above all else.

****

Betsy held back and had to be prodded as they neared the opening at the top of the ridge. There had been no opportunity for escape, but she had made a decision. She would fight until her last breath and make them shoot her if need be, or she'd run to the edge and jump to her own death if she had to, but she would not let this man have his way with her.

"This is close enough. Now it's time for that little treat I promised you."

"For God's sake, stop being so dramatic and get it over with if you must, Billy. But if you don't mind, I'll excuse myself. This is not going to be a pretty sight. Besides, I did my part. You can take care of this one."

As the woman headed, almost running, back down the thick trail, Betsy knew this was her chance. Billy was still holding the gun only inches from her, but now he was undoing his belt.

"What are you waiting for? Get those clothes off, all of them." He nudged her with the end of the gun.

Betsy slowly began unbuttoning her shirt, all the while stealing glances left and right, looking for the best direction to run. If she ran back down the way they had come, she would run into Julia. Her only chance was across the rugged and slippery razorback at the top of Hell's Canyon.

Betsy seized the opportunity when Billy glanced down to unzip his pants while holding the gun precariously in his non-dominant hand. Using her forearm, she knocked the gun from his hand, causing it to fly several feet away from him. Then she turned and darted up the hill. Running faster than she could have imagined possible, then climbing on all fours and kicking loose rocks as the trail became steeper, she clawed her way to the opening at the top.

All of a sudden Billy found himself in an awkward position. Not only did he have to fight the rocks plummeting down on him, he had to find his gun. His loosened pants kept falling around his knees, slowing him down, while Betsy was getting away.

"Damn!" Sliding back down to his starting point, he finally figured out he was making no progress. He quickly fastened his pants, found his gun, and bolted up after the girl.

She could hear him gaining on her as she made it to the top of Hell's Canyon.

"Don't look down!" She kept talking to herself as she leapt across the boulders that sat teetering near the edge. She knew she would be unable to take the extra precaution needed to prevent falling to her death, but she would not let herself be caught by this bastard. Just as she neared the other side of the opening, where she had hoped to head through the trees, Billy threw his full body as far as he could, knocking her to the ground.

He landed on top of her and had her hands pinned to the ground before she could stop him. She fought like a mountain lion, but it was useless against his strength. Her struggle ended as the murderer hit her across the face with his fist, knocking her out cold. He ripped her shirt open, intent on finishing what he had started.

"You crazy little bitch! Now you'll really get it!"

****

His name was Hawk, and his attack was swift and deadly. No amount of pain could stop him from killing the man who was hurting Betsy. He propelled his whole body from the trees, yelling like a savage, knocking the criminal off her and catapulting him into the massive rock cliff behind them.

Relentlessly, the half-blood hit hard and fast, not giving the would-be executioner time to figure out what was happening, much less a chance to fight back. Hawk held him in a headlock, thrashing his skull against the rock wall again and again, refusing to let up for even a second until blood and human tissue were flying in every direction. With his victim slumped and unconscious, Hawk dragged him to the edge of the canyon, still cursing him. In a rage, he lifted the assassin and tossed him mercilessly over the edge. There was no plea for mercy and no scream of horror, only the delayed thud of the body as it hit the canyon floor.

Turning his attention to Betsy, he knelt and cradled her in his arms, ignoring the blood once again gushing from his side. She came to and thought she was in heaven as she looked up and saw Hawk's face.

"I knew you'd come. I just knew it."

He lifted her to her feet and held her close to him, but their safety was not guaranteed yet.

"Now there's a scene from a movie." Julia pointed her gun at Betsy and Hawk as she carefully stepped across the razorback.

"Billy, I've got 'em! Come up here and help me, you worthless son-of-a-bitch," she yelled as she took quick glances around for her deadly partner. "Why do I have to do everything?"

"He can't help you, Linda. He's dead. Put the gun down." Hawk pushed Betsy behind him.

"Yeah, right. Name's Julia, not Linda. You must be one hell of a man to survive all that. What a shame; you're still going to die." She cocked the revolver, still waiting for her accomplice to show up.

"Billy!" She took quick glances down the trail to the side.

"Look down at the bottom of the canyon. He's dead. Give me the gun, Julia. It's not worth anyone else dying. You haven't killed anyone yet, so there's still a chance for you." Hawk began moving toward the woman, holding out his hand for the gun.

"I've killed plenty. One more won't hurt. Get back. You're lying. You're just trying to pull one of those cowboy tricks and make me look so you can rush me."

"I won't come any closer. Just look down." Hawk stopped, keeping a purposeful distance from Julia.

Figuring she would still have time to shoot if he rushed her, Julia took a few steps to the right and looked over the edge and began whimpering.

"Oh, God, no! You killed him! You killed my Billy! You'll pay for this, you bastard!" She raised the revolver to eye level and cocked it, holding firmly with both hands.

Hawk turned his back to the woman, covering Betsy to protect her from the blast he knew was coming.

The shot hit dead center. Julia fell to the ground.

Custer had not shot the rifle in years, but he hadn't lost his aim. There was no time to think about his sights being on a woman. His only consideration was Betsy and Hawk and the peril they were in. As his shot hit its target, he felt a burning in his chest that forced him down on a nearby rock.

As he clutched his chest, he looked up. "Thank you, Great One, for letting me make it in time. You can take me now. It's okay."

The clouds swirled over the Indian, and an eagle, Custer's animal spirit, squealed overhead as he peacefully fell back against the rock.

Chapter Ten

Nashville, Tennessee

Red, black, red, black, red, black!
The vintage Corvette kaleidoscoped down the embankment, reaching its final destination in a pile of shattered fiberglass, twisted steel, torn leather, and a volcano of blood. There were no signs of life from the stillness below except for the boom of late '80s hard rock vibrating through the void left by the once highly coveted T-top.

Curious spectators driven by their death instincts congregated on the rim above, but only one human being, a truck driver, had the guts to check for life in the tangled mass below. Without forethought, he had pulled the eighteen-wheeler to a halt and leapt from the big rig, never stopping as he thrust his way through the stupefied onlookers and bolted down the hill, sinking his pointed-toe cowboy boots into the soft dirt and gravel, half sliding, half running, proceeding steadily toward the carnage.

He could see little in the midnight hour and was guided only by his sixth sense, his obligation to help someone in trouble. With elevated adrenaline, his muscles swelled even more than normal as he thrashed his way through brush and vines, scything a path of mercy to the victims below. His tight western shirt, torn sleeveless, served as a showcase for the results of hundreds of hours of pumping iron and lifting heavy hand weights as he drove his endless routes with Hank, Jr. and Charlie Daniels riding shotgun.

"Damn! I should have grabbed the flashlight!" He spoke aloud to himself as he reached the 'Vette. "This mutha's darker than the hole in Grandma's outhouse."

Quickly, he pulled out his cigarette lighter, backing up several feet to check for fuel leakage before flicking the lighter dangerously like a blowtorch when lit.

Miraculously, the gas tank was intact. No puddles of fluid could be seen.

Holding the lighter as close as possible to the tiny mangled interior, he could see two people inside. The driver's head was slumped; his blood-drenched body draped the steering wheel jaggedly driven into the dashboard, oblivious to the custom-installed seatbelt imprisoning him in this death trap. The would-be rescuer hurried to the other side of the car, the only way he could see the passenger.

The passenger's long hair, soaked in crimson mousse, hung as a covering over her face, which had hit the dash. Her arms dangled disjointedly to the floorboard. Her seatbelt had held firm until the last rollover impacted the tree at the bottom of the ravine, setting the sports car upright again.

The truck driver turned his head and vomited. He'd seen many wrecks in his ten years on the road, but this was the closest he had been to the actual victims. He also had to deal with a sense of guilt, thinking he could possibly have prevented this horrific scene if he had not ignored what he overheard at the truck stop, if he had acted on his first gut instinct.

As he retched, he detected a soft moaning. The unbelievable reality of the moment settled his stomach instantly, and he felt for a pulse in the girl's neck. Feeling a slight pulsation, he reached across and did the same to the driver, with the same results.

"Call nine-one-one!" he yelled, his raspy smoker's voice straining to be heard over the useless chatter of the sightseers above. "Hurry! They're alive!"

Chapter Eleven

Montana

"Run over by an eighteen-wheeler" was the cliché that best described how Betsy felt as she sat in the hospital room by Hawk's side. Her jaw hurt, and she was covered in scratches and bruises, but she was alive, thanks to her protectors, and more importantly, Hawk was alive. The doctor gave Hawk a good prognosis, but he had lost a lot of blood and required transfusions.

No one could believe what he had done, given the shape he was in. In addition to the wound in his side, he had multiple bruises and three cracked ribs. Stubbornly, he refused the shots for pain, not wanting to be away from Betsy and his uncle, even if only in a semiconscious state.

Down the hall, Custer lay in intensive care. His heart attack was serious this time, and he lay silent as tubes and monitors tried to work their miracle to give him back to the people who loved him. Betsy's mother had flown in from Alaska and was sitting with Custer, allowed to stay there only because there were no other family members able to stand watch.

Jake had turned out to also be a hero in this horror movie. Seeing the fear on Custer's face as he rushed into the camp, Hawk's friend and outfitting partner had immediately grabbed the emergency bag containing the first-aid kit and the satellite phone the outfitters always carried and headed toward Second Rock.

He, too, had heard the gunshot, and he went from a fast walk to a run and actually saw what was happening through his binoculars at the two-path junction, but he was too far away to prevent it. Without knowing what he would find when he reached the top, he radioed the sheriff and the rescue unit.

Thanks to Jake and his quick thinking, the rescuers had gotten to Hawk and Custer quickly. It was a short flight by helicopter from Hell's Canyon to the hospital in Billings.

Later, Betsy sat with her mom in Custer's room, and even Betsy could see how her mother looked like an older version of herself, each of them with their long braid, although Sue Ann's was more gray now than blonde. As they watched Custer sleep, Betsy reached to take her mom's hand.

"Confession time, Mother."

"Oh?" Sue Ann cocked her head sideways and looked at her daughter, smiling. "Yours or mine?"

"Both. I read *The Half-Breed and the Lady*."

"Good! And what was your critical opinion of it? It's the favorite among my readers."

"All the way through it, I kept imagining Hawk as Cutter and thought you were warning me not to get too involved with him. But somehow it just didn't fit."

"Hawk would fit as Cutter as far as looks goes. He's certainly handsome and definitely strong enough for the character, and my, what a lover I bet he is, but we won't go there." Sue Ann squeezed Betsy's hand. "What changed your mind?"

"Watching you, sitting here watching Custer. I

wondered whose moccasins those were in the closet until I saw him at Hell's Canyon. He's not just an old friend, is he? He's Cutter. Am I right?" Betsy smiled.

"Very perceptive, my daughter. But it was a long time ago, a long, long time ago. Custer was there for me after I lost Shade. He didn't push me and would listen to me talk about Shade and our life together for hours. I had no idea how much Custer cared for me until one day he stopped me in the middle of one of my Shade narratives and said, 'Those passed should never be forgotten, but neither should they interfere with what can be happiness in the present. I can offer you so much more than just lending an ear, Sue Ann, if you will just let me.' "

"So you fell in love with Custer." Betsy watched for her mother's response.

"Yes, but I never really came to terms with it. I felt I was betraying Shade to love again, even though I knew he would want me to 'get on with life,' one of those clichés he hated, and I felt I was betraying Custer because even if I did have strong feelings for him, I could never love anyone as much as I loved Shade. Shade was my forever, and putting him completely out of my mind could never happen."

"So, getting back to *The Half-Breed and the Lady*, which one were you, Victoria or Soft-as-Deer?"

Sue Ann looked at Custer and sat silent for a few seconds.

"Both." She patted Custer's hand.

"How can you be both?" Betsy raised her brow. "One got Custer, rather Cutter, and the other went back to her old life."

"*Licentia poetica*—poetic license. It can be any

way I want, as a writer of fiction, and sometimes my readers won't even know." Sue Ann searched her daughter's face and saw the questions in her eyes.

"I worked hard to put memories of Shade aside, and I found myself falling in love with this handsome half-breed who was the same age as Shade. Custer reminded me of him in so many ways: his brute strength and courage; his unique way of life, though totally different from Shade's; the way he tried to protect me from the world…" Sue Ann cut her eyes at Betsy. "And, yes, the way he made love when I finally allowed myself to give in. He said he loved me, and he made me feel like I was the only woman ever in his life, and I guess I was."

"Then what was the problem, Mom? You know I loved Custer from the first day, when he made me confront my fear with the knife. He's always been there for me and for you. I would have approved even though no one could ever replace Shade for either of us, but Custer made his own place in our lives from day one." Betsy released her mother's hand and turned to face her, anxious to hear what she would say.

"The problem was that Custer seemed to love his life in that old cabin as much as he loved me, or maybe more, and wouldn't change for anything. I had a career—a doctorate, for Pete's sake—a daughter in college to provide for, and way too much pride to live like that." Sue Ann looked at Betsy and realized she was hanging on her every word.

"Besides, Custer could have crossed into my world much more easily than I into his. Did you know that old braided fart has a degree in forestry from Montana State? Anyway, he wouldn't move from his mountain, and I wouldn't move from Alaska."

"So that would make you Victoria, wouldn't it?"

"Yes, and no. Victoria was who I was, but Soft-as-Deer was who I really wanted to be."

"And the moral to this story is?" Betsy stared at her mom, waiting for her answer.

"Follow your heart, my daughter. Follow your heart. And as Custer always says, 'Don't play games with life, or life will come back…' "

"And kick you in the ass." Mother and daughter finished the saying together and laughed.

As Betsy left the room, she looked through the window and saw her mother take out a book and move to the side of his bed. It was a copy of *The Half-Breed and the Lady*. She held Custer's hand and began reading aloud, trying to stir in his subconscious the memories of why he should live. Victoria died that night when she thought she would lose Custer. Only Soft-as-Deer remained to hold his hand and read while praying the second man she could never forget would live.

Four days later, Hawk was able to leave the hospital. Betsy took him home with her to pamper him as much as he would let her. After almost losing him, she couldn't stand to be away from him for even a short time.

Hawk had begged to leave the hospital even sooner, saying he was afraid for Betsy to be alone when her life had been threatened. Even wounded he had proven he could protect her better than anyone.

While Hawk was recuperating in the hospital, the sheriff came by to give him and Betsy the news about their would-be killers.

"The man at the bottom of Hell's Canyon has been identified as William Townsend, an ex-convict who had a small spread in the mountains in Idaho. His neighbors didn't care for him and kept their distance, thinking—and rightly so—there was something shady about him. They said he seemed to have plenty of money but never worked, as far as they knew. They had seen the woman at his place but said she came and went, never staying long at a time."

"And the woman?" Hawk asked. "Who was she?"

"Julia Robinson was her name. She's alive but in critical condition. I've not been able to question her as yet, but the doctors will call me as soon as it's possible." The sheriff stood ready to leave the room but turned to Betsy before heading to the door.

"The black SUV you saw hidden on the forestry road was supposed to be used as the getaway vehicle. It's registered in Julia's name, with a false address given. She had no criminal record that we could find, but we know she and Billy were contract killers. Who contracted them is the question we all need answered."

****

Betsy thought constantly about what the sheriff had told them. She was the target. The homicidal couple had told her this much, but who would do such a thing, and what would they gain from it? She just did not believe Patrick was capable of such a heinous crime.

Angelique came to mind, but somehow Betsy just couldn't picture the beautiful young girl she had met in the boutique that day in such a despicable role, even if she was a husband-stealer. But really, she knew nothing about Angelique.

Lou was her best guess, but this kind of contract

cost a lot of money, and Betsy didn't think Lou could possibly raise it, especially now that Eddie was no longer a partner in the business. The sheriff had questioned Betsy for a long time, and she had given him her thoughts, but there was simply no real evidence.

One thing she knew for sure—whoever it was had to be from the South. No one in Montana knew Betsy well enough to hate her. The key to finding the answer lay in a guarded hospital room in Billings, and Julia might not live long enough to tell.

The day after she brought Hawk to the cabin, he became quiet and morose, a mood she had never seen in him.

"What's wrong, Hawk? Do you feel all right?" She was sitting by Hawk on the sofa and holding his head in her lap.

"Stop asking me how I feel, Betsy!" Hawk snapped at Betsy and rose to a sitting position, grimacing in pain from his quick move and placing his head in his hands.

Thanks to his actions, she left his side and moved out to the porch. A few minutes later, he followed her, slowly, taking his time more because of the cracked ribs than the gunshot wound. She was sitting on the edge of the porch looking up at Six Rocks. Holding to the post and groaning, he lowered himself to sit beside her. Pulling her head to his chest in an apologetic move, he began twisting her hair, which she had left down intentionally for him that day.

"Do you know what day it is, baby?"

"I know it's August and you have to start back to work on the reservation in two weeks. And I know I have to leave for Mississippi soon. There's nothing I can do about it, Hawk. If we're going to be together, I have to finalize this divorce."

"I'm scared, Betsy. I'm scared to death something will happen to you, and I'm scared you'll change your mind and never come back to me. I wouldn't let myself think about it until now, but it's tearing me up. I've got sick days built up. Let me go with you. I'll stay in the background—no one will even know who I am—but I need to be there to take care of you."

"I'll know who you are, Hawk. This is between Patrick and me, and I need to finalize it. Don't worry, my love." Taking his face in her hands, she kissed him. "I will come back to you. I will always come back to you."

"And what about whoever is trying to kill you? Where will you stay? Who'll watch out for you?"

"Mom is going with me. Custer should be okay by then. We'll stay at Parrish Oaks. Annie is close by, and the sheriff there and the police in Memphis are already working on the case. They'll send someone to watch out for me."

Hawk looked toward the mountains but didn't respond, obviously in deep thought.

They headed back to the hospital that afternoon, with Hawk driving, against Betsy's wishes and against doctor's orders. His mood had improved a little, but he was still edgy, and Betsy didn't want to risk another outburst from him.

She noticed he gritted his teeth each time they hit a bump on the forestry road, but she didn't say anything. Her patient had made it clear he did not want to be pampered, and no way would she deny him his masculinity; manliness was the wrapping on the gift of

Hawk Larson, and she loved the whole package.

Before they reached the hospital, Hawk swung by his place. When he returned, he had a small box in his hand.

"What's that?" Betsy eyed the package as Hawk put it in the pocket of the Jeep without offering it to her.

"You'll see later, when the mood is right. Something I got for you right before you became a guide."

Betsy stared at him with a half smirk, half frown.

"What?" Hawk's question was accompanied by a rascally grin.

"Became a guide? I don't think so." Betsy chuckled at the inference.

"Sure you are. Next summer I'll teach you to row the drift boat. You can get you some of those little-old-lady glasses that sit on the tip of your nose so you can see to tie number-twenties on."

She hit at him, and he ducked, jerking too quickly and pulling his side stitches.

"Ouch! Careful there, wild woman!"

She reached over and gently rubbed his wounded side and purposely let her hand fall lower.

"God, Betsy, quit, or I'll have to sit in the Jeep for an hour before I can get out at the hospital. You know how I'm built."

"Yes, I do, and I am very grateful. In fact, I was just thinking how I'd really like a big scoop of vanilla ice cream later. Are you up to it?"

"Oh, yeah!" Hawk shook his head, a smile covering his face as he took Betsy's hand.

****

When they walked into the hospital room, Custer

was sitting up in bed, letting Sue Ann stuff food in his mouth, the whole time complaining as if he actually minded. All he wanted was his pants and his cell phone.

"You're not eating enough, Custer. Now open your mouth." Sue Ann shoved the spoon at his mouth again.

"I'm not an invalid, Sue Ann." Custer protested but opened his mouth for the next bite.

"You two look like you're having fun," Betsy said, laughing.

"She's torturing me, Little One! Make her stop." Custer motioned for Betsy to come closer, and she knew he wanted his hug. Then he pointed at Hawk.

"Are you making him behave himself? Has he gotten on a horse yet?"

"Not yet, Unk," Hawk answered for Betsy. "Maybe tomorrow."

As Hawk moved to his uncle's bed to shake and pat his hand, Betsy's cell phone rang. She couldn't imagine who would be calling her, since everyone who usually called was in the room with her.

"Eddie? Is that you, Eddie?" Betsy looked from her mother to Hawk and shrugged her shoulders.

"Betsy, you have to come to Nashville. There's been a bad accident. We don't think Patrick is going to make it."

"Accident? What happened?" The room became deathly quiet, and Hawk moved to Betsy's side.

"He lost control of the Corvette and went down a deep embankment. Nobody knows how he survived." Eddie's voice cracked at this point, and Betsy could tell he was trying not to cry.

"Are you sure it was an accident, Eddie?"

"What do you mean? Of course it was an accident.

235

Patrick always drove that damn car too fast. You need to come, Betsy. You're still his wife, his next of kin in case—in case any decisions have to be made."

"How bad is he hurt?"

"His neck is broken. Even if he lives, he'll be paralyzed. Please come, Betsy. I need some support. I can't make these kinds of decisions. He's my brother."

"I'll be on the next plane, Eddie." Betsy hung up and turned to Hawk.

The look on Hawk's face showed he had heard the conversation.

"Patrick is in a coma. His neck is broken. Even if he lives, they think he'll be paralyzed." Reaching up, Betsy placed her hand on Hawk's face in reassurance.

"I have to go, Hawk. Legally, he's still my husband. Will you take me to the airport?"

****

They drove in silence, neither wanting to acknowledge the turn of events. There was a flight that night to Denver, the main hub on the trip to Nashville, and Betsy needed to go back to the cabin and pack.

Hawk sat on the bed, watching as she loaded her suitcase. Though he was silent, the look of despair and panic on his face spoke louder than any words.

Closing the suitcase, Betsy moved to the bed to sit beside him and pull his head to her lap, where she stroked his hair and kissed him. He closed his eyes and held tight to her legs, never wanting to let go.

"Make love to me, Hawk?"

He left the security of her lap and cuddled her in his arms, kissing the top of her head.

"Is there time?"

"We'll make time. I need you, Hawk, now more

than ever."

Once again, as she had done the second time they made love, she undressed him and claimed again for eternity all that was hers. She lingered at the wounds he had taken trying to protect her.

Following her lead, Hawk, too, laid claim to what was his. Then, together, they consummated their promise, sealing their love in a forever of passion.

A few hours later, as they walked into the terminal, Hawk waited until she had checked in and had her boarding pass in her hand before he said anything.

"Betsy, I know you have to do this, but…"

She put her fingertips to his lips stopping him. "I'll come back to you, Hawk. I don't know how long this will take, but I will come back to you. I took a vow with Patrick, and even though he broke his, I'm still bound by mine. I have to go. I am legally his next of kin."

By the moonlight, she could see the moisture in Hawk's eyes. It was hard to imagine her big guy crying, but she already knew he had a soft side.

"Betsy, promise me you'll be careful. I can be there as quick as I can get a flight, if you'll let me."

"We'll see," was all she commented, but she knew it would not be right for her lover to be there at such a difficult time.

"Oh, here." Hawk pulled the small box out of his pocket. "Open this when you get on the plane." Hawk paused as if trying to decide what to do or say next. Then he pulled her to him, holding her tight, afraid to let go, afraid he'd never see her again.

"Before you go, there's something I need to tell you. It's about my vision quest, what I said I'd tell you when the time was right."

"Yes, Hawk. What is it?" Betsy did not take her eyes off his.

"It was you. You were there with me. I know it's hard to believe, but the doe, my animal spirit, changed into human form, and it was you. I saw you sitting on the boulder at Second Rock, and you were dressed in white deerskin. You had wildflowers in your hair and, when I approached, you looked up at me and smiled."

"How do you know it was me, Hawk?"

"Golden hair like a palomino, emerald eyes that sparkled when you looked at me under the moonlight. You kissed me just like you do now, and you made me feel happy and secure like when we make love, the deepest contentment and passion I've ever experienced. It was you, Betsy. I saw you before we ever met that day on the trail. Do you believe me?" Hawk put his hands on Betsy's shoulders as she continued to look into his eyes. He was rewarded with her smile as she reached up and put her hand on his face.

"Yes, I believe you."

She gently outlined the scar on his cheek, and he took her hand and put it to his lips and kissed it.

"And that's why you know I'll come back to you, Hawk. It could be a while, but don't give up on me. Wait for me, my love. Promise me you'll wait for me for as long as it takes."

"I promise. I love you, Little One."

Their kissing was passionate but heartrending, as if marking the end to another sad chapter.

As Betsy sat on the airplane preparing for take-off, she took out the box Hawk had given her and opened it. Inside was a thick gold charm bracelet with several charms—a fishing creel, an ice cream cone, a drift boat, a hawk, a deer, and an American flag with July fourth on it. A note inside read:

Please don't forget our summer and all that made it special. Come back to me. Please come back to me, Soft-as-Deer.

I love you,
Hawk

Chapter Twelve

Nashville, Tennessee

Betsy took her bag with her to the hospital, not taking time to check into a hotel in Nashville. The first person she saw as she entered the waiting room for intensive care was Eddie.

Hugging her, he broke down and cried immediately, as if he had been waiting for his sister-in-law's arrival to release his emotions. He was alone and Betsy was glad, not wanting to see Lou until she was sure she was not the criminal who plotted her death.

"Is there any change?" Betsy sat on a couch and Eddie sat beside her, holding her hand.

"No, he's still in a coma. They'll probably let you see him if you tell them you're his wife. God, Betsy, how he loved you!" With these unbelievable words, Eddie began to cry again as Betsy put her arms around him and tried to console him.

It was hard to believe it was Patrick lying in the hospital bed. His head was encased in bandages, and metal brackets held his neck and head in place. Tubes ran everywhere, while a monitor gave an unnatural beeping noise, indicating there was still life, though barely, in what was once a handsome, successful man.

Betsy cried as she looked at him and felt guilty because she could only feel sadness and not love for this man who had been her husband for ten years. The nurse told her she could stay only a minute. Bending over Patrick, she patted his arm and whispered to him.

"Patrick, it's Betsy. I'm here. Fight, Patrick! You can do it." Out of devotion gone awry, she kissed him on the cheek.

In the waiting room, Lou now sat by Eddie, faking concern for her husband. Only one remark entered Betsy's mind as she looked at her with disdain. "That creep of a brother-in-law of yours" was what she had called Eddie on the phone. Betsy hated the woman and knew she would not be able to pretend otherwise.

As she came closer to the couple, Lou got up and hugged her. Betsy stood rigid, refusing to return the hug. No way would she be part of Lou's charade of sincerity and caring. She knew her too well.

"Betsy, you need to come and sit down. We need to talk. There's a lot you don't know." The three of them were alone in the room, and Betsy prepared for the worst as she sat on the other side of Eddie and ignored his wife completely. "Patrick was not alone when he had the wreck. There was a woman with him."

This was not a surprise to Betsy, and she immediately thought it must have been Angelique.

Eddie looked at Lou before he continued. "It was Susan Carson."

"Susan Carson? The secretary?" Betsy's eyes took on a look of concern as she waited for Eddie's answer. "Is she all right?"

"I don't think you understand, Betsy. Patrick was having an affair with Susan. It's been going on for almost a year. And there's more."

Betsy's face must have shown her shock, because

instantly Eddie put his arm around her as if she needed consoling.

"I know Lou told you I was having an affair with Susan, and that's what she thought. I never told her any different because I didn't want her to know it was Patrick, for fear she'd tell you."

Betsy suddenly remembered her glimpse of Susan's body profile in the Little Rock office. "The baby...the baby was Patrick's?" The realization brought a look of horror and disbelief to Betsy's face as she spoke aloud what she already knew was true.

"The baby is Patrick's." Eddie emphasized the word "is." "Susan is still alive, but barely. She had severe trauma to the head. The doctors say she's brain-dead. They're keeping her alive through life support to save the baby. Surprisingly, the baby seems to be all right. Susan's sister is flying in from New Zealand and should be here tomorrow. She's the only relative Susan has and will have to be the one to say if life support is stopped. The medical team is monitoring the baby closely, and if at any moment it appears Susan is dying, they'll take the baby."

This was too much for Betsy. Susan was having the baby Patrick had denied her, and this young girl, his mistress, would never even live to see it. It wasn't fair, not for her and not for Susan, whom her husband had seduced and whose life he had cut short.

Betsy could feel the emotion welling up in her, and she ran from the waiting room. She had to get away and think. As she rounded the corner in the hallway, she saw the one person she needed most at the moment.

"Annie!" Betsy fell into her friend's arms, and together they wept.

Annie led Betsy into the hospital chapel, where they could be away from curious bystanders and together could try to make sense out of this catastrophe. After letting her friend cry for a few minutes and express her pent-up rage, Annie decided it was time for Betsy to face reality.

"You've got to get control and figure out what comes next, Betsy. I know it's a shock, but regardless of what that girl did to your marriage, that's Patrick's baby that is in a position of life or death. You need to talk to a lawyer. We can call Dad and ask him, but I believe, by law, if Susan dies—and from all indications she will—the baby is Patrick's as long as he is alive. Even if Susan does live, she's brain-dead, Betsy. She cannot be a mother. Do you catch my meaning?"

"You mean I need to take care of some other woman's baby until my unfaithful husband can take over as a father. Where is the justice in all this, Annie? I'm childless because of Patrick, yet he allows another woman to have his baby." Betsy looked to her friend for an answer.

"I know Patrick, Betsy, and I don't think it was planned parenthood. You'll have to wait and see what the sister says when she gets here. She's the only one who can remove life support, but she really can't make the decision about the baby. That decision is Patrick's, and if Patrick is in no condition to make it, you will have to make it for him. You are still his wife."

"I need to see her, Annie. I need to see Susan. Will you come with me?"

They told the nurses they were friends and were allowed to go into Susan's room for five minutes. The lifeless body looked nothing like the friendly and beautiful girl she had met in Little Rock.

Once again the *beep, beep* told the story of life and death, but there was another life being monitored, and from all indications on the monitor he or she was very much alive and waiting for a chance to enter the world, albeit a sad and confusing one.

Betsy stepped to Susan's side and patted her still hand. She could bear no malice for her, this young woman who had no family to support and love her. As contradictory as it sounded, she hoped Patrick had been good to her even to the point of showing her some love and caring in her otherwise loveless world.

Before leaving, she put her hand on Susan's abdomen. As if trying to communicate with her, the baby kicked hard against her hand, causing Betsy to draw back in surprise. Then she put her hand back.

"Hang on, Little One. Hang on a little longer," Betsy whispered to the child before leaving the room.

Annie had come prepared to stay with Betsy for a couple of days. Sue Ann had called and asked her to be there since she was unable to come just yet. The two friends talked way into the night in the hotel, and Betsy told her everything about Hawk and the attempt on her life.

"This is serious, Betsy. I'm calling Dad so he can get with the sheriff to see what he can find out. You don't need to be here alone. Can you stay with Eddie and Lou?"

Betsy told Annie that Lou was high on her list of suspects and also mentioned Angelique again.

"I know it doesn't seem possible for that sweet-looking girl to be part of such a nasty plot, but now that we know Patrick was having this serious relationship with Susan, maybe Angelique needs to be investigated. Maybe she went psycho and decided to try to kill off everyone in Patrick's life. It still seems like too much of a coincidence for me to be almost murdered in the same week that Patrick careens off an embankment with Susan. I wonder if they've checked the Corvette to see if it was tampered with in any way." Betsy wrung her hands as she talked about the possibility of hits on Patrick and Susan being connected to the attempt on her own life.

"I'll give all this information to Dad when I talk to him. In the meantime, we need to make sure you're safe."

At the insistence of Betsy's mom, late that afternoon the Nashville police posted a guard with Betsy. The hope was that the person who had contracted her daughter's death would be apprehended soon. Betsy figured Hawk had a part in demanding this protection.

****

There was no change in Patrick or Susan the next day. Shortly after Betsy and Annie arrived, an attractive woman who looked to be in her forties came into the waiting room. From her accent, Betsy knew immediately it was Susan's sister. Awkwardly, Betsy stood and extended her hand to her as she introduced herself and Annie.

"Oh, Mrs. Wingate, I am Carol Wilson. I'm so sorry about your husband and for the heartache my sister caused you. I do hope he will be all right."

"Please call me Betsy. I'm really sorry for Susan. She looks so helpless lying there."

"Yes. It's hard to see her like that. The last time I

saw her she was a teenager, full of life and full of problems like a lot of teenagers. If I had taken her with me to New Zealand, maybe this wouldn't have happened, but she threatened to run away again."

"Carol, I want you to know I have no ill feelings toward Susan. To tell you the truth, I only met her once, in the Little Rock office, and I liked her at that meeting. Of course, I had no idea what was going on, at that time."

"My sister told me about meeting you. I remember she said she thought Patrick was still in love with you and she was afraid of having the baby alone. Such a sad case, my dear little sister, and now she lies dying. This is a terrible decision for me to have to make. I wish someone else could make it for me."

"I'm sure you'll make the right decision. Just know I'm here for you if you need support." Betsy looked at Annie, and Annie nodded her head, giving Betsy the support she needed for her next question.

"I do need to know if you've had any thoughts about the baby, Carol. I believe that, legally, it will be Patrick's child as long as he's alive. The one thing I don't want to happen is for the baby to become a ward of the state if Patrick and Susan never recover from this horrible accident." Betsy took a seat by Annie in the waiting room.

"Oh, my! I hadn't thought of that. Susan was very excited about this baby. It was all she talked about in her letters and the few times we talked on the phone. She told me the father was married but that he was getting a divorce. Are you still planning to go on with the divorce?" Carol kept her eyes locked on Betsy's.

"I really haven't thought about it, to tell you the

truth. I'm committed to seeing Patrick through the worst, and that's as far as I've gotten. The doctors say he'll be paralyzed, but they're not sure what the extent of the paralysis will be yet. They seem to think he has a good chance of coming out of the coma as the swelling goes down in his brain."

"How do you feel about this baby?" Carol asked, pulling her chair close to Betsy. "It's obvious Susan has lost her battle with life, but the one thing I know is she would want this baby to be loved and have a good home, something she never had. As much as I would love to, I can't raise the baby. My husband and I talked about it before I left New Zealand, and we are just not financially or emotionally able to start over at this point. We've raised five children of our own, with three still at home. At the risk of sounding callous, Betsy, could you love the child of your husband's extramarital relationship?"

Before Betsy could answer, the nurse's station became abuzz with activity.

"Paging Dr. Pitcock! Paging Dr. Pitcock!"

Both women rushed to the hallway to see where the activity was coming from. It was Susan's room, and Betsy held to Carol's hand as they realized they were wheeling her quickly out of her room and down the hall to surgery.

"Oh, God! She's dying!" Carol whispered through her tears.

Betsy hugged Carol as she cried, knowing her prayer had been answered in the cruelest way possible. She would not have to make the decision that was so hard. Betsy hoped she would not have to make such a decision either.

Dr. Pitcock came to them a few minutes later and asked who was Miss Carson's family. Both women knew immediately Susan had lost her battle with life as they recognized the look of sympathy on the kind doctor's face.

They were directed to go to the nursery and wait, and they would be able to see the baby boy who had entered the world as his mother left it.

Carol and Betsy put on the hospital gowns and masks required of those who are about to be introduced to new members of their family. Annie stood at the nursery window, watching.

Carol held the baby boy first and told him his mother would be so proud to know she had such a beautiful, healthy son. Betsy stood anxiously by her, not knowing what emotions she would feel, if any, but knowing she had to judge for herself if she was to play a part in this child's life.

As Carol placed the baby in Betsy's arms, she cradled him close to her. As if he knew he had to impress this person, he opened his eyes and looked directly at her. He balled up his little fists under the sleeves covering them and waved them as if frantic for attention. Then he kicked Betsy again, just as he had from his mother's womb, as if telling her in the only way he knew, "I'm here; love me."

At that moment, the tears began and dropped down on the son she already loved. Smiling under her mask, she held the baby up to the nursery window so Annie could see him, but Annie was not looking at the baby. She was looking at her friend, a mother at last.

Chapter Thirteen

Patrick came out of his coma the next day with Betsy standing beside his bed. He tried to talk, but his words were not audible. She could read his lips and knew he was saying, "I'm sorry."

"Don't think about anything now, Patrick, but getting well. You have a son, and he's beautiful. He looks like his daddy." She smiled to let him know everything was all right, but she knew it wasn't. The next word she read from his lips was "Susan."

Betsy looked questioningly at the doctor who stood on the other side of the bed. He gave her the nod of okay, and she knew she would be the deliverer of the bad news.

"I'm sorry, Patrick. Susan didn't make it, but the baby did and is perfectly healthy. He's a tough little guy, a survivor. Susan would be happy to know that."

Patrick's eyes glossed over, and Betsy reached to take his hand. She squeezed his fingers, not knowing if there was any feeling, but there was no reaction. Only time would tell if he would be able to move his upper body, but she already knew he would never walk again. Her minutes were up, and she allowed Eddie to take his turn visiting his brother.

Betsy had not told her mother about the baby. She wanted to be sure she would be able to have him as her own before she did. Her cell phone rang and she answered it, hoping it would be Hawk but knowing he would never call her. She had made it clear to him this was between her and Patrick, and she could only hope and pray he would wait for her.

"I couldn't stand it any longer, Betsy. How is Patrick?"

"He came out of the coma this morning, Mom, but he doesn't seem to have any feeling in his body anywhere. The best-case scenario is paralysis from the waist down. How's Custer?"

"He's fine. He'll be back at his cabin in no time. You know how hardheaded he is." There was a lull in the conversation, and her mom knew she wanted to ask about Hawk.

"What can I tell Hawk, Betsy? The man is dying inside. I've never seen anything like it. Custer is really worried about him and is terrified Hawk will start drinking again even though Hawk has assured him he has nothing to worry about."

"Tell him…tell him I miss him and reassure him I'll be back some day. Mom, I've got to see Patrick through the worst, and that's all I know for sure right now, and the worst could be months. Just tell Hawk to wait for me."

Betsy wanted to say, "Tell him I love him," but she had never said those words to him in person and decided they were not words to be spoken secondhand. She looked down at the gold charm bracelet and smiled. It was a treasure, and she never took it off, but she didn't need it to remind her of Hawk. Her dreams were sufficient for that.

The next day, Betsy went shopping for something to send Hawk. She found a gold deer, a doe, and had it put on a thick gold rope chain. With it, she put a simple note that read:

Wait for me, Hawk. Please wait for me. I'll come back to you.

Soft-as-Deer

****

On the second day of Patrick's return to consciousness, he was able to speak enough for Eddie to question him about the accident. Patrick had no recollection of losing control of the Corvette, nor did he remember going over the embankment. The only thing he remembered was leaving his apartment late that night with Susan and going to check on the night shift at the job site about twenty miles from the city. This was his usual routine when in Nashville and was always the last thing he did before retiring for the night.

Betsy told Patrick not to try to talk any more when she could see what a strain it was for him, and how tired he was becoming with the oxygen tube in his throat. But he refused, requesting that Eddie come closer as he spoke in a whisper.

"Get Fred Burkes."

Fred Burkes was the lawyer for Wingate Constructors and had an office in Nashville.

"Patrick, this is not about the divorce, is it? Please don't think about that now. The important thing is for you to get well." Betsy put her hand over Patrick's.

"No," he whispered. "No divorce."

The next morning, the attorney had to get right up to Patrick's face to hear what he was saying, and even though Betsy and Eddie were straining to hear, they could not understand him. Finally, the lawyer turned to them.

"Patrick wants you to have the baby, Betsy. He wants me to fill out adoption papers and act as his power of attorney to see to it this takes place as soon as possible. Are you in agreement with this?"

Betsy's smile was her answer. In the days following, every minute she was not with Patrick she spent at the nursery window. At every opportunity, she put on the required gown and mask and fed the baby boy. He was small, weighing only four and a half pounds at birth, and would stay in the hospital longer than usual to make sure there were no unforeseen injuries from the accident. A cruel twist of fate had made her a mother, and she would not take this responsibility lightly as she cared for her son.

A few days later, Patrick called her to his bedside and in his hoarse voice told her again he was sorry for everything and he still loved her. Betsy did not respond but smiled at him to at least let him know she cared. Feeling responsible for the death of the baby's mother, he told her to name him whatever she wanted but not to name the baby after him.

As Betsy held the boy later that day while feeding him, she looked down, smiled, and said, "Trapper Tobias Wingate, my little man. That's who you are. Someday you'll live in the mountains, and I'll teach you to fly fish." Trapper looked up at his mom as if he understood every word she said and once again gave her the kick of approval. Trapper was a name she had always wanted for a son, especially after living in Alaska, and Tobias was the name her mother had given Betsy's twin brother who had died shortly after birth. Now Tobi could live through Trapper.

Two weeks later, Trapper was ready to be taken

home. Betsy knew it was time for her mother to find out she had a grandchild.

"Mom, I know you're ready to get back to Alaska, but I really need you to come to Nashville."

"When, Betsy?"

"As soon as possible. I really need you here, Mom."

"Is anything wrong? I mean, other than the fact that you're caring for a man that any normal woman would pull the plugs on."

"Mom, that's so cruel."

"I've never been one to hide my feelings about my son-in-law. I know you mean well, but I'm ready for you to have some happiness. Patrick is not getting any better, and that's not your fault. I see no need for you to stay there any longer. There's a man in Montana who really loves you like you deserve."

"Just come, Mom. Today, if possible."

Late that afternoon, Annie picked Sue Ann up at the airport.

"Annie, what in the world are you doing here? Surely you haven't stayed away from those babies the whole time Betsy has been in Nashville."

"Oh, no, the kids are with me. You'll see them in a few minutes."

"Aren't we going to the hospital?"

"No. Betsy rented a small apartment close to the hospital. We'll meet her there. There's a little party going on."

"She got the divorce?" Sue Ann spoke in an excited voice, forgetting the gravity of the situation into which her daughter had been tossed.

"Oh, something better than that, Sue Ann. Be

patient." Annie pulled into the parking lot of a small apartment complex. "Well, you're about to see." Annie gave her a huge smile, obviously excited about the surprise for Sue Ann.

The apartment building was comfortable, but nothing fancy. It was right next to the hospital and used mainly by families of patients with long-term care requirements. They took the elevator to the third floor, and Annie continued smiling as they walked down the hall.

"What is going on, Annie? You look as giddy as you girls used to look when you were in elementary school."

Annie knocked on the door. Burt, Annie's husband, opened the door and was also full of smiles as he kissed Sue Ann on the cheek to welcome her. The apartment was decorated in streamers and balloons, and there was a cake and more decorations on the table.

"Whose birthday is it? I know it's not mine. What's going on here?"

At that moment, Betsy entered from the bedroom, carrying a bundle.

"Mom, I've got someone I want you to meet. His name is Trapper Tobias Wingate. Trapper, meet your grandma."

As Betsy held the baby out to her mother, Sue Ann stood back, not knowing what was going on. She knew better than to ask questions and just took the baby, smiling down at him, oohing and ahhing with the group while looking at her daughter for answers.

Once Betsy explained what had happened, her mom just hugged her with her other arm and cried.

"My God, Betsy, you're a mom! The son-of-a-bitch came through after all—even if it was with another woman—but do we care?" Her voice changed to baby talk. "No, Trapper, we don't care. We're gonna love you and watch you grow in spite of your old man." She turned her attention back to Betsy. "And you named him after Tobi. This is wonderful, Betsy!"

In the next instant, her voice changed to the serious adult version again. "You need to call Hawk, Betsy. He needs to know about this turn of events. Does it change how you feel about him?"

"No, but I'm scared to death it might change how he feels about me. As much as I care about Hawk, there is no choice between him and Trapper. This is what I've dreamed of, and Trapper needs me even more than Hawk does." Betsy took the baby and held him close. "How can you love someone so much from the first time you hold him?"

When the celebration was over, the guests had all left, and Trapper was tucked into the bassinet, Betsy sat by her mom, who was still smiling.

"Mom, is this wrong? Is it right for me to be this happy when Patrick is a cripple, probably dying, Trapper's mom is dead, and I'm in love with a man who is not my husband even though I'm not divorced?"

"Well, I wouldn't take that one to confession, if I were you. Thank God we're not Catholic. I don't know, Betsy. All I know is this is one lucky little boy to have come out of this disaster with nothing wrong with him and to have found a mother who will love and care for him like you do. What you do need to decide, my darling, is what you're going to do about the two men in your life. I've hated Patrick for the unhappiness he's caused you, but at this point in his life it's not fair for him to think you're going to stay married if you don't love him anymore. Not that fair is the word that comes to mind when I think of my son-in-law. And if Hawk is to be part of the celebration of this little fellow's life, you need to call him, Betsy, and tell him."

"Patrick keeps telling me he's sorry and he loves me. Where is that coming from?" Betsy stared at her mother, anxious for her answer.

"I'm sure he's sorry. Look what grief he's caused. I think Patrick is in love with the idea of loving you, but you don't hurt someone you love the way he hurt you." Sue Ann waved her hand and left her daughter sitting on the sofa. "That's all I'm saying, Betsy. You have to make your own decisions from here."

"Mom, don't tell Hawk about Trapper. I want to be the one to tell him."

Her mother left at the end of the month, heading back to Montana, not Alaska, to continue the role she had assumed as caretaker of Custer, a role she had almost waited too late to play. But she knew she would be coming often to Nashville now that she had a grandchild.

Chapter Fourteen

Hawk sat in his rental car at the Nashville airport, studying the city map he had picked up. After getting his bearings, he headed in the direction of the hospital. It had been months since Betsy had left, and he could stand it no longer. Would he confront her and demand to know if she was coming back to him? Or would he just hide in the background like a stalker, watching and waiting? These were decisions he would make later, but for right now, he had to see her again, even if it was from a distance.

****

Betsy sat by Patrick's bed, silent. He was sleeping, something he always did, or perhaps it was his way of avoiding talking. She tried to look at Patrick through different eyes, knowing he was the biological father to the little boy who had captured her heart with that first kick of his tiny foot. As she stared at the man who breathed only because of the tube in his mouth, her mind began wandering.

I am so thankful I have Trapper, the answer to all my hopes and dreams, but what now? I look at you, Patrick, through sad eyes full of pity but not through eyes of love. My heart, that part of my heart, belongs only to Hawk. When I think of Trapper with a daddy, it's not with you, Patrick, and I'm sorry it turned out this way, but I see Trapper with Hawk, learning to ride a horse and to fly fish—a pint-sized cowboy just like the man I want to raise him. I see Trapper growing into a caring, loving, responsible man, but not because of your teaching, Patrick. I do not see the three of us together as a family. God forgive me, but it is true!

Betsy was brought out of her reverie when she heard Patrick's whispered voice calling her.

"Betsy! Betsy!" His voice became strained, almost panicky, and she moved quickly to his side.

"I'm here, Patrick, right here beside you." Betsy leaned down where he could see her and patted his hand. "Do you need something?"

"I was dreaming." Patrick took a deep breath through the tube. Tears filled his eyes and trickled down his cheeks. "I dreamed you were with me." He gasped for breath. "When I went over…" As he took another breath, he began wheezing, unable to breathe. Terrified, Betsy rushed out of the room to find a nurse.

****

Hawk stopped at the desk in the hospital entrance to ask what room Patrick Wingate was in and was told he was on the fourth floor, a floor for long-term patients. Hawk stopped at the elevator and hesitated when it opened. A couple got on and asked if he was going up, but he shook his head and walked away. He was dressed in jeans and boots but had left his hat in the car, not wanting to draw attention to himself. After seeing a few other men with cowboy boots and hats, he remembered he was in Nashville, the country music capital, and figured he would wear it from then on— that is, if he stayed. As he stood looking out a window in a small sitting room on the first floor, he began to reconsider his trip.

What if she doesn't want me anymore? Maybe she and Patrick have reconciled. Do I have the right to find Betsy, to pin her down and demand an answer?

Hawk headed back to the elevator, entered it, and pushed button four.

****

Betsy stood outside the door while the doctor and nurse worked with Patrick to help him with his breathing. When they opened the door, the doctor stopped beside her.

"Mrs. Wingate, he seems to have gotten upset, and it affected his breathing." The doctor paused, as though thinking maybe Betsy could explain what happened.

"He dreamed about the wreck," Betsy offered. "Then he just started gasping for air."

"We gave him a sedative, and his breathing is back to normal. He'll sleep for a good while now, but we'll monitor him closely." The doctor put his hand on Betsy's arm. "Don't worry, Mrs. Wingate. This happens frequently with patients in your husband's condition."

After the doctor left, Betsy returned to Patrick's bedside, stopping by the window, where her chair had been moved. His breathing was even now, and his eyes were closed. Betsy felt guilty for her thoughts before Patrick woke up and vowed not to think about Hawk anymore when she was in the room with Patrick, but she knew that would be almost impossible. Out of guilt, Betsy leaned over Patrick, pushed the hair from his eyes, and kissed him on the cheek.

****

Hawk stood outside the door to Patrick's room and watched through the open door. The man looked nothing like he'd thought, with all kinds of tubes and hookups to monitors and his head and neck held firmly in a brace. Hawk moved out of sight as he heard movement inside the room. When he got up the nerve to look inside again, he saw her. Betsy leaning over Patrick, looking down into his face. Hawk wanted to move away, but he couldn't. It was his first look at her in months, and it was all he could do to keep from barging in, grabbing her, and holding her tight, never letting go. But as he watched, she leaned over, put her hand on Patrick's face and kissed him.

Hawk's heart was breaking, and he knew he should not have come. He darted away from the door and headed back to the elevator. The nurses stared at him as he stood waiting for the elevator. He could feel them smiling, but he refused to look up and return their smiles. All he wanted to do was get out of the hospital. What he would do then, he didn't know, but in his heart he knew that, whatever it was, it could not include the woman he loved.

****

Betsy stood looking out the window in Patrick's room. It was late afternoon, time for her to pick up Trapper at daycare and head back to her apartment, where she would hold her son and play with him until bedtime. She lived for this part of the day.

As she looked down on the street below, a man caught her eye. He was dressed in cowboy boots, jeans, and a western sports jacket just like the one Hawk had worn the night he took her to the Windmill to eat. She pressed her face to the window, trying to get a closer look, and watched as the tall, dark-haired man walked briskly to the parking lot. He stopped at a sedan, unlocked the door, and started to get in when he stopped and cast his eyes up toward where she stood looking down at him.

It can't be! Not Hawk here in Nashville!

The man got into the car and drove away. Betsy watched until the car was out of sight and shook her head in denial.

No way it was Hawk. Just my imagination, but I wish it had been. If only he was here.

****

Hawk drove to the tallest hotel he could find in downtown Nashville and got a room on the twelfth floor. He felt empty, and, just like before his vision quest, he no longer wanted to live.

Two hours later, Hawk sat in the bar in the hotel. He tried to talk himself out of breaking his promise to First Maker, but the old demons resurfaced and seized control of his mind, convincing him First Maker had broken a promise to him. Getting a bottle of whiskey to take with him, Hawk staggered into the elevator and made his way to the floor where his room was located. After struggling to get the key in the door, Hawk finally entered the room but did not turn the light on, preferring to let darkness hide him from himself.

Hawk pulled off his boots and socks and then all his clothes except for his jeans. Sitting Indian style in the middle of the bedroom floor, he reenacted the vision quest where he first saw Betsy. He drank straight from the whiskey bottle, not wanting to be civilized and drink from a glass. The more he drank, the more he cried, until the bottle was drained and no tears were left, leaving his soul parched and lifeless. He had hoped to pass out, but when he didn't, he stood clumsily and held on to the furniture that made up the sitting area of his suite. Clumsily he made his way to the sliding glass door that opened onto the balcony.

The cold air took his breath when he stepped out, and he knew if he lost his nerve and couldn't throw himself over the wall that separated him from the escape he sought, he could pass out and maybe freeze to death. Either way, his life was over. Betsy was gone. Hope was gone.

****

Betsy held Trapper, rocking him until he fell asleep. She kissed her baby boy and placed him in the crib she had bought for the small apartment.

Returning to the rocking chair, Betsy could not get Hawk out of her mind. Could he have come to Nashville to see her and then changed his mind? Was that him she had seen in the parking lot?

Betsy pulled her cell phone from her pocket and dialed the number she swore she would not call until she could go back to Hawk for good.

****

Hawk swayed and fell against the balcony rail. He ran his hand along the ledge that was at least a foot wide and pulled himself upright again. Before he had time to talk himself out of it, he crawled up and stood, his bare feet freezing against the cold concrete. He held his hands up toward the sky obscured by the reflection of city lights, but no words came to him from the ancient spirits, except for Custer's words that day almost six years ago when he had left his nephew in the wilderness to begin his vision quest.

"I'll die, Uncle," Hawk had said, pleading with Custer not to leave him.

"Better to die trying to live than to die trying to die." Custer had turned from his nephew and walked out of sight, leaving him to find his way.

And now here he was, again seeking death.

****

Betsy heard Hawk's phone ringing, ringing, ringing, but he did not answer. When his voice mail picked up, cold chills covered her body as she heard Hawk's voice, the first time since she left months ago, asking for the caller to leave a message. When the beep sounded, she hesitated and then softly asked, "Hawk…Hawk, where are you?" Then the phone fell silent.

****

Hawk steadied himself on the ledge as the cold wind threatened to take over, pushing him to jump. His head was swirling, but he kept his eyes closed, hoping the wind would take him.

"Better to die trying to live…Better to die trying to live…Better to die trying to live…"

Hawk grabbed his head with both hands and screamed, trying to make Custer's pleading stop. All he had to do was move an inch closer and all his troubles would be over. Then Custer started tormenting him again.

"Pursue only those that capture your heart…capture your heart…capture your heart…"

Hawk held tighter to his head, moving it from side to side, trying to make the voice, Custer's voice, leave him. As his toes moved closer to the edge, another voice rang out—a voice he could not ignore.

"Hawk! Hawk! Where are you?"

Betsy's voice cut through the cold wind—cut

through Custer's pleas—cut through Hawk's drunken, crazed state. He stepped back, tumbling off the ledge, and rolled onto the balcony floor. Sobbing, he half crawled, half pulled himself back through the doors and onto the bedroom floor, where consciousness left him.

Chapter Fifteen

Montana

One morning while Custer and Sue Ann were sitting having coffee, looking out at the wonderland of the first big blizzard winter had created, they were interrupted by a knock at the door.

"Hawk! What a nice surprise! Come in and sit by the fire with Custer and me. It's a coffee morning. How about a cup?"

"Thanks, Sue Ann. Coffee sounds good."

After removing his coat and hat, Hawk made his way to the table where he and Betsy had shared coffee so many mornings an eternity ago. As Sue Ann poured his coffee, she noticed him looking around, searching for ghosts in a mental haze of nostalgia. His stare came to rest on the bearskin rug, bringing back to her a reverie in her own mind of a time many years ago when she had experienced the soft contentment the old grizzly offered as she held on to a handsome half-blood of her own.

As she placed the blue mug in front of him, Hawk was startled back into reality and looked at Sue Ann. Seeing the know-all twinkle in her eyes, the one copied right off Betsy's face, he looked away in shy embarrassment like a small boy caught with his hand down his pants.

Redirecting his focus, he glared at the mug as if it were some monster about to leap up and take a chunk out of him. Custer watched as Hawk became jittery and quiet, rubbing his hands on the upper leg of his jeans like Custer remembered him doing as a boy scared because of some trouble he had found himself in. Oblivious to his audience, Hawk continued to stare unabated.

"You've lost a lot of weight, Hawk. Are you well?" Custer was looking at his nephew with concern written all over his usually stoic face.

Hawk looked up uneasily when he realized his uncle had asked him a question. "I'm fine, Unk. Just been working out pretty hard after school." He still seemed to be trying to ignore the cup in front of him.

"Is something wrong with your coffee, Hawk?" Sue Ann saw the look on Custer's face and knew he had sensed Hawk's discomfort.

"No! No! It's fine." He took the cup by the handle but released it without taking a sip. Looking up at the two of them, seeing them both staring at him, he felt foolish and embarrassed and pushed away from the table.

"Hell, no! It's not fine!" Hawk left the table and headed for the door. "I'm sorry, Sue Ann, Unk. I thought I could do this, but I can't."

As Hawk grabbed his coat and hat and headed out the door, Sue Ann got up to follow him.

"Wait, Sue Ann. I'll talk to him."

Custer grabbed his coat from the hook and stepped out onto the porch. Hawk stood there staring up at Six Rocks.

"Sit down, son. You need to spill your guts, and

I'm the right one to listen." Custer took his place in the rocker and motioned for Hawk to sit in the other one. "Now, what's really on your mind, as if I don't know." It was several seconds before Hawk answered.

"I'm scared, Uncle Custer. I can't do this anymore. I don't think I can keep my bargain."

"What bargain is that, son? Do you want to tell me about it?"

"The one I made with First Maker, God, whoever the hell He is. The day I got shot, I promised never to drink or have to test myself again if He would let me get to Betsy in time. I promised, but I'm going insane here. She's not coming back, and I'm a fool to think she is." Leaving the rocker, Hawk walked to the edge of the porch and leaned against the pole, still looking at Six Rocks with despair crying from his heart.

"To tell the truth, I've already broken my bargain, but it's not something I'm ready to talk about. I wanted to die, Uncle Custer, just like before my vision quest. Do you remember?"

"Yes, son. I remember well. I thought I had lost you, but you came back to me." Custer took on a worried look at hearing his nephew had backslidden and had contemplated ending his life.

"All I can think about is getting paralyzing drunk, just to be free from thinking about her, relief for a few hours, or days. Months would be even better. Most days, I wish I'd died up there on that mountain. Then I wouldn't have to suffer like this. Do you understand the hell I'm going through, Uncle Custer?"

"Better than any other man alive. You've had six months. I had eighteen years without Sue Ann. I wish I could tell you it would get easier, but it doesn't. You just learn to deal with it in different ways."

"How, Unk? How the hell do you deal with it and stay a man?"

"Even a man can love beyond the bounds of reason. Don't be so hard on yourself, son. I know how unbearable it feels. Remember, Sue Ann left me and went back to Alaska. I did get to see her periodically during all those years, but most times it was longer than six months between visits. I never knew for sure she'd be back until I'd see her coming down the path.

"It was kind of like being in prison and having conjugal visits, but don't tell her I told you that. I never gave up on her, and you shouldn't give up on Betsy, Hawk. Those two are just alike, two blooms of Indian paintbrush growing off the same stem."

Custer moved to stand beside his nephew, placing his hand on his shoulder. "You need to talk to Sue Ann. Find out what Betsy's all about. She knows her better than anyone, and she won't steer you wrong. Trust her, Hawk."

Reluctantly, Hawk followed his uncle back inside.

"You still got that coffee for Hawk, Sue Ann?"

"Made a fresh pot hoping you'd come back, Hawk." As Hawk sat down at the table, he noticed Sue Ann had poured his coffee in the brown mug Betsy always poured for him. He looked up at her, his eyes questioning how she knew.

"I know. The blue one is Betsy's. Figured it out as soon as you left. I'm sorry, Hawk. That was insensitive of me."

"I know it's silly, Sue Ann. I just couldn't… It just wouldn't…"

"It's okay, honey. I understand." Sue Ann patted

Hawk's hand. "How about some breakfast? Custer hasn't had any yet, but don't expect steak and eggs. I've got your uncle on a low-cholesterol diet. Want a bran muffin with light butter and some scrambled egg whites?"

"Now you sound like your daughter. Betsy stayed after me about eating too much red meat. Funny. I'd gladly eat chicken and yogurt, even that cottage cheese shit, for the rest of my life just to hear her nag at me one more time." Taking a drink of coffee, Hawk got the serious look in his eyes again as Sue Ann placed a muffin in front of him.

"Be careful what you promise, son. You might have to eat your words like your old uncle is doing." Custer leaned toward Hawk. "Egg whites are not the real thing, no matter what women tell you." Custer whispered the last part to Hawk as Sue Ann handed him a plate of anemic-looking scrambled eggs to go with his bran muffin.

"I heard that!" Sue Ann called from the stove. "You want eggs, Hawk?"

"No, thanks. The muffin is plenty."

Hawk forced down the muffin slowly, grateful to be able to talk about Betsy with someone who knew and loved her like he did. There had been too many months of silence where she was concerned, something that only magnified his misery. After pouring himself another cup of coffee, he took down the blue mug from the cabinet.

"Betsy holds her coffee cup different from anybody I've ever seen. She never holds on to the handle but sticks two fingers through the opening like this and wraps both hands around it and drinks from the side opposite the handle. Don't know how she holds on to it, it's so hot. I used to pretend I was jealous, accuse her of making love to the brew the way she embraced that mug, always holding it close to her like it was precious. Sorry, Sue Ann, guess that wasn't a very good analogy to be describing to her mother."

"It's a perfect analogy. Don't be surprised if you see it in my next novel. And yes, I know exactly how Betsy holds her coffee cup. She embraces life, every aspect of life that's important to her, the same way. But Betsy's passion sometimes gets in the way of her judgment."

"I'm not sure I know what you mean, Sue Ann. Is Betsy passionate about Patrick?"

"No, I don't mean that. I know you don't understand why she's still watching over him, and I'm not sure I do either, but I can assure you of one thing, Hawk. It has nothing to do with loving him. Betsy has the keenest sense of right and wrong I've ever seen in a person, to a fault, and she somehow thinks this is what she is supposed to do, what's right. You will just have to trust me on that."

"If she would just call me or write, I'd have enough to give me hope, but there's been nothing except for this." Pulling the chain out of his shirt, he showed Sue Ann the gold deer. "It's actually something we shared from one of your books."

"Let me guess. Soft-as-Deer."

Hawk nodded his head as he put the chain back inside his shirt, looking down. His melancholy had returned, and Sue Ann felt helpless, unable to offer him anything but sympathy.

Guiltily, Hawk looked down at the table, rubbing

his finger on the rim of his cup, unable to look at Sue Ann.

"I've been seeing someone else, trying to get my mind off Betsy." Pausing, hesitant to look up, it was several seconds before he continued. "But it's no good. If I can't have Betsy, I'll just be alone. I can't love anyone else."

Looking up at Sue Ann, his sad eyes begged. "Do you think there's a chance in hell she loves me, Sue Ann? I need something, anything!"

"Well, let's see if I can give you some hope." Sue Ann took a long sip of coffee and then smiled at Hawk, patting his hand again.

"Betsy wears this gold charm bracelet, and I don't have a clue where it came from, but it must be important. No, wear is not the right word. Betsy embraces it like a blue mug full of coffee, fondles it constantly, looks at each charm as if she's seeing it for the first time—and she doesn't even know she's doing it. Never takes it off, not even to shower. Pretty nerve-wracking, if you ask me, but I never asked her where it came from or what the charms mean. I figure if that annoying little tic gives my daughter any pleasure at all, I could live with it, seeing as how her joys are few and far between at the moment. Any idea where that bracelet came from, Hawk?"

Hawk smiled for the first time since he'd entered the cabin. Leaving his chair, he hugged Sue Ann.

"Well, now. That's something!"

"Hawk, there is another development in her life, but I have sworn to Betsy I will not tell you about it. She says she wants to tell you herself, so I know she's planning on coming back. When you find out about this, I think this whole thing will make more sense to you. I wish I could give you more, Hawk."

"That's a hell of a lot more than I had when I came here. Thank you, Sue Ann."

Sue Ann and Custer watched from the window as Hawk pulled away from the cabin.

"I never told you, Sue Ann, but Hawk went after Betsy a couple of months ago. I knew he wanted to and thought I'd talked him out of it. He said he was going to drag her back if he had to. He doesn't know I know, but I found out by accident...saw a hotel receipt in his rig for two nights in a fancy hotel in Nashville. He told me on the porch he broke his promise to First Maker, and I'm sure it had something to do with going to Nashville."

"Do you mean Hawk drank again, Custer?"

"Yes. He said as much. I guess I thought he was stronger, but at least he lived through it."

"You don't think he'll start back drinking, do you?" Sue Ann looked worried.

"No. He'll be all right now. You did good, Sue Ann. I know. A man just needs a thread every once in a while to hold on to, and he can make it a long time, even eighteen years."

Sue Ann smiled at Custer and left her chair. Standing over him, she put her arms around his neck and kissed his cheek.

Chapter Sixteen

Tennessee

The months dragged on, but Betsy had not contacted Hawk after the one message on his answering machine. Things were too unsure, and she just didn't know what to say to him.

Patrick was not getting any better but had been moved to a convalescent center in Memphis, where he would be closer to Eddie. Betsy and Trapper moved into the condo on Riverside Drive, to be close enough to check on Patrick.

Every day Betsy's conversation with Patrick was the same, until the day he finally put an end to it.

"Patrick, don't you want to see your son? He's beautiful, and he's growing so fast."

"No, Betsy. You might as well stop asking." Patrick had to stop and take breaths from the oxygen tube every few seconds. "He will never know me. There won't be any pitching baseball or hanging out at dirt bike tracks for him and me."

"But Patrick…"

"Stop it, Betsy! Don't ask me again! You might be fooled, but I'm not. I will never be his father. Do you understand?"

After that day, Patrick stopped telling her he was sorry and no longer told her he loved her, probably because he never got the reaction he desired, she figured. He had become more and more despondent as his therapy continued with no results.

As time passed, Betsy put her fears behind her, almost forgetting the person who wanted her dead was still free. There had been no more threats, and the police had stopped watching her apartment, at her request. Julia had survived but refused to give any information at all. She was awaiting sentencing in Montana, having pleaded guilty to attempted murder.

Betsy's days were absorbed with caring for her son and watching the changes in him. She thrived on his cooing and smiling and was amazed at how quickly he passed through each baby phase, from infant to toddler.

Each day, she walked her six miles, carrying Trapper on her back, knowing—hoping—some day soon she would be able to take him to the Beartooths, and also knowing she would not leave her son behind for any reason. As he grew, her strength would grow, enabling her to carry him well into his toddler phase.

As she walked one day, her cell phone rang. It was a man's voice she did not recognize.

"Ms. Wingate, Ms. Patrick Wingate?"

"Speaking. Who is this?"

"Ma'am, you don't know me, but I've been living with some information that's eating me up, and I can't deal with it anymore. I don't think your husband's wreck was an accident at all, and I thought you ought to know about it."

"How did you get my number?"

"I got it from the police in Nashville. Told them I was the first one at the crash site and had some things from the wreck I'd been meaning to give you. It was partially true, but it's information, not actual things."

"Are you the truck driver the police said got to the Corvette first?"

"Yes, ma'am; that's right."

"Why didn't you go to the police? It's been months since the accident."

"I didn't because I know the guys I think ran your husband off the road. I wasn't for sure, since I didn't actually see it happen, and I kept telling myself not to get involved, but like I said, it's eatin' me up."

"What makes you think these guys ran him off the road, if you didn't see it?"

"I was at a truck stop not far from where the wreck happened, and I overheard 'em talkin' to somebody in the booth next to me. They was bein' paid five thousand dollars to run him off at that big drop-off. I was going that way, so I hurried up to see if it was true or not. I think it's too much of a coincidence not to be planned."

"Did you know the person in the booth offering the money?"

"No, but I could identify her if you could show me some pictures. I bet you know some ladies that wanted to do him in."

"What's your name?"

"Joe's good enough. I'll go to the police, but not unless I can tell them who paid these guys to do it. Way I figure, it ain't right for them to go to jail and her to go free."

"Where can I meet you to show you some pictures?"

"I'd ruther you just leave me some pictures and let me call you back. You know where the truck stop is down at Senatobia, Mississippi?"

"Yes, I know that one."

"I'll be through that way late tomorrow evening. Leave 'em in an envelope with my name on the outside. Give 'em to the waitress named Trudy. She knows me good."

"I'll have them there tomorrow, Joe. And thank you."

"Yes, ma'am. I'm just sorry it took me so long."

Women in Patrick's life who might want to do him harm—and maybe kill off his wife, too?

Betsy went to the built-in cabinet in Patrick's condo to see if she could find any pictures. She had the clipping of Angelique but needed a picture of Lou. There was a box in the far corner of the cabinet and, pulling it out, she found it was full of family photos, mostly of her and Patrick but some of his family.

"Pay dirt!" There was a wedding picture of Lou and Eddie, with Lou looking just the same as she did at the present, all ninety-five pounds of her.

As she started to put the pictures back in the box, she noticed pictures of Patrick's family in a separate envelope. There he was, playing big brother to Eddie, teaching him how to hold his bat.

Another picture showed the whole family after Mona married his dad, looking like the all-American family they obviously were not, considering how Patrick turned out. Looking at Mona, she wished again her mother-in-law could have stayed around longer. Mona would be one family tie she would never break if she were alive.

The last picture was one of Mona with Patrick's dad, both dressed for a fancy night out. Patrick got his looks from his dad, and perhaps some of his personality and bad habits, too, but she didn't know this last for sure. His dad had on a tuxedo, and Mona wore a silk-flowered cocktail dress. She was beautiful, and she could see why Patrick's dad was gloating in the picture.

As she reached to put the box of pictures back in the cabinet, Betsy saw a box containing a small video camera.

"Look here, Trapper. It's kind of obsolete, but at least I have it here for when you really start doing tricks. It'll do until we can get a digital camcorder. I'll leave it out and let it be charging."

The baby cooed and smiled as if he understood every word his mother said. Conversation was going on constantly in the condo, whether Trapper understood it or not, and Betsy counted her blessings every time she looked at him.

The next afternoon, Betsy and Trapper were on their way down Interstate 55 to leave the envelope of pictures at the truck stop. Trudy was a big-busted woman in her fifties, with thin bleached hair and too much makeup. Expecting the envelope and Joe, the woman smiled more than was necessary as she folded the envelope and put it in her pocket.

"Bet I know who takes her home when the dinner shift is over." Betsy talked aloud as if Trapper understood what she was saying.

Out of habit, Betsy almost turned on the southbound ramp heading toward Parrish Oaks, but turned north instead. Trapper began whining and rubbing his eyes.

"I know, Little Man, you'd like to go see your Auntie Annie, but you've got the sniffles, and we don't want to give them to Michael. Close your eyes, my little Trapper. We'll be home soon." As John Denver sang "Annie's Song" softly in the background, the baby leaned his head against his car seat and closed his eyes.

"That's right, Baby Boy. You'll grow up listening to John Denver just like your mommy did, and soon I'll show you the Rockies and the man I want you to grow up to be just like. His name is Hawk, and I hope some day he'll be your daddy."

Chapter Seventeen

Pacing, strolling, looking at the phone to make sure it was working. This was how Betsy passed the time waiting for the call from Joe. The morning after she'd delivered the envelope to Trudy, the call came.

"Ms. Wingate?"

"Yes, Joe, did you get the pictures?"

"Yes, ma'am, I did. That's her, all right."

Her heart began its maddening race, knowing the identification of the attempted murderer of Patrick and probably her was about to be disclosed.

"Which one is she, Joe, the photo or the newspaper clipping?"

"The newspaper clipping. I'd remember that face anywhere. Just couldn't see how any woman that beautiful could be so damn brutal. What now, Ms. Wingate? Do you want me to go to the police? I'm back in Nashville visiting my kids for a couple of days."

"Yes, Joe. Ask for Lieutenant Bowling. He's in charge of this case and another case that's connected. Go to him and give him the information. I'm leaving it up to the police at this point."

Angelique! The beautiful, angelic other mistress! Betsy's thoughts were mixed at this point. How many women had there been in Patrick's life? How many young women's lives were ruined because of him? However many there were, she'd harbor no regrets about his affair with Susan, for look at the blessing that had resulted.

As she held Trapper in her arms, she knew she could not further delay the divorce from Patrick even though she had nothing but pity for him now. There was nothing more she could give him other than care and love for the boy child he had helped to create.

Later that day, Lieutenant Bowling called.

"Mrs. Wingate, I guess you know the truck driver has identified a woman who he claims paid two thugs to run your husband off the highway the night of his accident?"

"Yes, Lieutenant. I told him to go to you. What's the next step? Will you arrest her?"

"Not yet. I'd appreciate it if you would keep this information to yourself. We're going to pick up the two guys in the pickup that did the dirty deed. I'm sure they know by now they're responsible for the murder of Susan Carson, so they're probably on the run. Of course, they'll deny it, so it could take a while to get the proof we need. It certainly helps having an eyewitness. I just wish he had come clean sooner."

"What about the attempt on my life? Do you think she is the one who got the contract on me?"

"More than likely the person who tried to kill your husband is the same one who tried to kill you, but we won't know that until the evidence starts coming in. I'll keep in touch, Mrs. Wingate. As soon as I know anything, I'll call you."

"Keep busy."

Betsy told herself it was way too early to think this mess was over, and began busying herself with anything she could think of to take her mind off the new developments. Her daily six-mile walk turned into seven, and Trapper got into a routine of sleeping in the back carrier rather than his crib. The condo sparkled, never having been this clean even when her eccentric, left-brained husband lived here.

Though she had made up her mind to go ahead with the divorce, Betsy had not told Patrick yet. Every afternoon when she visited him, she would start to tell him and then change her mind. He never mentioned Trapper, as if he didn't exist.

A daycare was attached to the convalescent center and made it easy for Betsy to visit her soon-to-be ex-husband each day. She hoped one day she would be able to bring the baby to Patrick's room but would not unless Patrick asked.

They talked small talk if they talked at all. Patrick was becoming more and more despondent, and his therapist said he refused to have anymore physical therapy; he seemed to have given up. He was especially quiet this afternoon, and Betsy had the feeling he had something on his mind.

After ten minutes of silence, he told her to come to the side of the bed where he could see her. It was hard for him to say many words at a time since he constantly had to take puffs of oxygen.

"You look good, Betsy. I don't think I told you."

"Thank you. No, you never said anything."

There was a long silence, as if Patrick was trying to get up the nerve and energy for what he really wanted to say.

"Betsy, I don't want to live. I won't live!"

"No, Patrick! You can't give up." Betsy took Patrick's arm, forgetting he had no feeling.

"Give up? As if I have a choice? Damn it, Betsy! What can I do? I can't even scratch my own ass if I could feel it itching. I can't pull a trigger, couldn't pick up a fucking cyanide pill if one was staring at me from that god-forsaken food tray they shove in front of me when they shovel mushy shit in me like a baby. But if I could, I'd end it this second. I've even tried to get Eddie to hire someone to finish me off, but he gives me the brotherly love shit and won't do it."

"Patrick, you can't mean that. There are new developments in medicine every day. Look how long Christopher Reeves lived."

"Just be quiet and listen. This is not me. It's some dead locust shell with a brain. I know I've been a bastard of a husband and shouldn't be able to read your mind, but I still can."

"Oh? And what am I thinking, Patrick?"

"You want the divorce. I killed your love and I'm certainly in no position to win it back." He paused, seeming to wait for a response that did not come. "You pity me, and I hate it. Nobody ever pitied Patrick Wingate. I was on top of the world, and now I'm trapped in this piece-of-shit nothing body. It's way past September first. I gave you my word."

"I'm not sure, Patrick. I made a vow, 'in sickness and in health,' and I feel it's my duty to stay with you. Maybe it's the baby that makes me feel this way."

"Don't! Please don't. If you feel any obligation at all toward me, you'll get this divorce. My lawyer has everything ready. You just need to sign. You and the boy will be taken care of for the rest of your life. You've earned it, Betsy. Take it and run."

"It's not the money, Patrick. I've never been about

money, and you know it. I need to think about it."

"No, this is not your decision. It's mine. Don't you get it, Betsy?" Patrick took several puffs of oxygen before he could go on.

"I want the divorce. No more visits not knowing what to say. No more looks of 'poor Patrick the cripple.' Do it, Betsy! For me."

For some reason, Betsy could not hold back the tears. She was unsure whether they were tears of relief or tears of sadness for the end of this terrible chapter. Not knowing what to say, she just turned and left. When she reached the daycare, Trapper looked up at her with his usual big grin while reaching for her, and her mood changed instantly.

That night as she rocked him in her arms, not wanting to put him down, she reflected on what Patrick had said. Yes, she would go ahead with the divorce. It was the only thing left he could feel he had any control over, and she would relinquish this to him. But she also made a decision, one that he would not be happy about at first.

The next day, Betsy signed the divorce papers at the lawyer's office. The marriage that had been a curse and a blessing would be over as soon as a judge finalized it—within the week, the attorney had said— and she would be free. Her first thought was of Hawk.

The snow was deep in the mountains by now, and weekend fishing trips had been over for months. Did he visit the cabin, think of her, long for her as she did him? She could only hope so. If it had not been for Trapper, she would have gone insane thinking of Hawk, not being able to touch him, have him hold her and call her "Little One."

As she turned the gold bracelet on her arm, she looked again at each charm and remembered.

Soon, my beloved, soon. Please wait for me.

****

The divorce was final, but Betsy remained in Memphis. Every day she visited Patrick as if nothing had changed. He still wished for death, planned for it in his mind, but she could tell his spirits improved, if only temporarily, when she visited each day. Neither of them really understood why she remained close to him, but he never asked her to stop coming, now that he knew she came by choice and not out of obligation.

With her newfound freedom, Betsy decided it was time to do something commemorative, but she'd wait so Annie could be part of it. She got her chance a week later.

Betsy told Annie she needed her to go someplace with her. After dropping Trapper off at the daycare, Betsy drove down the street, parking on the curb.

"Oh, no, Betsy! I was kidding that day we got our belly buttons pierced. There's no way. Burt likes my belly button ring, but he'd kill me if I got a tattoo. Besides, I've heard horror stories about people getting hepatitis and all kinds of things from tattoos."

"I've checked it out thoroughly, Annie. This artist is a female registered nurse. She comes highly recommended."

"By who? Hell's Angels?" Annie hung back, refusing to go any closer to the tattoo parlor.

"Okay. You don't have to get one, but I am. Just come with me and hold my hand."

"So what are you getting?" Annie started walking again. "A butterfly? And where are you getting it put?"

Betsy turned and faced Annie before opening the door.

"No, a hawk. Right here." Betsy turned, pulling her jeans down slightly, and pointed to a spot about two inches below her waist at the top of her hip.

"Well, see? There you have it." Annie held her hands out and shrugged. "There's no way I could get a tattoo anyway, if we're doing the men we love. It just wouldn't be quite as dramatic, you with a hawk and me with a muppet."

****

While Trapper played in the kitchen cupboard, pulling out pots and pans and smiling like a mischievous angel, his mom sat at her laptop. Every once in a while she would look up at her son and grin and then would begin typing again.

She was writing what she could only describe as the greatest love story since the Song of Solomon. The box of tissues had a permanent place on the kitchen table as she reflected on the past year, pouring her thoughts and feelings onto the computer screen.

The clank of the gold bracelet on the keyboard formed the background music that kept her thoughts flowing like the waterfall where she and Hawk had first made love. Before she realized it, she had three hundred typed pages of manuscript. The title was *The Hawk and the Deer*, and it was the easiest and most rewarding accomplishment of her life.

Her mother was coming that weekend but did not know her daughter was writing. Betsy planned to surprise her and to get her expertise in editing and putting the finishing touches on it. Getting it published never entered Betsy's mind. The story was for her and

Hawk, with the final chapter remaining unwritten until she was in his arms again.

When the phone rang, she jumped awake from her nap on the sofa with her little boy snuggled next to her.

"We've got 'em, Mrs. Wingate!"

"Lieutenant Bowling? You mean the men who caused Patrick's accident?"

"Yes. They're not talking yet, but if I can judge bad character, they'll be chirping away before much longer."

"And the woman? Are you going to arrest her now?"

"It's still a little too early, but we're watching her every minute. When the time comes, we'll move in. I'll let you know when that happens."

Relief flooded through Betsy as she realized the long ordeal was almost over and Angelique would get what she deserved.

A few days later, Betsy was typing away when a little hand pulled at her knees and a little voice said, "Mama."

"What was that? Did you say 'Mama'?"

As if wanting to make sure she understood, Trapper stood up, holding to her knees, and babbled, "Mama, Mama, Mama," as if his CD was scratched.

"Oh, my precious boy! You are so smart! I can't wait to show your Sudi when she gets here this weekend. I need to get a movie of you today, Little Man, 'cause this day will go down in history and be preserved in the Trapper Baby Book."

As she dug the video camera out of the cabinet, she hoped it still worked. The camera had probably been in the cabinet for ages, but it looked brand new. True to

Patrick's calling, it was still surrounded by its original Styrofoam and carefully placed back in its original box. The camera was obsolete, but Betsy knew she could get a video copied onto a DVD. By using her computer, she could take still shots from the DVD. She had charged it not long ago, getting it ready for just such an event. Trapper's baby book was full of pictures taken with her phone, since her mother required new pictures be sent every week, but this would be Trapper's debut movie. Trapper held on to the sofa and babbled "Mama" as if practicing for his first major movie production while his mom opened the camera, ready to insert a blank video.

"Oops! Looks like it's not new, Trapper. There's a videotape already in it."

As she pulled out the tape, she noticed a small portion of it had been taped on and wondered what Patrick had captured for posterity. Probably another million-dollar project he had been working on.

"I can reuse this and take your picture, Trapper, but I better check it out first."

Betsy put the tape into the VCR/DVD player attached to Patrick's TV. While waiting for the tape to rewind, she went to the kitchen and poured a cup of coffee. Pushing play, she began backing toward the sofa as she waited for the recording to start.

Betsy never made it to the sofa as her cup dropped and coffee spilled across the carpet. Never even looking down, she stood motionless, staring at the video. On the screen was a familiar red bedroom with a white satin round bed, and on it sat a dark-haired Italian beauty posed and smiling as someone entered.

She wore a flowered silk cocktail dress with the spaghetti straps hung sensually off her shoulders. It was hiked up past her thighs as she sat poised with one knee up, disclosing black silk stockings held up by a garter belt.

"Come in, darling. I've been waiting for you." She spoke in a soft, seductive voice, moving on to her knees and pulling the straps off her shoulder, allowing the dress to fall below her breasts.

"Don't do this, Rosanna. I told you we're through." Betsy heard Patrick's voice before he moved into view.

"I'm Mona, Patrick. Mona from your dreams, and you know you can't resist me. Come, lie here, and I'll help you undress like I did when you were seventeen. Remember, Patrick? It's the night of your seventeenth birthday, the first time I came to you in your bedroom. I knew you wanted me then, and I know you want me now."

"No, Rosanna! Stop!" Patrick stood beside the bed looking down at Rosanna. "It's over. I told you. I'm going to get Betsy back as soon as Susan has the baby. I've got a million dollars to buy Susan off, and Betsy will want me back for the baby. We'll raise it together. I was wrong to start this. I don't love you. I never did. You reminded me of Mona, nothing more."

"I can be Mona, and I'll stay with you forever. We're the same, you and me. You need me, not those young ones who'll leave you." At this, the woman pulled her dress over her head, leaving only her garter belt and hose as she pulled Patrick to her.

"Mona, Mona! I love you. I've always loved you." Patrick seemed frozen in time as he kissed her and then attacked her breasts as the woman began tearing at his shirt.

Betsy stood ready to stop the horrible scene, unable

to watch anymore, when suddenly Patrick jerked away and threw the woman hard against the headboard as he yelled, "No! I'm getting out of here. Don't come near me!" He put his arms up to keep her away. "You're not Mona. You're nothing but an old, worn-out whore. We're through. I'm shutting this apartment down, and you're leaving. Get your clothes on and go. Now!"

The woman stood facing Patrick, furious at his outburst, and pushed him until they were no longer in view of the camera. Their voices were still audible as they became louder and more hostile.

"I'll leave, all right, but you will always be mine! Do you hear me, Patrick Wingate? You're mine, or nobody's! I'll kill you before I'll let Susan or Betsy have you! I'll kill them, too. No one can have Patrick Wingate but me!"

As Rosanna continued to scream threats in the background, Patrick returned to the bed, picked up the remote, and aimed it at the camera, clicking it off. The look on his face was pure rage, and he looked like he wanted to kill.

"That dress!"

The TV spewed static in its imageless screen as Betsy rushed to the cabinet and pulled out the box of pictures. Throwing pictures right and left, she found the packet containing Patrick's family pictures, and there it was, Mona in the flowered silk cocktail dress, the same dress she had found in the closet the day she played detective.

"Oh, Mona, how could you? I trusted you and loved you as a mother-in-law." Tears ran down Betsy's cheeks as the betrayal became real.

It all made sense to her now, why Patrick missed

Mona more than his own mom. Mona had seduced him at seventeen and kept it up until his dad found out about it when Patrick was a grown man, and married.

The two men had fought, and his dad had disowned him. The pain and the need for denial had caused Patrick never to disclose to her the reason for the fight. And Mona had died and left a big insurance policy—not for the son she never had but for the young lover she'd hidden from both husbands.

Betsy knew what she had to do as she lifted the receiver.

"Lieutenant Bowling, please." Nervously, she clutched the receiver, standing in shock and disbelief at the terrible revelation.

"Lieutenant, this is Betsy Wingate. About the picture the truck driver identified, do you know who she is yet? Was it the young girl in the front of the picture from the newspaper clipping?"

"No, Mrs. Wingate. It was the older lady in the background, Rosanna Cavalera. I believe she is the aunt of the young girl in the picture. Why? Do you know her?"

"Yes, I'm afraid I do, and I just found evidence she threatened to kill Patrick as well as Susan and me."

****

The five o'clock news was filled with the arrest of Rosanna Cavalera, and pictures of the demolished Corvette were shown again and again as it was being pulled from the embankment where it had plummeted Susan Carson to her death and Patrick to his life of misery.

Once Rosanna was arrested, Julia began to sing from her prison cell in Montana, confirming the woman was the same one who had hired her and Billy to kill Betsy.

Eddie told Patrick the news, but Betsy never mentioned it to him. He had been punished enough for his transgressions, and she saw no reason to burden him further.

Patrick began a hunger strike that day, refusing food and demanding no life support. His lawyer was beckoned to his bedside to prepare his will. Eddie and Betsy could not convince him to eat no matter how hard they tried, but they both understood.

****

Trapper was the center of attention when his Sudi arrived, as if he needed any more pampering, and before the first day was up, he was hissing the "s" sound as he attempted to mock the word being thrown at him constantly. On the second day of Sue Ann's visit, Betsy presented the manuscript to her mother.

"What's this?" Sue Ann took the box.

"My first attempt to follow in my brilliant mother's footsteps."

Sue Ann opened the box and gasped. A big smile covered her face, and Betsy knew she couldn't wait to start reading. The younger mom figured there would be no more visiting until the older mom had devoured it cover to cover. Trapper got to take a long, late walk with a detour by his favorite ice cream shop.

When Betsy returned, her mother was curled up on the sofa and didn't even bother to look up. Betsy was dying to know what she thought and started to say something to her, but her mom just held up her hand to stop her.

"Not now. I'm busy."

After bathing Trapper and getting him to bed, Betsy returned to the living room and found her mother bawling, something she thought was a good sign. Again without a word, Betsy got the box of tissues from the kitchen table and handed them to her mother.

Sometime after midnight, Betsy awoke as someone shook her.

"Get up, Betsy. I've got the coffee made."

A mountain of used tissues stood beside the empty tissue box as Sue Ann sat on the sofa holding her cup, waiting for her daughter to sit down. She still had not said a word, and Betsy was beginning to think maybe her mother didn't think her writing was very good.

After putting her cup on the coffee table, Betsy sat by her, waiting. A big smile crossed her mother's face, and she began crying again.

"That's the most beautiful love story I've ever read. And to think my daughter wrote it as a first effort." The two swayed as they held tight to each other and cried.

"You really did like it, didn't you, Mom? You're not just saying that because I'm your daughter?"

"Betsy, get serious. Look at me. I'm a mess. If you can make a reader laugh and cry, it's more than good. Oh, my gosh, that waterfall scene! It took my breath away. I know that waterfall, and I don't just mean seeing you splashing under it as a silly adolescent. And that beautiful Neapolitan man…" Sue Ann shook her head and then looked at Betsy with her best imitation of being serious. "Do I know him?"

"I think you've seen him around." Betsy took her mom's hand and gave it a squeeze. Neither of them could stop smiling.

"Question is, where's the ending?" Sue Ann took on a serious look this time.

Betsy paused. "To be continued."

"When, Betsy? What's stopping you from rushing to Montana and grabbing that cowboy you obviously are in love with, and pushing him to the altar? You're not married. Patrick has given you his blessing to go, and you've got a precious little boy who needs a daddy."

Betsy turned away from her mother and sat silent as if in deep thought about her answer.

"One reason and one reason only, Mom." She paused again. "I don't want Patrick to die alone, and he is determined to die. It may sound silly to you, but it's the only reason I've stayed. Dying alone is a million times worse than just dying, and no one, not even Patrick, deserves that. I'm terrified Hawk will find someone else and won't wait for me, but if we're meant to be, he'll be there when I get back. I really believe that with all my heart."

"Well, you know what they say. Never argue with a hopeless romantic. What's next for the book? It's not all fiction; it's more of a memoir of the last year of your life. You need to send it to my agent. You will send it, won't you?"

"You really think my writing is good enough, Mom?"

"It's brilliant, full of passion and intrigue just like your life has been. I know she'll agree, but you will need an ending, Betsy."

"I know, but I need help with that, and I don't mean an editor. I thought about mailing it to Hawk, but I'm afraid I might find it back in my box 'return to sender' since I haven't spoken to him since I left Montana eight months ago. Hawk needs to read it first. Will you take it to him, Mom?"

After editing one more time, Betsy put the manuscript in a notebook and gave the box to her mother to be delivered to Hawk. The note she put with it read:

Hawk,

Take this to the cabin one weekend soon, build a fire, make yourself a pot of coffee, and wrap your heart around memories of us.

Please wait for me.

Soon, my beloved, soon,

Betsy

Chapter Eighteen

Montana

Sue Ann did as she had promised and called Hawk to come to the cabin the weekend after she returned. He stared at the box she placed in his hands.

"What's this?"

"Betsy asked me to give it to you. She also requested you spend the weekend here at the cabin."

"Stay here? I don't understand." Hawk shook his head and looked from Sue Ann to Custer.

"Don't ask questions, son. You wanted answers, so listen to Sue Ann." Picking up the suitcase by the door, Custer headed for the Jeep.

"Trust me, Hawk. Things will make more sense to you. You might not agree with my daughter's decisions, but you will understand a whole lot more. Now, your uncle has promised me a weekend of shopping, eating out, and even a movie in Billings, and I'm calling in the promise. There's plenty of food and coffee, so help yourself. The cabin is yours." With these words, Sue Ann and Custer left, leaving Hawk sitting on the sofa by the fire, staring down at the unopened box.

****

As Hawk left the cabin at the end of the weekend after reading and rereading the book Betsy had sent him, his heart was full. But he had to get back to the reservation, back to start another week of counseling, the only thing that had saved him from himself after she left.

As he turned onto the highway that would take him back, he thought about the promise he had made to First Maker. Allowed to regain his strength and save the woman he loved, he had promised never to drink again, nor would he ever have to test himself even if she left him. And she had left him. His pain had never let up, in all these months, and in a moment of weakness he had broken his promise to First Maker, trying to give himself the courage to end his own life.

With her words refusing to leave his mind and heart, Hawk did not go to the apartment he rented during the school year. He needed someone to comfort him and assure him everything would be all right, someone who loved him as much as he loved Betsy.

Turning into the driveway at the old doublewide, he practically ran onto the porch, bolting through the front door. The old woman sat in her chair and smiled at him with outstretched arms as if she had been expecting him. Hurrying to her, the cowboy took off his hat and fell to his knees, burying his head in her lap and sobbing. Nana stroked his hair and let him cry for a long time. Then, lifting his face to look in his eyes, she smiled as she wiped his tears with the skirt of her dress.

"I told you the Great One would provide your answer."

"But he did, Nana! She is the one, but she left me. Why am I still being punished?" And he put his head back in Nana's lap and continued to sob.

"Sometimes our punishments can lead to even greater rewards." Nana lifted his head so his eyes met hers. "Be patient, Grandson, and have faith."

****

Tennessee

As Patrick grew weaker, Betsy knew it was time to make the move she had been planning. The therapist and other specialists no longer attempted to work with him, knowing it was useless. Even though Patrick was being given nourishment intravenously, his organs were shutting down, just as he willed.

Taking a deep breath, she quietly opened the door to his room. As usual, he was sleeping. Betsy moved to his bedside.

"Patrick, Patrick?" She spoke quietly not wanting to startle him. "Someone is here who wants to meet you."

His eyes batted as if he was not sure whether to open them or not. Slowly, Patrick opened his eyes and stared at the boy, his baby boy, who was wiggling and trying to get to the bed just below his mother's arms.

"This is Trapper. Trapper, this is your daddy."

The dark-haired toddler stared at the stranger as if wondering why he didn't reach for him like everyone else did. Patrick kept his eyes focused on the boy but said nothing. Trapper gave him a big smile and pointed to Betsy and said "Mommy," his favorite new word, as if an introduction were in order. Then, having made the first move, the boy reached for Patrick, opening and closing his fingers and giggling.

A faint smile came across Patrick's face, and the expression in his eyes changed.

"He's…my boy is beautiful. Thank you, Betsy." The frail man spoke in a whisper as he closed his eyes, giving Betsy her cue to leave. As she started out the door, she changed her mind and returned to his bed. Puddles of sadness had formed in the corners of Patrick's closed eyes. Leaning down, she gently kissed his lips. Then, as she had done so many times before, she pushed the hair away from his eyes.

Chapter Nineteen

Montana

The Indian paintbrush was beginning to bloom in June, signaling it was time for the few patches of snow in the aspen groves to make their getaway. Trapper had come alive on the rough forestry road and laughed every time the Jeep hit a bump. His laughter was infectious, and it was a happy ride for mother and grandmother.

When Betsy took Trapper out of his car seat, he squirmed until she put him down, and he took off running on his wobbly legs, heading for the porch steps like he knew he was home.

The cabin door opened and a braided, smiling Custer looked down at the active little boy who looked up at him and smiled before pushing past to climb an even bigger set of stairs he had spotted.

Custer went after the boy, grabbing him from behind and lifting him high in the air, making the boy giggle. "Little One's little one is gonna be a mountain climber, huh?"

Trapper giggled like he was being tickled and swung on Custer's braids as he lowered him to the floor.

It was a match from the start, and Betsy knew she would not lack for a babysitter, or a teacher for her son.

But Custer was not the most important man she wanted in Trapper's life. Hawk knew about the boy from the book she had sent him weeks earlier, but there had been no response. Perhaps she was too late.

"Did Hawk know we were coming?" She was hesitant to ask but could stand it no longer.

"I told him," Custer replied.

"Oh." Betsy dropped her eyes to the floor.

Seeing her pain, Custer hugged Betsy.

"Give him some time, Little One. He hasn't gotten over the fact you left in the first place. He'll come around."

"It's been over ten months. There's no one else, is there, Custer?" Betsy kept her arm around Custer's waist, looking him in the face as she awaited his answer. Custer only shook his head, leaving her with no real answer. After unpacking for both herself and Trapper, she walked to the porch, ever gazing toward Six Rocks.

"Need some fresh air, Daughter? You haven't walked your six miles today. Custer and I will entertain the boy wonder." Sue Ann picked Trapper up and gave him a hug. "Go on. I know you're dying to get up there."

Betsy changed into shorts and hiking boots, kissed Trapper, and headed out the door, grabbing her Winston cap on the way out. As she walked, she began to feel alive again, even with the emptiness.

As she sat at Six Rocks drinking water, she replayed in her mind a cowboy tipping his hat, smiling, and saying, "Morning."

I can't stay here if Hawk doesn't want me. As much as I love the Beartooths, I'd see him around every rock, and at every sunrise and sunset.

Her thoughts became a prayer, and even though she knew she shouldn't, she bargained aloud.

"Are you there, God? You used to be. Please, Heavenly Father, I know I've messed up a lot, but you've still blessed me with the child I never thought I'd have. You've given me so much, and I've done so little in return, but I need your help. I love Hawk. I promise it will be my last time to love if you just give me one more chance."

Instinctively, Betsy turned down the trail that led to the waterfall.

****

He sat on the rock, throwing rocks into the pool at the bottom. His hat lay by his side, and he seemed to be deep in thought. She could see the gold chain shining in the sunlight under his open collar and knew he was wearing the deer she had sent him.

"Too cool for a shower, cowboy?"

Turning, he looked up at her. Though she smiled down at him, he did not return the smile and turned away from her gaze saying nothing. His silence was purposeful and cut to her heart.

Being careful not to slip, Betsy approached and sat on the rock beside him and looked at the waterfall. The silence roared louder than the falls, but neither would break it. After a forever several minutes long, he spoke, still refusing to look at her.

"Why'd you do it? Why'd you shut me out, Betsy? You could have called. You could have written. Now you just two-step back in like it's last July."

Choosing carefully what she would say, her only response was, "It had to be that way, Hawk. I didn't want it to, but it had to be."

More silence.

"I can't do this again, Betsy. I just can't. It hurts too damn much. I'm leaving here. Got a job with some outfitters out of Bozeman for the summer."

"I see." But really, she didn't. Her heart hurt, and Hawk was the only one who could stop the pain.

Putting on his hat, he walked away from her but stopped before reaching the trail, keeping his back to her.

"What's he like?"

"Who?"

"The boy."

"Trapper. His name is Trapper. He's beautiful, full of life, took his first steps at nine months, smiles constantly, and runs everywhere he goes."

"I'm proud for you, Betsy. I know how much you wanted a child." Hawk continued walking away from her.

"He needs more than me." Her words caused him to stop again. Hooking his fingertips in his pockets, he kept his back to her.

"How's that?" he asked, so low he was barely audible over the waterfall.

"He's going to need someone to teach him how to ride a horse and tip his hat and be a man. I can't teach him that."

Hearing these words, Hawk turned and faced her. For the first time, she could see the dark cisterns of his sad eyes, and she wanted to dive into them with her whole being. He remained wordless, looking at her as if in deep contemplation of what she had said. After several seconds, he spoke.

"Did you mean all you wrote in the book?"

"Every word of it."

Looking down, he hesitated before responding. Searching her eyes again, he continued, "There's a lot you haven't said."

Betsy stood and walked up to him and stood in his shadow, looking directly up into his eyes. Uneasy with their closeness, he dropped his eyes, turning his gaze away from her. She grabbed his chin with her left hand and turned his face, holding on until he repositioned his eyes to look directly into hers. His hands left his pockets, and he waited for her to speak.

"Why are you always doing this to me?" She sounded angry. "Making me turn around and retrace my steps? It's time we had a heart-to-heart, big guy, and got some things out in the open. No mealy-mouthed 'friend' shit, either. We're more than that. I feel something when I'm with you, something I can't let go of, and it's time to stop playing games. Somebody once told me if you play games with life, life'll come back and kick you in the ass."

"Betsy, I…"

"Be quiet, Hawk. I'm not through. I don't give a damn about the past. It's over and done with. You're here and I'm here, and this moment is what counts, nothing else. Do you understand what I'm saying? Now, if you don't want to be a part of this, part of me, then now's your chance to get rid of me forever. Just turn around and take your gorgeous butt back up that trail. But listen good, Hawk, 'cause I ain't saying it but once. If you think there's a chance in hell there could be something wonderful to come out of all this, then get your horse out of the trees, 'cause I know you didn't walk up here in those boots, and take me home. And don't plan on leaving, not ever. Do I make myself clear?"

"I, uh…"

"And another thing. I love you, Hawk Larson, like I've never loved anyone in my whole life. I need you with me, and Trapper needs you to be his daddy. You are my forever."

Staring down at her, a smile crept across his face as he took off his hat and threw it. Lifting her up, he kissed her like he'd never let go. With her arms tight around his neck, she wrapped her legs around his waist in anticipation of his next move.

Without putting her down, he walked, still kissing her, to the edge of the waterfall.

Chapter Twenty

It was July fourth, and a crowd had formed around the waterfall just down the trail from Six Rocks. They didn't look like a wedding party, dressed in shorts and hiking boots, baseball caps and sunglasses, but they were all there for the same reason. Annie and Burt, Darlene and Mack, Jake and Cindy, and many others from Red Lodge were there to watch as Hawk and Betsy joined lives.

Even Amanda was there, but only as a devoted friend—really all she ever wanted to be with Hawk in the first place. By her side was the new man in her life, Buzz, who had finally found a woman who would take the lead and put him back on the dance floor.

The only real cowboy at the gathering was Trapper, with his big hat falling over his eyes and wearing the cowboy boots Hawk had bought him. His soon-to-be grandmother Isabel tried unsuccessfully to restrain the boy as he hopped around on the big flat rock, stomping his boots and laughing at the noise they made.

The bride carried a bouquet of Indian paintbrush and had wildflowers in her hair, worn long at Hawk's request. Her dress was two-piece and was made of white deerskin by Hawk's mother, who had embellished it with white beads and fringe. It had the traditional look of a Crow wedding dress, but with the split skirt of the Old West, a symbol of the union of two cultures. White moccasins covered her feet, and she stood smiling, thankful for the beautiful man standing by her side, who was going to be her husband at last.

Hawk's bride was exactly the same as in his vision, and, just as Nana had assured him, the Great Spirit had provided the answer for the part of the vision that had not fit—the animal spirit of a fawn who was always with the doe. In human form, it was a small boy with dark hair and eyes.

The groom wore no cowboy hat over his thick, black hair. Instead he'd chosen the headband of his Crow ancestors, which he wore with a moose-hide shirt hung long over moose-hide pants and moccasins like those he had worn the day he saw her for the first time, while on his vision quest.

Two people stood in attendance—Sue Ann and Custer. When the minister asked, "Who gives this woman," they spoke together saying, "We do," for they, too, were as one.

The rings the bride and groom gave each other were also symbols of their united cultures: his, a wide, gold band inlaid with turquoise; hers, identical to the groom's but with a large solitaire diamond mounted in the center.

When it was time for their vows, Betsy turned and looked up at Hawk and smiled, laying her hands on his chest. With his hands around her waist, he looked deep into the emerald eyes he loved. Their vows were passages from The Song of Solomon in the King James Bible, the greatest love story ever told, with small changes to make them truly theirs.

Betsy spoke first: "The voice of my beloved! Behold, he cometh leaping upon the mountains, skipping upon the hills. My beloved spake, and said unto me, 'Rise up, my love, my fair one, and come away.' "

Betsy moved one hand, placing it gently on Hawk's cheek, where he took it in his hand, moving it to his mouth and kissing it tenderly before he responded: "Thou art beautiful, oh, my love, as Tirzah."

Taking both her hands in his, Hawk looked into Betsy's eyes, speaking with the wonder befitting the words: "Who is she that looketh forth as the morning, fair as the moon, clear as the sun?"

Betsy blushed a little, and her voice grew shaky with emotion as she responded: "Awake, O north wind; and come, thou south; blow upon my garden, that the spices thereof may flow out. Let my beloved come into my garden, and eat my pleasant fruits."

"Behold, thou art fair, my love; behold, thou art fair." Hawk's eyes shone, reflecting his bride's love as, together, they proclaimed their vow: "I am my beloved's, and my beloved is mine, forever."

With the vows over and every woman weeping out of control while their men tried to comfort them, the minister pronounced, "May I present to you Elizabeth Ann and Hawk Thomas Larson." The couple was far too busy with their wedding kiss to acknowledge the presentation, and the crowd clapped, whistled, and cheered their approval.

As the wedding party began disbanding a few minutes later, Hawk lifted his bride and set her on his horse to ride behind him as they had done the first time they went to the waterfall together. After he'd mounted to the saddle in front of her, she put her arms around his waist as he turned and kissed her.

A miniature cowboy, struggling to be free from his grandmother, briefly interrupted the scene. The little one pointed, his arms outstretched, whimpering, "Mommy! Daddy!"

Smiling, Hawk reached out his hands to signal the youngster's release. Custer took the boy and placed him in front of Hawk. With a grin the size of Montana, Trapper grabbed the saddle horn as if an old pro already.

"Hold on, Son." With his free hand, Hawk held tight to the boy and turned the horse down the trail. "We're going home."

As they disappeared over the hill, a hawk dipped its wings beneath the clouds and called its approval of the scene below. The final chapter was written.

A word about the author…

Dr. Sue Clifton is a retired principal, fly fisher, ghost hunter, and published author. Dr. Sue, as she is known, can't remember a time when she did not write, beginning with two plays published at sixteen. Her writing career was placed on hold while she traveled the world with her husband Woody in his career, as well as with her own career as a teacher and principal in Mississippi, Alaska, New Zealand, and on the Northern Cheyenne Reservation in Montana. The places Dr. Sue has lived provide rich background and settings for the novels she creates.

Dr. Sue now divides her time among Montana, Mississippi, and Arkansas and enjoys traveling with Woody as well as with her 8000-plus fly fishing group Sisters on the Fly. She loves all things vintage, including her 1950 camper and her 1951 Plymouth Savoy "Woodie 2."

Dr. Sue is the author of eight novels, four in her "Daughters of Parrish Oaks" series with The Wild Rose Press, Inc., three paranormal mysteries, and one young adult paranormal mystery written in collaboration with seventy-one high school English students.

Visit Dr. Sue at:
http://www.drsueclifton.com.

Thank you for purchasing
this publication of The Wild Rose Press, Inc.

If you enjoyed the story, we would appreciate your
letting others know by leaving a review.

For other wonderful stories,
please visit our on-line bookstore at
www.thewildrosepress.com.

For questions or more information
contact us at
info@thewildrosepress.com.

The Wild Rose Press, Inc.
www.thewildrosepress.com

Stay current with The Wild Rose Press, Inc.

Like us on Facebook

https://www.facebook.com/TheWildRosePress

And Follow us on Twitter
https://twitter.com/WildRosePress